CATACOMBS OF HELL

CATACOMBS OF HELL

MARY A. LONERGAN

CONTENTS

ISBN 978-1-0879-9372-0

CHAPTER 1

CATACOMBS OF HELL

The gathering of the dark and stormy clouds, suddenly, let lose a split second bolt of lightning along with a sudden thunderous crash, splitting apart a tree that left a loud vibrational noise startling Madeleine, who earlier passed out from exhaustion and was resting her tired, battered and bruised body against a trunk of an unknown tree.

In a state of panic, she jumped franticly with her eyes wide open looking around only to realize, that she was finally outside sitting under a tree. The trees umbrella branches were not enough to protect her from the harsh weather elements, yet, she was shivering and soaking wet from the cold spring rains usual heavy downpour.

Feeling her hot tears spilling over against her cold and bruised cheeks, while feebly thinking to herself, *'oh my God, at last I made it out, and I can't believe it, YES! I'm still alive, ohh the rain; ohh it feels so good'* as she eagerly stretched out her hands, weak and trembling, grasping and cupping her palms to catch the rain waters, began quickly drinking while letting the cold water flow down her parched throat, each time reaching out for more rainwater to quench her thirst, she didn't care if her hands were dirty or not, she needed water.

She hadn't eaten any foods or drank any liquids in the last forty-eight hours or more. With just barely enough water to satisfy her thirst, she tried to make sense if she had to fall asleep or fell back into unconscious this, it didn't matter, she had finally made her way out of the Catacombs of Hell, somewhere below the beautiful City of Lights – Paris!

Nor could she tell the time because her watch, a birthday gift from her parents was broken, the crystal glass face had been shattered during one of her recent falls against the rocks and now, the digital time was stuck at seven-thirty most likely in the evening, the last she remember it to be, she knew by the dark skies that it was much later.

The pains in Madeleine's body reminded her that she immediately needed medical attention; she knew it was important for her health to get out of the cold rains and fast before she went further into shock. Feeling weak and trembling, unsure, if she could stand up and try to make a run before kidnappers somehow, managed to find her. Forcing her back against the tree, she slowly edged herself upright, at the same time, forcing her wobbly legs to stand up, just then, the sudden sharp pain pierced through her left knee.

Gently massaging it and looking through the heavy rains to see where she was. Just up ahead of her, she saw the glow from the city lights, her memory came flooding back reminding her that she was still in Paris. *But, where about in Paris, am I?*

Through the downpour, she immediately looked around for any recognizable buildings or structures of any kind that would stand out to her, disappointed, it didn't. Just over forty-eight hours ago, the vast catacombs of Paris's underground networks and the realms of the cavern complexity had plunged Madeleine into total darkness. Her memories came flooding back, to those entrées of the Paris Catacombs that one early morning.

And so the adventure begins with Madeleine and a certain gentleman.

The previous year, Madeleine Windsor, age twenty-five years old and still unmarried, while some of her friends were planning their weddings. Already she had been a bridesmaid at two different weddings. Glancing at her calendar, July 21st is another friend's wedding coming up in a couple of months that she planned to attend. Only this time, she is not going as a bridesmaid, but as a guest. She didn't mind being a bridesmaids; it was the walk down the aisle that made her felt uncomfortable. She felt all questionable eyes on her. *Her time was coming*; she would reassure herself. The trouble with summer weddings, she found them too hot and stifling. Especially when they wore gorgeous long flowing gowns that would cling to the sides of their already damp legs while she listen to the other bridal parties all complaining about the same problem too. At least she wasn't the only one feeling the summer's intense heat.

Since then, she had made up her mind with the right man by her side, their wedding would most defiantly be a late fall wedding, perhaps even a Thanksgiving one would be a nice change for everyone or even a Christmas wedding with all the gorgeous colors of reds, whites and greens.

With her best friend, Donna Wilson's wedding being twelve weeks away, she needed a new outfit and what a perfect time to do some clothes shopping with her parents in the downtown heart of Paris. Her father, Fred who was requested to attend an urgent meeting overseas, in France, not only did he have the plane tickets already lined up, he also had three tickets for them to the Opera house.

In Paris, the Opera Quarters are the famous district where all the opera houses were located. Everyone who lived in Paris knew the location of every large or small opera house; it is one of the Parisian's major pride and joy. No tourist, in their right minds would dare to leave Paris without first, taking in one of more famous Opera performances. It was one of their main entertainment cultures as well as, scattered about in the parks, were the many new hungry artist water colors and oil painters begging to do your portraits while sitting in the sunshine.

Tourists loved having their portrait done out in the open fresh air for all to see. Their foods were the Parisians pride and joy, many famous chiefs topped the world with their delicate pastries, many different kinds of cheese and their chocolate croissants, were to die for. The elegantly and fashionable clothing that French people wore daily, made the trip itself, well worth going to Paris. Next, stepping up to the popular plates are Parisian chocolates. The largest majority of the visitors brought home their famous "melt in your mouths" chocolates and candies galore. There were many, many more attractions in Paris too numerous to mention, not to mention, perfume factories, museums and stone churches.

Madeleine had always wanted to see the famous landmarks, art galleries and the Eiffel Tower was one of them, she was eagerly looking forwards to her first trip to "The City of Lights" as known to the world, Paris, it was as the people's expression quoted, 'is every girl's dream comes true.'

Her father, Fred Windsor, the CEO of one of the largest charter banks in Canada. He had met and fallen in love with his wife Courtney, while attending a seminar for all Canadian branch managers from across the country. Courtney was a very striking and well-dressed banker in the same city of Lansing. Well on her way up the corporate ladder and after her marriage to Fred; she too became a CEO at a different branch, but at the other end of their city. The small city of Lansing's population was back than 120,000, but now at last count, over 350,000 and still climbing.

Madeleine, a young seamstress, also a fashion designer and had no problems taking the week off work once she convinced her boss, Albert Hugo: with promises that she would bring back to his office, Paris's latest fashion designs.

Their staff would copy, makeup and sell to their elite customers. His business had been trickling down for some time. Madeleine, not once had to worry about her boss trying to take advantage of her or any of the other ladies in their workplace; Hugo was gay and with a lover waiting at home for his nightly arrival.

Hugo and his partner were well known in the gay community and together they did a lot of volunteer and charity work. He was not a good looking man by any means, he stood just less under five feet tall, with short red curly hair and squinty baby blue eyes that peeped through his thick black-framed glasses, whereas his partner, Tom was an inch taller and a much better-looking man.

Madeleine could have sworn that Hugo was going blind. The staff's open-style warehouse was bright enough to light up a whole football stadium, but no one complained.

She excitedly told her closest friend, Donna all about her upcoming trip to Paris. The ladies have known each other since kindergarten days and their friendship was still growing by leaps and bounds.

Together, they had split the cost of buying a three-bedroom condo on the seventh floor; theirs was a corner unit with a wraparound balcony exposed to the entire city. Not only did they live there, they also shared the condo with a Persian cat named 'Ginger,' a two-year-old female, the color of spice. It was both Donna and

Madeleine's parents who one day; surprised them with 'Ginger' as a "housewarming gift," they told them.

Their downtown condo was also in the city of Lansing, nestling on the waterfronts of the great Lake Ontario. With promises to each other, whoever married first, will be giving the other partner, the first opportunity to buy the other half at face value but, no mentions of who might take 'Ginger' to their new dwellings!

Madeleine had saved enough money on her parent's advice. Her father invested any of her spare savings into stocks and bonds; in the course of two years they lived there, she had more than enough saved up should Donna decided to sell out. She kept this little secret to herself in a special account, on her father's advice.

She knew it was a matter of time before Donna and her boyfriend Greg Walters of more than two years were about to announce their engagement and knew that Donna was planning on a Christmas wedding, along with her bridesmaid all wearing red dresses while she would wear a white wedding gown, carrying red and white rose bouquets. Her bridesmaids will be carrying the traditional Christmas colors of red and green bouquets as well. The reception dinner will be a traditional Turkey event with all its fixings and trimmings.

The red-eye plane ride to Paris had been smooth with very few air pockets bumps, on her father's advice; the family managed to get some shut eyes known that it would be late morning when they all would arrive at the airport. Remarking, "They would be up all that day."

She was used to traveling with her parents in and around Canada and the USA, she knew all about jet lags, but she had never been on a trip with them to Europe, this was her first trip to Europe.

On their arrival in Paris, with the late spring in the air, they noticed that already the tourists were quickly filling up the city. The taxi ride to their hotel was a little rushed and Madeleine had to close her eyes a couple of times, she thought for sure this wild reckless driver was accidentally prone. They crossed over bridges, past museums and tall cathedral churches and Fred pointed out the Eiffel Tower which flashed past before her eyes, *thanks to the driver!*

Once inside the de Grand Hotel, Madeleine breathed a sigh of relief that they indeed had arrived in one piece. Looking around and studying the interior of the hotel's famous de Grand lobby. The feeling was magical with all the soft colored granite floors and high columns of marble making the hotel look much bigger on the inside than did from outside when first stepping out from the taxi cab.

Next, she studied the fashionable customers all wearing designers' brand-name clothing. She could smell all around her the many different French perfumes and colognes waffling through the lobby's air.

With registering taking care of, they took the elevator up to the fourth floor to where their rooms were waiting to greet them. She was glad to have her own bedroom. Her parent's room was next door to hers, along with a doorway adjoining each other's rooms. There was no need to go out into the hallway and both rooms had their own private bathrooms – a bonus.

After putting away the clothing and toiletries and freshen herself up, she notice the closed heavy drapery on the tall windows. Needing some fresh air, she pushed aside the heavy drapes filling her room with bright sunlight. She was surprised to see, instead of windows she saw a single wide French glass door leading out to her own private balcony. Excited to see the city below and without hesitation, she swung open and stepped out through the doorway; the sudden splash of breezy air welcomed her body, she began to admire the cities majestic tapestry sights. Breathless, she was about to call out to her parents to quickly come and see when suddenly from somewhere below; she faintly heard a rapid session of a gun firing.

Quickly scanning her eyes around not known what direction the shooting was coming from then spotted what looked like a well-dressed man, running in between one of the buildings across from her hotel; following him was a trail of police officers not far behind him.

The running man in question turned and looked behind him, seeing if the officers were gaining on him, satisfied that he was still ahead for the moment, till something up high caught his the corner of his eyes. Concentrating on the hotel's front building, up on the fourth floor, was the shade of blue that made him looked up to that particular balcony.

There stood the silhouette of a woman with long black flowing hair, flown gently in the spring's breeze. It took his breath away.

Today was his lucky day to see sight while running from the law. Without known who she was and without hesitating with his right hand he threw a kiss, saluting upwards to her with a mischievous grin, turned and continued on making his getaway.

Madeleine smiled at the thought of a dashing mad Frenchman flirting with her in the first hour on Paris soil, when suddenly; she felt a tight grip on her upper arm as she was being pulled quickly back into her hotel bedroom, swung around coming to an abrupt halt, faced to face with her panicking father.

"Madeleine, what are you doing out there, didn't you hear the gun fires?" loudly questioning her father. He quickly stepped away from her and closed the French door behind him, returned, wrapping both strong his arms around her thin body, after complete inspecting, he was satisfied that she was ok.

"Don't panic father, I'm fine."

Not wanting to tell him that the man below had the nerve to flirt with her instead she said coyly, "Do you think we should find somewhere to dine, the food on the plane wasn't filling enough?"

"I agree with her Fred; if we are ready, let's check out the dining hall downstairs, shall we?" suggested her mother, Courtney, who had earlier fallowed on her husband's heels.

Fred also agreed with them. He made a quick phone call, said a few words in French and hung up. "We have a lunch table for three in thirty minutes," in his now calmed voice.

The two days they had been in Paris had been blissful, magical and exciting for Courtney and her daughter while Fred attended his urgent business meetings. Both mother and daughter, walked along the city's famous streets to admire the arts and did some high fashion clothing shopping till they almost dropped.

The weather was cooperative on the evening of the opera, beautiful and warm with the Parisians people suddenly came alive, filling the air with electricity and excitement leaving the world of troubles behind them. All thoughts of the mad dashing man had left Madeleine's mind, for now.

Up in the balcony facing the National de Paris Opera stage, the Windsor family were truly enjoying the Opera sounds and sights of 'Verdi' until Madeleine, began to glancing around taking in the scenes around and below her, she wanted to mentally sketch any fashionable clothing's the other elegant ladies were wearing. Then in one of the lower rows, somewhere in the middle, she spotted a man starring back up towards her balcony.

Satisfied that she saw him; he nodded his head to acknowledge to her, having seen him.

With a sudden recognition of him, she felt a searing flash of heat rushing up to her face, she quickly look away towards the opera stage and didn't look back again to where he was sitting. *The nerve of him* as she wondered to herself if all the Frenchmen were as brazing as he had been, was he intentionally following her, *I highly doubt it,* she thought.

The man in question is in fact, Jack Holt, with soft hazel eyes with striking jet-black wavy hair in his mid-thirties with his broad shoulders neatly tucked back; wearing a black suit and starched white shirt with black mother of pearl buttons and black bow tie. His bristle-free square chin was scented with lightly woodsy cologne. Not like most men wearing heavily scented cologne, which you could smell coming from a mile away.

Jack was still single, a most legible bachelor not ready to settle down type; in fact, he was quite the opposite, a ladies man who had trouble keeping the women at bay. Some of the ladies were married, some were divorcée with a ton of baggage and some were looking for a rebound relationship. None, of which, bothered Jack.

He was a wealthy, above average and flamboyant fun type of guy who knew just what women wanted, which left him, in no hurry to tie the knots any time soon.

His idea of entertainment was expensive gifts and dinners nights in popular clubs that towered high in the evening skies, overlooking the city lights or a quiet evening in his downtown condo. It would be just the two of them alone, dancing to a soft jazzy music coming from his CD/radio player.

Jack Holt was the playboy of the year to some of his jealous male friends. Once he held the ladies attention span, he would take advantage of their loneliness by whispering sweet words while nogging his nose against their soft perfumed hair, just enough for them to barely hear what he had in mind for them. His chosen guest would be caught up in the moment letting out a throaty laughter or giggling like a schoolgirl on their first date. And them, of course, would take the advantage of going out for the evening or going home with Jack Holt the city's most eligible bachelor of the year in hope of tying the knot, but none of them succeeded.

With the condo towering in the Paris city of lights, the top floor penthouse overlooking the Seine River but, very few ladies knew that his real home, his real treasure; was somewhere out in the countryside. His home was an ancient castle, one of the smaller ones sitting by the private lake that he purchases just over two years ago, and just less than an hour's drive outside of Paris, near-by a town called Chalone-En-Champage.

His faithful butler, Wilbert an English gentleman who had been with his family from the time of Jack's birth never married and loved Jack like a son; had promised Jack's father that he vowed to remain by his side till death came knocking at his door. Yet, to this very day, he had always been and still is Jack's advisor and confidence when it came to his wellbeing.

Wilbert was very intuitive when it came to Jack's needs; and at times, was able to read his mind. He knew just when the next road trip was coming up even before Jack told him. Yet, somehow even knew on which days Jack would arrive back to the castle.

Jack's clothing would be all pack and waiting by the staircase at a moment's. Wilbert was also the castles private chauffer. Whether it was business or an enchanted trip with one of the cities' ladies;

Wilbert never question Jack. What Jack did was his private business and no one else's.

But, tonight out of the blue, Jack was one trumpet up on poor Wilbert who was baffled and began to think he was losing his magical touch.

"Wilbert, where is my opera suit?" demanded Jack when he came running inside before the front door slammed shut behind him, echoing throughout the castles hallways.

The poor butler had rarely seen Jack so rushed, he usually was calm and composed, but today something was up in the air, *must be love in the spring air again,* and thought as Wilbert sigh.

On seeing Wilbert, "Please have my suit ready by five o'clock, I'm going to the opera tonight," then he quickly ran up the staircase two steps at a time, to shower and shave.

A short time later, Jack was dressed and down at the hall's entrance checking his wallet to make sure he had the printed out, opera ticket and some cash on hand for champagne afterward.

"Sir, I didn't know you had tickets to the opera tonight or I would have had your suit laid out for you," looking questionably at Jack?

"That's alright Wilbert," with his wide grin at having out-foxed him for once and proudly announced that "with my good ole cell phone, I manage to hack into the hotel's computer to check to see who was registered up on the fourth floor out front and when I found out their names, next, I checked the Operas computers to see which day and their seating plan the Windsor family are attending the opera!"

With that info, I ordered my ticket, good thing I did because, this ticket was the last one!"

"Good Lord Jack, how in the world did you guess they were going to the opera?"

"Because my good man, have you ever known a tourist coming to Paris and not seeing an opera before leaving?"

"Jack, I am afraid that one of these days someone will be able to trace your cell phone back to you, so please, for the sake of your name, be careful!"

"Don't worry so much, I plan to meet this Madeleine Windsor tonight!"

"Beg your pardon sir, did you say, Windsor's, are you saying that the Queen's family from England are here, staying here, in France?"

"Good gracious Wilbert, had they been here the whole dam countryside would be having a fit right now, wouldn't they?"

"As a matter of fact, the Windsor's I'm talking about are Canadians and I have no idea how long they will be here for or if they are just touring Europe."

Jack said his goodnight and began his drive his brand new two-seated 2015 Voir La Gamme Peugeot to the opera house. During the drive, he kept thinking of the lady in the blue dress, why did she not run back inside her room, but, stayed during the entire gun tooting commotion, unlike most women he knew, would have been terrified and screaming their fool heads off but, not her. *Who knows, just maybe I'll run into her during intermission and strike up a conversation, maybe invite her out for a late night dinner.* Jack thought.

Settled into his seat and as the Opera house lights began to dim, the atmosphere had suddenly quieted own, with the curtains already open, the singer began her performance. Jack glanced over to the balcony to where the Windsor's were sitting. He knew the layout of the opera house; he has been there numerous times with his ladies of the evening. He notice the lady in question was sitting between an older gentleman and an older woman. *Who are these people to her*, he wondered to himself?

He quickly glanced around the audience and did indeed notice that men of all ages were stealing quick glances up to the balcony where a beautiful young lady was sitting, this made Jack a tab bit jealous, *eyes off you ideates, she is mine*, he thought quietly to himself with a slight smug.

At the same time he did notice the young lady was concentrating and enjoying the performance wholly and he was quite pleased to see that she is indeed is very beautiful from a closer distance. He could tell that she was very elegant.

Three-quarters of the way into the first part, Madeleine began to look around the house till she had spotted him. Saw that he was smiling up at her.

Their eyes locked momentarily and he nodded his head in acknowledgement but she quickly turned away ignoring his glance, shocking him as he was not used to women ignoring him; this was something new to him. So she is one of these women who like to play hard to get, he thought.

He planned to make it his mission to accidentally bump into them. Perhaps even offer to buy them a glass of France's finest champagne during the intermission while they waited for the second half of the performance to begin. He would like to learn more about these Canadians, especially the mysterious woman in blue.

The light inside the opera house became brighter as the curtains closed down, signaling the end of the first part of the performance bringing tears and shouting were heard everywhere by everyone.

Fred, along with the rest of the audience shouted, "Bravo, bravo" to the singers who were leaving the stage, slightly embarrassing Madeleine.

"Come ladies, let's beat the crowd and get ourselves a nice tall glass of champagne, shall we?" while Fred walked behind while ushering the ladies out to the hallway and down a flight of stairs towards the waiting bar.

While the three Canadians were savoring their bubbly Champagne and discussing the opera, a tall blonde handsome-looking gentleman who was about to step up to Madeleine, Jack with his quick steps intercepted and stood next to Fred and politely interrupted their conversations. "Monsieur que pensez-vous de l'opera?"

The tall blonde man on recognizing Jack took his cue and politely bowed his head and quietly took his leave.

Fred turned to face him and was pleased that the gentleman in question had to take the time to speak directly to them and decided instead of responding back in French language he spoke in his English, proud that they were out of town people coming into their city.

"Ahh, yes, yes sir, the performance was excellent and we are looking forwards to seeing the second half of this magnificent performance." hoping that the gentleman also understood English.

Jack on hearing the English spoken words took it to pond himself, to speak English as well.

"Oh, you are not French residents I take it, may I ask where a bouts are you and your lovely lady friends are from?" hoping to entice them into a full conversation, without giving away his curiously for the younger lady.

"Certainly sir, please allow me to introduce ourselves, I am Fred Windsor and this is my wife, Courtney and this is our lovely daughter, Madeleine, we are from Canada and may I kindly ask your name, sir?"

On seeing Madeleine's face up close for the first moment, time suddenly stood still for a brief second, he almost stuttered his words.

"Oh please excuse my manners, I must admit this evening has been very enchanted, my name is Jack Holt and it's a pleasure to meet a family all the way from Canada enjoying one of our Opera plays, and by any chance are you related to the Queen of England?"

"Absolutely no connections, not, that I am aware of Mr. Holt," chuckled Fred.

After shaking hands with both her parents and when he did turn to extend his hand out directly to Madeleine, challenging her to take his hand hoping that she did not recognize him from the chaos the other day.

She, who hesitated for a brief second longer than both her parents, did. Madeleine was not sure she wanted to shake his hand, instead, decided on a no-nonsense type of hand shake after all, *I probably won't be seeing him again and may as well get it done and over with, b*ut she was wrong, this was the beginning of their story!

She reached out and firmly shook his hand and with a slight tilt forwards of her head while starring hard back into his hazel eyes, not saying a word to him, just a simple nod.

Jack was even more stunt at her beauty, almost taking his breath away, making him eager to get to know more about her, who held his attention. He did notice her slender hand felt warm and her skin felt very soft.

"Please to meet you mademoiselle," impressing her with his French accent while starring back into her capitation eyes. With the Opera hall's lighting, he could not help but notice they were almost a deep violet shade of blue that sparkled back at him, setting his heart beating harder and faster something no other women have done.

Madeleine only smiled back, *and I'll bet you are*, she thought to herself.

Both her parents were surprised to see a certain igniting spark, coming from Jack and decided to take the opportunity to invite this stranger who was taken aback by their daughter's beauty, out to a late dinner, hoping to encourage the couple to perhaps, go out for a day with someone of their age group people, just so they too have some time on their own.

Clearing his throat, "Mr. Holt, after the opera we planned on having a late light dinner, would you care to join us or do you have other plans for later this evening?"

Jack decided to seize the opportunity, "please call me Jack and no, I have not had any dinner tonight and yes I would be honored to join you and your lovely family. I would love to hear about Canada, shall we all meet, say, by the hall's front doors." Not wanting to be caught off guard staring at his daughter who by then was seething at her father's suggestion.

"Then, it's set; we shall meet you by the front doors and we will all go out for dinner, oh I do believe the show is about to restart, shall we return to our seats, ladies." Pleased at himself playing matchmaker tonight and even more so, at having to beat Courtney at her own game.

Back at her seat, Madeleine was by now furious and with every fiber of her being turned to speak to her father hoping to discourage the dinner invitation. But, the show had already begun and both her parents were deeply embossed on the singer. She wasn't paying much attention to the rest of the show, she had to figure out a way of getting out of the dinner date tonight and decided on to cornering this "Jack" directly and give him a piece of her mind. As for her parents, perhaps she should tell them the truth about their so called new founded friend, who the other day, was the man being chased by the policemen. Thinking, they won't have anything more to do with Jack.

Madeleine looked down to where Jack was sitting and was surprise that instead of watching the show; again, he was looking up at her.

This time, he turned the tables around, with a quick nod; he suddenly turned to concentrate on the performance, almost ignoring her. And Madeleine thought that was a bit odd.

They didn't see each other again until they all met by the front doors of the lobby where Jack was already there waiting for them. After they all acknowledge each other and debated the performance of the singers. It was Jack who suggested the Windsor's being new in town that he would like to have the privilege of buying and escorting the family to a fine dinner club high atop the condo and so they could see for themselves that Paris never sleeps.

With Jacks car having only two front seats, he hailed a taxi cab and gave the driver the address and opens the door for his guests. He then sat in the front with the driver. The ride was a short one to the downtown's hotel La Grange where the dinner club was on the top floor. On arrival, Jack quickly hopped out of the cab, paid his fare and held open the taxi door for Madeleine and offered his arm, but she refused and stepping out on her own, and quietly out her parent's earshot, "Don't flatter yourself mister," and walked ahead of him and waited for her parents to catch up with her.

A little amused and miffed that he was turned down; again, something he is not used to, he knew that he had his work cut out for him, *this was just the beginning of a cat and mouse game, the night is not over yet my dear lady,* Jack thought to himself.

Once inside the dinner club and seated at the reserved table by the window, Jack who sitting next to Madeleine politely asked her, "Can you see the Eiffel Tower just past that bend?"

She didn't respond to his first questions of many. *Is she always this rude, what is her problem*? He wondered, he didn't see a wedding or an engagement ring on her finger.

Madeleine did not knowing him but kept looking out the window, she was assuming that he was chatting to her father and chose not to pay any attention to him till she heard her mother's voice.

"Dear, Jack has just asked you a question."

Turning to her mother, "I am sorry, what do you just say, mother"?

Again Courtney repeated the same question.

Fred who was used to saving their daughter when she had been caught off her guard, spoke up for her.

"Jack, Madeleine is hard of hearing and wears a hearing aid, I am sorry, we should have mentioned it earlier on but, I leave that up to her discretion to tell people or not," almost apologizing to him.

Jack turned and starred back at Madeleine and thought, *but how could someone as beautiful as she is having a hearing impairment.* He knew all about hearing impairments, his father, due to his age, wore a hearing aid for a long time before his death, so he was told. He learned over the years that, it was important to face the people so that they could read their lips should they not hear their words very clearly.

"I am so sorry to hear that but, Madeleine were you able to hear the performance ok." looking straight at her with questioned her with a serious look. She detected a moment of tenderness but, didn't care.

"Why yes, of course Mr. Holt I heard the singing and the music, it was loud enough and I thank you for your candor," feeling rather perplexed that her father had brought this up to this total stranger and that she must remember to prim him to ever do this again.

She wanted to yell out to her father, *don't be so blinded by this gangster*, and to tell him about the policemen chasing him instead, she played it cool, waiting for the right moment to pounce on Jack.

Jack cleared his throat and spoke up a little clearer for her to hear, "I would like it if you were to call me, Jack," he told her with a polite smile. *A little Miss Snooty*, he thought to himself, *hearing impaired or not!*

Meanwhile, Fred glanced at the menu and saw that it was all in French but, he decided to give Jack the opportunity to please his daughter who, he noticed was unusually quiet tonight. Did he think perhaps she was a little shy or was it jet lag? He asked Jack to suggest something light for them to eat and Jack gladly suggested a special blend of soup along with their famous homemade fresh baguette and a glass of chilled Chablis white wine to go with the soup.

The conversation during dinner was light mostly about Paris and about the Opera. Fred decided to question Jack and praying for the two singles to strike up a conversation of their own.

"Have you lived your whole life in Paris and what do you do for a living here in this beautiful city of yours, if you don't mind my asking Jack?"

"Why, not at all Fred," speaking up so Madeleine could hear him as well, whether she was paying attention to him or not.

This should prove interesting, I wonder is he dare tell us the truth, she thought to herself.

"I have lived in Paris for more than half my life now, my deceased parents moved us from Tipperary, Ireland, when I was young as my mother was a French-born lady who met my father, they married in Ireland and came to France to start a food chain store. And as for my line of work, I do coffee and chocolate imports; actually I have my own coffee/chocolate shop just down the next block from here."

"I also, own and operate my own Vineyard, I purchase it two years ago from an owner who has badly neglected his vines, I had to remove, wait a full year to disinfect the grounds, replant all the new grapes vine plants, starting it all up from scratch once again. It was the money from the coffee/chocolate shop has helped to keep me out of debt. And to be honest with you, this is my first wine production coming up this fall; it has been a lot of long hard work."

"You mean to say that you have had to rebuild the whole she-bang?" question Fred.

"Did you rename the vineyards?"

"Yes as a matter of fact I did, it's called: Holts Vineyards," said Jack proudly.

"Also, as we speak I am in the middle of negotiating a deal with a Champagne vineyard plantation that is going into bankcruptcy. I hoped to own two vineyards."

"Oh really, a coffee shop, chocolates and vineyard, perhaps before we leave Paris we can all come by on our last day and buy some of your products for our Canadian friends back home?"

On hearing *the last day*, Jack felt a sudden hollow pit in the middle of his stomach; he did not want them to leave, not just yet, anyhow.

"Then, may I suggest we all take a short walk to work off this meal, I have the keys with me to open my shop and perhaps I can give you a personal grand tour?"

"Also may I suggest that we skip coffee here and I'll make us fresh pot of coffee for us?"

"Why that is a lovely idea, isn't it Madeleine?" suggested Court-ney.

Oh great, now he is assuming, that we all drink coffee, probably try to poison us, thought Madeleine.

"Then, please let me take care of this bill and we will be on our way," said Jack.

Madeleine tried not to walk alongside of Jack but, somehow she did.

Once they arrived at the front door of Jack's shop, she noticed the rich colors were mostly gold and black lettering with a sage shade of green exterior. The Bristol-style patio table and chairs were still sitting outdoors on the front walkway.

Jack had unlocked the double narrow doors, went inside turning on the inside lights. He invited his guest to step inside and locked the doors behind them; he did not want to be interrupted tonight.

While his guest was looking around, Jack skillfully start up the coffee machine, added water and added the correct amount of coffee beans and proceed to set out the cups and saucer on the tray. The coffee's amour began to tickled his guest's nose, "hummm, this smells delicious, now, I know why everyone raves about the Parisian coffees." said shyly Courtney who was eyeing the rows of chocolate bars.

Sitting at one of the nearby Bristol tables savoring their coffees, Jack explain everything to his guest about coffees beans and choco-late imports of how, where and why he got into this business ven-ture. He was particular about Madeleine's hearing, he made sure that he was facing her, and did notice she was mostly lip-reading him most of the time.

Dam, her eyes are beautiful almost haunting, making him feel special when she stared at his lips like that, to the point, almost making him want to lean across the table, take her head between his hands and kiss her lips. He wanted nothing but to take her in his arms and savory her plump lips and protect her from the evil world.

Fred set his cup down and thanked Jack for his hospitality and suggest to the ladies they should be getting back to their hotel. Jack felt a mild panic, "Fred, may I ask what your plans are for tomorrow?"

"Well, actually we were thinking of bringing along picnic baskets and taking advantage of the countryside fresh air, I did rent us a car for the length of time being here. Is there someplace you could recommend for us?"

Jack jumped at the chance, "I certainly can Fred, I know of a perfect spot and please allow me the honors of picking all of you up and driving, I promise you will not be disappointed."

Without consulting with his family, "What a brilliant idea, you know your countryside better than we do, what time shall we expect you Jack and please, what can we bring?"

"No, no I don't expect my Canadian guests to bring anything; I'll pick you up at your hotel here say, eleven a.m.?"

"Then its settle, we will see you in the a.m."

Again Jack hailed down a passing taxi cab and took the Windsor family back to their hotel, said their goodnights.

Back at the hotel Madeline followed her parents into their room and Courtney was surprised to see that her daughter who has not been on her usual shelf and chalked it up to jetlag was still lingering about the room.

"Dear, are you not going into your own room?"

"No, not just yet mother and besides, I think we need to talk about your Mr. Jack Holt!"

"Why yes, he is such a fine gentleman, something so rare these days."

"No mother he is not a gentleman!"

By this remark, both her parents looked stunned at each other.

"What is it Madeline, I have notice you have been unusually quiet tonight?" surprising Fred.

And so Madeleine began her story from the start to the finish on Jack Holt leaving her both parents standing shocked.

"And furthermore, I don't think it's a good idea to go on the picnic with this gangster, who knows what he has in store for us!"

"For god sakes, why didn't you say something earlier?" questioned the furious Fred.

"Because father, Jack saw that there was no time to cut in, you both were wrapped up in his...how should I say it.. his candor!"

"Then by all means, I trust your judgments dear, and I think you are right.

"What I'll do is. I'll call down to the front desk and leave a note for Jack telling him that we changed our minds. Meanwhile why don't we stick to the original plan of having the hotel make up our picnic basket and we will drive ourselves out to the countryside?" suggested Fred, who was feeling a little disappointed.

After the agreements, Fred called down to the front desk leaving instructions for the picnic basket and to have their car ready for ten-thirty tomorrow morning. Next, he sat at the desk and proceeded to write a quick apology note for Jack.

Back in her bedroom and feeling smug, *this will teach him a lesson!*

Hours later, Madeleine was having a fitful sleep, *dam him*; she thought to herself and decided to put him out of her mind. Something about Jack was bothering her and she could quit putting her finger on it. He did look handsome in his tuxedo suit and was very mannerly for a gangster. No doubt he had won both her parents' approval, *well no more, Mr. Jack Holt, my parents know all about you and the policemen fiasco!*

She put him out of her mind and took her hearing aid out placing it in the little container, setting it on the night table, turned over and puffed up her pillow and finally went off to deep sleep.

CHAPTER 2

Earlier, on the second day in Paris, Fred had rented a four-seated convertible car from the car rental company and had it delivered to their hotel for their remaining length of stay in Paris. This was Madeleine's first time in France and he wanted to show her all around and what the beautiful country had to offer, he had a surprise waiting for her back in Canada. *Today is a good day to tell her all about it,* thinking quietly to himself.

After they picked up their picnic basket from the lobby's front desk and were on the road driving out to the countryside. Madeleine sat in the front seat next to her father while her mother had chosen to sit in the back. During the driving, Fred, who prides himself in France's history, pointed out the L'arc de Triumph which was in the center, with many streets all branched away from the center, reminding her of a wagon wheel and its spooks. He also pointed out other famous structures.

In his louder than normal voice, he told her all about the cathedral churches, the story of France and World War II and reminding her that his own father had served the war in Dieppe, which she had already, heard the story for the tenth time. The drive out to the countryside was what she needed to take her mind of Jack and she was glad that her parents agreed not to have anything more to do the gangster. *For all they knew he could be the main ring leader of a gang or a notorious murdering, worst yet, dealing drugs to young children.*

Her concentration on the drive began to settle her rattling nerves; the sun was shining and the air was warm with a slight breeze, *a perfect day for a picnic,* she thought.

On the narrow slightly curvy road, they passed through a couple of small towns before her father had decided to settle somewhere inside of the regional town of Chalons-en-Champagne.

He knew the vineyard region to be France's world's famous champagne making and wanted to introduce this to Madeleine. *But, what he didn't know was that Jack Holt's castle was somewhere nearby.*

They found a perfect picnic spot by a narrow riverbank, leaving their car parked on the side road; the ladies carefully climbed the grey weather-beaten wooden fence and set out the blanket under the tree's umbrella.

Fred got out the picnic basket out from the car's trunk bringing it back and setting it down on the blanket at the same time, whispering to Courtney, "let's have lunch before we tell her the news, ok." Courtney agreed.

Madeleine called her mother to come to see the river; she didn't hesitate in joining her.

From a distance, Fred was admiring his wife and daughter walking along the river's bank and decided to leave them to themselves while he would catch some shut eyes, the drive there had tired him, not to mention the disappointments in Jack Holt. Through his light napping he could hear the ladies giggling till he heard a screech coming from their way. With quick reflexes he was up and by their side in no time.

They point out towards the opposite side of the river was the mother fox and her two babies cubs trotting gingerly behind her.

On seeing the action, Fred pulled out his cell phone from his pocket and began shooting a short video.

"Shhh, don't move and stay quiet, she will go on her way," commanded Fred.

They stood still and watch the mother marching her tribe down the river bank. To their relief, they were gone.

"Come now, let's have our picnic and then we will go into town, I like to buy a couple of cases of Champagne to bring back home to Canada." suggested Fred.

It was during their picnic lunch that Fred decided the timing was right to surprise Madeleine; he looked for Courtney's approval who mouthed the words, NOW," to him while Madeleine was looking the other way.

She decided to take the first lead.

"Dear, we have something to tell you, I'm going to let your father explain everything."

Fred set his glass of red wine down on the picnic blanket and cleared his throat.

Seeing that he had her attention, "Madeleine, your boss Hugo came into my office a couple of weeks ago regarding his company's mortgage loans."

"Oh really father," surprised that she did not hear of it, everyone in the office always knew what was going on.

"Yes, it seems this is the fourth time that he has missed his mortgage payments in the last eight months and I have to admit that he was generous enough to come into see me personally, to tell me that he was putting his business up for sale."

"WHAT, Hugo is selling his business; surely he would have told us all?"

"Well that is just great; now I have to find myself another job."

"Well no dear, you won't need to find yourself another job,'" smiled Courtney.

"Listen to the rest of the details your father is going to tell you."

And so, Madeleine began to concentrate harder on her father's lips, she did not want to miss one word coming from him.

"What your mother and I have to tell you is this; we bought out Hugo's company for a modest price and transferred it all into your name, dear!"

"You did WHAT?" said the now, wild-eyed Madeleine.

She wasn't sure if she heard her father correctly or not.

"Yes, the company is now yours, to do, what you will with it; you can keep the company's name or give it a new name, whichever you prefer, it's all yours."

"The building is your, the employee is yours, you are their new owner, it's all yours!" pipped in Courtney!

Madeleine was stumped, she didn't know if she wanted to cry or protest.

"I-I-I don't know about this father, I-I mean, being hard of hearing and all, how will I ever hear what the customers are requesting or hear what they are asking me on the telephone, WOW, I don't even answer the phones at work now."

Seeing that she was about to knock herself down.

"Listen Madeleine," grabbing hold of both her hands to help steady them still.

"Hugo is going to stay with you for at least two months to teach you more of the business end of the ropes, I've no doubt you can run this operation on your own, instead of you answering the phone, I have to take the liberty in hiring you a personal secretary or I should say an assistance that will be taking care of your hearing needs.”

“OF MY GOD, what about ordering all the materials from France and Italy where Hugo buys them from?”

“No worries, give Rachel your orders and she will take care of the rest.”

“And who is this Rachel; do I know her, father?”

“No dear, you don’t know her.

“Rachel Holt, is your new personal assistant, she will look after the phones, the ordering and she will be traveling with you to and back from France or another country and she will be present at all the meetings, by your side.”

“In other words, she will be your right-hand lady,” piped up Courtney who was beaming with pride.

Then a horrifying thought came to her, *the staff!*

“Does the staff know that I am their new owner, now?”

“Yes, they do by now know, and as a matter of fact, they are look-ing forwards to some new changes. Also, for your information, no one is losing or leaving their jobs.”

“And my dear, Rachel is already at Hugo’s getting your new of-fice set up for your returning.” Courtney continued.

Madeline looked at her father, “So is it a done deal, it’s for real?”

“Yes dear, it is a done deal and it is all for real,” starring back at her with his wide grin. Fred reached into the picnic basket sitting beside him and pulled out a large thick brown envelope.

He kept hidden behind and covered with a napkin; he carefully placed it onto Madeline’s lap.

She slowly picked up the brown envelope and hesitated.

Courtney whispered to her “go ahead dear and open it.”

"Come Courtney, let's give Madeleine some privacy," while helping his wife to her feet. Together they walk arm in arm over to the river bank, proceeded to watch their daughter open up the envelope.

Madeleine's hands began to tremble as she slowly opened the envelope, carefully sliding out the contracts and began to read each page, absorbing them one by one. Warm tears spilled down onto her flushed cheeks, for a girl who never attended university when all her friends did, she is now, the owner of her own dress-making company, along with her very own staff of twelve employees. After reading pages after pages she carefully folded and put them back inside the envelope, stood up and joined her parents by the river bank.

"What did I ever do to deserve this?" holding up the envelope.

"You just needed a chance to prove yourself, besides dear, in spite of your hearing impairments, you have no idea what you are really capable of until you take chances," smiled her mother.

"How can I ever thank you mom and dad?"

"No need to," just make sure you keep it running smoothly and please don't go bankrupt," chuckled Fred.

Fred and Courtney took turns hugging their daughter with warm embraces.

"Look, if you have any problems, just know, that we have your back; just give us a call, ok?"

"But, father, how do you know that I could make this company work?"

"Let me tell you, one night your mother and I went after hours to Hugo's, we met with both him and his lawyer, it was then he took the liberty to show us some of your work, your designs, Madeleine, my God, they are out of this world!"

"We knew there was an artistry side of you but, we had no idea you are that talent. While Hugo showed us some of your designs, he was saying that you have a very impressive talent for designing your own outfits and you are a quick learner too."

Madeleine hugged both her parents, "I can't wait to get started, I have so many new ideas" she whispered.

"By the way dear, are you planning on keeping the same company's name?" questioned Courtney.

"HUGO'S," no I don't think so.

"Than do you have a new name in mind"?

"How about this one, CITY OF LIGHTS" suggested Madeleine?

"And care to explain why you choose that name?"

"Because mother, my designs are all about Paris, Italy and her fashions, it's because of Paris that I am now the owner of, CITY OF LIGHTS."

She was testing out her new company's name and hardly contain her excitement.

"I love this new name," clapped excitedly at Courtney who at that moment had her wheels grinding into motions. With all her ladies friends and customers, she plans to give a helping hand to make her daughter's new business a success!

"Uumm.. The City of Lights, I think we should christen it with a bottle of France's finest Champagne!" suggested Fred.

"Quick, let's pack this up and go into town now, not only am I ordering two cases two cases but four cases of France's finest Champagne!"

"Why Fred, why on earth are you ordering four, you usually order two cases at a time!"

"Because my dear lady, now, that our daughter has her own business, she should have a couple of cases of her own, wouldn't you agree?" winking at her.

"Well, I was hoping to have a look at the castle just beyond the trees."

"Let's save the castle for another time, besides, it's too close to closing time, I doubt they would be giving any tours or if they do for that matter!"

"Oh by the way, Madeleine, we have a very important appointment for ten o'clock tomorrow morning. One is with the textile company and later at one o'clock to meet with the bankers." Starring back at her father and feeling the panic already beginning to set in, "What do you mean by, WE?"

"Well after all honey, aren't you are the new owner of The City Of Lights?" questioning her with his broad smile.

"Well, yes tactically I am, but I am nowhere near ready to take on the big, bad corporate world just right now, I've so much to learn yet!"

He sensed panic in her already, "don't worry I have explained the situation to everyone, and they are looking forwards to meeting you."

"And to be perfectly honest, they didn't much care for your old boss, Hugo; now let's get ourselves back into town before everything closes up, shall we?"

While the ride into town had been short, Madeleine didn't pay any attention to the scenery or a small castle standing by the lakeside. She already had her wheels in motion and at the same time a little excited, yet, a little panicky. She was sure her parents meant well but, she wished they had invited her in on the decision-making, but now it's too late, she was the new owner of City Of Lights.

At the vineyard warehouse, Fred introduced his family and ordered not only four but, six cases of their very finest Champagne to go, shocking the ladies. With all the celebrations and grand re-opening, he planned to invite everyone that the Windsor's knew, hoping to encourage more business for her new company. He had taken the liberty to let his wife drive back them back to Paris under his watchful eye. He then turn to look at Madeleine sitting in the back seat and asked her, if there was a color scheme that she likes for her new building, without hesitation and without thinking; she automatically told him, gold with sage green background.

He then got on his cell phone and contacted the printers; a small company his bank uses when reordering batches of business cards and stationary. Because of the time zone difference he left a message on their answering machine with instructions on the color schemes and designs of the new company; the address and the phone numbers were to remain the same and asked the bill be sent directly to his office; the first of many gifts for his daughter. Then he called Rachel to let her know that her new boss will be coming to work soon and left her further instructions on the catering, they were going to have a surprise party for its new owner on her first day back!

With the convertible top being down, Madeline did not hear who her father was talking with; *it's just his banking business* she thought to herself. Sitting behind her mother while she drove, told her of the many new designs that she planned to introduce to City Of Lights.

Back at their hotel, the three of them had an exhilarating dinner while they talked and planning new ideas for her new business. She knew that tonight was forever memorable, as excited as she was, she said her goodnights, giving both her parents long hugs and kisses before turning in for the night.

Madeleine opened her laptop to email Donna a quick note, telling her all about her new business and what name she decided to name her new company.

Donna, my dearest friend,

I just found out that I am now, the new owner HUGO'S, Yes, Hugo's old company, he planned to put it up for sale till my parent bought him out!

And, to think that all of us at the company could have lost our jobs and standing in the unemployment lines! Well, not if I could help it!

Anyway, I am changing the company name to; 'City Of Lights!'

I'll be home soon with tons of stuff to tell you. Oh yes, I have to tell you about a mob gangster having dinner with us, OMG, that what I said, a gangster....ok, ok girl, hold onto hold your britches till I get home and I'll tell you all about it. Oh yeah, give Ginger a hug for me?

Chat later, Maddie.

Morning came fast for her and with anticipation she hardly touched her breakfast. The meeting at the textile company proved to be successful. The company's sales representatives wanting her business and treated her with the upmost respect.

They took the Windsor's on a grand tour explain every detail of the company and educated them on the textiles. Before leaving, Madeleine signed all purchasers' contracts. Fred then opened his wallet and producer a cashier's check for one hundred thousand dollars and handed to be put directly into 'City Of Lights' new account.

This stunts Madeleine and she planned to question him later on the money. She had plans to borrow from either parent banks to start-up small not wanting to be like Hugo, getting herself future into debt.

Next, they met with the president of the Bank of Paris and after a round of introductions, they open an account, again signing more documents for 'City Of Lights' with Fred Windsor handing him, again another cashier's check for twenty five thousand dollars. Madeleine could not believe that she is now one hundred and twenty-five thousand dollars in debt to both her parents. She made a mental note that she would not spend it so extravagantly and hope to be able to give some back to them.

During dinner back at the hotel she seized the opportunity, again thanking both her parent for the generous gift of a lifetime and promised to make them both proud.

"Tell me something father, this emergency meeting was not about your company but all about my business, wasn't it?"

Fred smiled, he knew that once the cat was out of the bag it was a matter of her put together two and two, she always was a smart thinker.

"Yes, dear, the meeting was all about your business.

"Your mother and I wanted to make sure that should one day you find yourself on your own; you had something to keep yourself busy, be happy and not relying on a company going downhill putting you out of a job."

"We have known for a very long time that if it were not for your hearing impairment, you would have been in your own business with the talents you have otherwise we would not have bought this investment of Hugo's company."

"As for your hearing impairment, you might just be surprised at how well you can do, never take life for granted, my dear!"

"Your mother and I will help and back you up just until things get rolling, after that, you are on your own."

"What about payments that I now owe to you, I mean you have invested one and twenty-five thousand dollars, isn't this yours and mom's retirement fund?"

Courtney seeing her daughter's worry look, "No dear, that money is your rightful inheritance from your grandfather Windsor."

Madeleine was taken back by her last remark.

"You see, this money was meant for your university fees and since you did not go, well, your mother and I have decided on buying Hugo's company for you as your own."

"Oh, I didn't know grandfather was that wealthy?"

"He wasn't, it was his farmland of three hundred acres, plus a herd of one hundred mixed cattle, I put it all up for sale immediately after his death, I am, no farmer!."

Courtney chuckled out loud, "We both know your father is not a farmer type.

"And well, that is how the money came in."

Fred adding his two cents worth, "I sold it all for four million dollars, invested all in stock for the last year and a half which brought us to a total of just over the six million dollar mark, so now you can see, we are set, it is you that we worry about!"

"So are you saying that I bought out Hugo with my own inheritance money?"

"Yes, you did dear."

"Wow, you both must have a lot of faith in me, I mean, what if I didn't want the business?"

"That is the chance we had to take and, don't forget, with your mother and I being bankers, who else takes chances more than us!"

The last couple of days for Madeleine had been a whirlwind experience of any young ladies' lifetime, and she had forgotten all about, Jack Holt.

Jack went to the hotel's front desk to collect his guest for their planned picnic lunch, instead he was curtly handed a note. He quickly tore it opened to read,

Dear Jack,

I am sorry but, we have changed our minds and once again I like to take this opportunity to thank you for your generous hospitality. We will never forget your kindness.

Best regards,

Fred Windsor

When Jack read the note, he was furious. He crumpled up the note and jammed it into his blazer pocket. *No doubt she told her parents about me, dam her, well Madeleine, I am not someone to trifle with,* he thought to him as he stormed out of the hotel. He got into his sports car and used his cell phone to call Wilbert to cancel the surprise lunch he had planned for them. No women in his lifetime have upset Jacket the way she had.

Next, he drove to his condo with the intentions of getting himself drunk, but instead he drove around hoping to get a glimpse of them walking somewhere along the busy streets. He drove past all the churches and art galleries as well as Pyramid Du Louvre and the Eiffel Tower still no sight of them. He checked his watch and noticed the time; he may as well go home.

Back at his condo slowly savoring a whisky in his hand; the rattling of the ice clinking against the crystal rock glass had helped to calm down his temper enough to think. In the morning he planned to go to their hotel and without announcing himself and knock on their door.

His intention was to first tell her parents the truth and then have a few words with Miss Madeleine. After that he wasn't sure what will happen. This is one lady; that Jack could not put out of his mind. Her dark-haired, violet-eyed woman starring at his lips, *Dam her, why is she still haunting me,* hard as he tried, *hell, even her name was enchanting!*

The more Jack drank the more dunker he got, soon his room began to spin sending him passing out on the sofa where he was sitting, whispering her name, *Madeleine where are you?*

CHAPTER 3

On the plane flight back to Canada, Madeline felt bad about Jack Holt, she only wished that she had not seen what she saw that day on the balcony. *If only things had been different, oh well it's his problem, not mine and still not my time yet!*

With a sketch pad on her lap, she busied herself sketching new designs she had seen while in Paris, with some alterations here and there. While her parents were both catching some shut eyes; they both knew the next couple of weeks were going to be hectic with their daughter's new company and Jack Holt was the farthest person from their minds.

They landed safely at Lansing International Airport in the mid-afternoon and gathering the family's luggage, Fred suggested on the way home that they drop into Hugo's to meet Rachel Newman. Madeleine's protest was not heard. "You have to meet her sometime dear and today are as good as any, right Fred?"

On pulling up, she was shocked to see the company's building front allready painted from the traditional burgundy and black coloring. Fred pointed out her company's new name; *'CITY of LIGHTS'*

The background interior was painted from burgundy to sage green with the company name in large bold letterings painted in gold, highlighted with bold black forcing the gold paint to stand out even more, had taken away Madeleine's breathe away.

It brought back memories of the night at Jack's coffee shop. Why she picked that color scheme was beyond her wildest dreams. Yet there are thousands of colors out there to choose from.

Hugo met the Windsor family at the front door with a glass of Champagne in each of his hands.

"Welcome back Madeline," he shouted out to her, handing her a glass of the bubbly and the other to her father. Grabbing a couple more from the serving tray, he handed one glass to her mother and the other he kept for him. The atmosphere was alive with excitement and everyone was trying to congratulate Madeleine all at the same time, overwhelming her.

Hugo, after chatting with Fred, put his arm through Madeleine's arm.

"Come Madeleine; let me introduce you to your new personal assistant, Rachael Holt."

Rachel had been standing in the corner chatting with Courtney who was giving her a quick education rundown on hearing impairment.

"In the future please call me Rachel, I'm sure we will be constant in touch and not worry, Mrs. Windsor, my father was himself hearing impaired and we got along just fine."

This pleased Courtney who let out a sigh of relief. The ladies were now on a first name basis.

Madeleine met, Rachel Holt; she took a liking to her immediately. She was a slender woman in her early to middle forties; soft brown eyes with her black hair pulled neatly back into a tight bun, sporting short bands and she wore fashionable reading glasses. There was something about her that she couldn't put her finger on.

"It's my pleasure to meet you Miss Holt." Extending her hand outwards.

"Hello Madeleine, the pleasure is mine and in the future, please do call me Rachel. If you would like to see your office, I would be more than happy to show you what has been done so far."

"If this is not to your liking, please let me know and we will do something about it." Making sure to face Madeleine, specking each word clearly so that she can read her lips, should she miss hearing any of the spoken words?

Together, both ladies along with her parents who followed close behind, walked down the hallway and Hugo had already made his way up ahead of them quickly sprung open the double wide wooden doors for Madeleine.

In one sweeping eyeful, she scanned her new office; she could see the decorators had been very busy putting everything quickly together while she was away in Paris. With money being no objection, her office was big and sunny; there stood a large glass table in front of the window, tucked neatly behind was a high back taupe leather chair, along with two shorter taupe leather chairs facing the desk, *for her guest*, she thought.

All the **colors** were neutral with warm tones. Tall tree-like plants was sun tanning by the wide office windows. Madeleine saw art deco sitting in the double-wide bookcase along with her many of her own books of designs and fabric samples from many parts of the world. In the final corner was a large designing drafting table. All this left her speechless.

"Well, Madeleine, what do you think of your new office?" Question Fred.

"I don't know what to say; I mean even Hugo's' office was never this big!"

Fred laughed out loud, "don't worry, you will get used to it."

"Now come, let's crack open the bottle of Champagne that we brought back from France shall we?"

Madeleine suddenly felt a light tap on her left shoulder, she turn around to see Donna standing there beaming through a gift box of Ivy vines at her. Donna quickly handed her a large box of plants. "Here, you better help me with this thing, it's really heavier than I thought," while laughing out loud.

A couple of her employees stepped up and took away the box putting it on one of the other tables. Once they gave each other's affectionate hugs, "by the time I read your email, you were already on your way back home." She chuckled.

"Donna, I'm so glad you are here!" in an almost panicky voice.

"I knew all about the company purchase, your parents called me for a dinner meeting one night to discussed the pro and cons, they also ask if I would help out with the inside decorating and color schemes, oh the fun we had?"

"And I said, of course I would, I couldn't pass up this chance to help out a good friend, could I Maddie?' using her nickname that none of her employees have heard before.

Hearing her nickname for the first time, "I love it, why didn't you tell me Maddie?" chuckled, Hugo.

Madeleine could only scrunch up her nose at him, "in the work place, I prefer my real name, thank you."

"Umm, don't worry Maddie dear, I took a week off work to help you get started, and besides that, do you think I'm going to miss out on all the fun around here, not a chance." pipped up Donna.

For this reason, she felt a little relief that Donna was going to be there to help out. Hugo came over and handed Donna a glass of

Champagne, while he stepped up to the front with his loud pitchy voice.

"Can I have everyone's attention here please and thank you?"

Satisfied that all eyes were on him, rising his glass upwards towards Madeleine,

"I would like to congratulate and propose a toast to your new owner, Madeleine Windsor and may 'City Of Lights' be named the business of the year."

After a sip of his cold bubbly drink, Hugo then handed Madeleine a large ring with all the companies' different keys; she could see the identification tags were already tied on each of the keys. *How thoughtful of him,* she thought.

Cheers and applauding were heard all around the room. Champagne began flowing like crazy and finger foods were being served by the hired catering company, the atmosphere was joyful and relaxing all at the same time.

What Madeleine didn't know was Fred had another surprise for her, he had to take the liberty to have his printers publish a short notice in the local paper of a brand new fashion designing company that was opening up in a couple of weeks. He wanted to give Madeleine a chance to get her employees and as well as herself more organized. Courtney also had taken an extra couple of days off work and planned to pitch in to help her as well.

The first year passed quickly by and, Madeleine surprised the public with her newest designs, hence establishing her name. Word got around fast. Everything was working out perfectly and Rachel Newman with Madeleine's hearing impairment had taken her under her wing. She made all the phone calls, all the arrangement for meetings and she handle the clientele's orders. She also traveled from and to Paris and Italy; always by her side.

At meetings, Rachel learned very quickly to step in for Madeleine when she spotted her little frown, a tattle tale sign that she was having difficulties hearing their words clearly. She would speak up louder, thus encouraging the speaker to speak up more so. In most cases, Madeline did a lot of lip reading.

And if Rachel saw that Madeleine was able to handle conversations well without any hearing problems, she would leave them be, but always kept one ear glued to their conversations, just in case Madeleine verbally didn't pick up, more so, when it came to dollar figures. She understood Madeleine was able to hear the women's higher tone voices clearly more so than most men's baritone voices which was too deep, unless she was lip reading them.

And she clued in on which sounds that she could hear more clearly than other sounds. She finally understood and mechanical voices coming from the telephones and radios were the most troublesome for her.

Most days Madeleine would be found buried under a pile of work with many deadlines to be met. She was always the last to leave and the first to arrive at the City of Lights. Her company had grown from the staff of twelve working members to the staff of twenty-eight workers and still growing.

He father earlier had taking the liberty to fire Hugo's old book keeper who he suspected of scamming and hired a trusting legally licensed booker keeper and to keep him informed as well at all times.

Madeleine was thankful for Rachel and one day during her email to Donna, "Rachel reminds me of a tigress with a whip in one hand and loudspeaker in the other when it concerns the employees, she does keep them in line for me, thank God."

Her most popular clothing lines are the wedding party dresses and evening gowns, mother, future mother–in-law outfits and business suits as well. All were designed and all made on her premises, but their meeting was always on separate days to keep the suspense a secret. And when the wedding line ordering and adjustment fittings had quieting down, it was usually the high school parties and graduations gowns that followed as well as beautiful gowns for special occasions.

She once tailor made the cities mayor's wife her compete attire while traveling. Orders coming in kept them busy, not to mentioned the numerous alterations.

During the quieter times, both Madeleine and Rachel would be off to Paris and Italy checking out the newer fashion lines of fabrics and clothing styles to bring back to her company.

Then one day it was pouring rain and the winds were blowing stronger than normal that early fall day and Madeleine felt the chill running deeply into her bones. She put on her blue cardigan and went back into the kitchenette to make her some pot of Chamomile tea. The only other staff member in early that morning was Rachel.

She went into her office with good intentions to see if she would like share a pot of tea with her only to be stopped at the doorway and surprised see a man's back facing her. He was sitting in the chair facing and talking with Rachel.

"Oh I am so sorry Rachel, I didn't know you had an early meeting this morning," she apologized, turning to walk back out.

On seeing Madeleine at the doorway, "no problem dear, come on in, I want you to meet my brother, he just arrived from the airport and I was giving him the house keys and directions how to get there." She laughed.

The man in question spun around faced to face with Madeleine to offer out his hand was shocked on seeing who he came face to face with.

"Madeleine!" Wide eyed, suddenly pointing his finger directly at her.

"Jack Holt," she said suddenly turning pale.

"Oh, I take you know each other," when she saw they were each staring.

"Yes Rachel, we do know 'OF' each other" in his sarcastic voice.

"Am I Right, Madeleine Windsor?"

"Uhm, yes I believe so," was all she could mustard up at the moment.

Jack had not taking his eyes off her, "and I see you are still wearing blue, but a different shade," pointing his finger to her cardigan sweater. Madeleine's face flushed with a crimson colour, remember that day in Paris out on the balcony.

Turning her eyes away from Jack, "Rachel, I came in to ask if you care to share a pot of tea with me," not looking back at Jack. And before Rachel could speak up,

"That is very kind of you to offer and as a matter of fact, yes, I would like some tea please" in his still sarcastic voice, "and by the way, please don't leave any notes in the cup," smiled Jack, challenging Madeleine and he quickly turned his back on her to face the NOW confused Rachel.

Madeleine turned and quickly stormed off to the kitchenette with her heart pounding, *the nervy baster!* Thinking to herself with trembling hands, she placed the teabag into the teapot and set out the three tea cups on the tray, and then waited for the kettle to boil the water.

I know he is toying with me, too bad I don't have any rat poisoning, I wonder why Rachel didn't mention to me that she had any siblings, I guess it's largely my fault for not asking! She thought.

She made a mental note to get to know her personal assistance a little better the next time and proceed to take out her notepad that she always kept in her pockets then scribbles in big, bold letters "Welcome to Canada, Jack!"

She folded up the note and place into one of the tea cups. Without knocking on office door, she marched in and set the tea tray on Rachel's desk and picked up the tea pot and poured herself a cup.

"Rachel, I'm going to leave you to your guest and I'll take my tea to my office."

"I have some catching up to do before the gang arrives," as she turned to face Jack with a little nod to him, she continued to walk out the door.

Whoa, lady, what a cold exit, Jack thought.

He turned to face his, "Is she always like this?"

"No, but I have a strong hunch that somewhere you pissed this lady off!"

The hot Chamomile tea helped to calm Madeleine's nerves while she went over and made some minor adjustments on her latest sketch. Rubbing her tried neck till she looked up and saw Jack leaning against the door frame with both his arms crossed over on his chest, standing there starring at her.

Jack has been missing Madeleine like crazy and hard as he tried, he could not get her off his mind. He even dated other women but his feelings for her would not go away. Even when he was drunk, he would always think of her.

He went back to their hotel and was deeply disappointed to find out that the Windsor family had already left to return home to Canada. He even tried to bribe the hotel manager into giving him their forward address, but due to the hotels privacy policy, would not give him any forward information on the Windsor family. He went so far as to calling the Canadian telephone operators only to find out that there were hundreds of Windsor families all living in everywhere in Canada and some of them had unlisted phone numbers. He finally decided to try and forget her.

Jack came over to Canada pertaining on some business meeting regarding his Champagne vineyard and decided to call his older sister to let her know that he would be dropping for a visit, and she encouraged him to stay with her at her house, "we have tons of stuff to catch up on Jack."

After arriving at the Lansing airport, he gave the taxi cab the address instructions to Rachel's place of business, *The City of Lights*. *That is odd*, thought Jack when he saw the company building; *it's pretty much the same colour schemes as my coffee shop.*

Jack was enjoying his conversation with Rachel till he turned to see Madeleine standing in the doorway leaving him utterly speechless. He couldn't believe his eyes; there she was, alive in person and still wearing that same shade of blue, making her eyes even more beautiful. He wanted to jump up and take her into his arms, never, letting her out of his sight again, but he knew he had his work cut out for him.

She look even more beautiful than the last time he saw her, he did noticed she had lost some weight. The pounds that she lost, gave away to her shapely figure. And when she offered Rachel some tea, he wanted to talk with her about what happened back in Paris and saw that she didn't seem at all pleased to see him again.

Well, things are going to change Madeleine Winsor! He thought to himself.

When she left to make the tea, he asked his sister if Madeleine was one of her employees.

"Good heavens no, Jack; Madeleine is the owner of this establishment,"

"WHAT, how can that be, she is hearing impaired?" shocking Jack.

"Yes, she is hearing impaired Jack and that is where I come in, I work for Madeleine Windsor, I am her personal assistance."

"Gezzz sis, you never once mentioned your boss's name!"

"And you, dear brother have never asked and for your future information."
"I take care of all the phone calls, the ordering and I travel with her as well, basically you could say that, I am second in command chief."

Jack was stumped, "then by any chance, the last time you called me where you both in Paris back in August?" he questioned her seriously.

"Well as a matter of fact, yes we were in Paris a couple of times, why?"

"Then, why the hell didn't you tell me you were with Madeleine?"

"Because you didn't ask and if you remember correctly, you told me that you were on your way out of town with some bleached bimbo, remember!"

"And future more, I believe you were drunk the night I called you."

"I am sorry sis, but this past year has been hell, I have been busy with my coffee shop and the winery as well."

"So I am guessing that Madeleine was the woman you told me about, "the one who got away," am I correct?"

"Yeah, she is the one, dam her!"

Madeleine walked in at that moment and poured herself another cup of tea and nodded her head to him and walked out.

This set the motion with Jack as he was determined not to let her slip away from him again, *enough is enough of her games, time to play fifty questions with her and I intend to get all answers,* he thought.

Jack stood up from his chair, asked Rachel which office was Madeleine's and said that he had to take care of something and he will be back to get the keys. He then marched down hallway and found Madeleine's office and without knocking, he leaned against her opened doorframe.

He noticed her office was much bigger and brighter than Rachel's office and she was sitting at her drafting table working away. He cleared his throat; she still had not heard him or was she playing games?

In his louder serious tone of voice, "I believe an apology is order, don't you think so Madeleine?"

Madeleine looked up suddenly with a startled.

"Now, what do I have to apologize for?" returning his sarcastic demand.

"Well let's see," counting on his fingers and slowly walking towards her.

"Number one, you let me pay for dinner, taxi cabs, and coffees all in that order."

"Not my fault, you offered, remember and besides, you were only trying to impress my parents!"

"You have a point there."

"By the way Jack, I did tell my parents of your gangster activities," said Madeleine.

"I figured as much when I read the note back at the hotel."

"Rather a cold callus note I'd say," snared Jack.

"Well take it up with my father; he is the one who wrote it."

"Hey, I like the note you put in my tea cup, thank you, and for your info, I love Canada already, now that I have found you."

"And before you give me the fifth degree, I like you to hear my side why the police officers were hounding after me."

"Talk all you want, but it's not likely I'll even care!"

Jack wanted to break the thick ice that she had surrounded herself with. He thought for a moment while starring at her, *how in the hell am I going to melt this ice princess?* He decided to give it all he had and in his calmed voice.

"Madeleine, if you don't mind, I like to explain myself, as I can understand why; we got off on the wrong foot to begin with."

"Oh we did, excuse me, I didn't know 'we' were an item?"

"Oh for crying out loud, at least pretend to show some compassion, will you?" raising his voice.

This shocked Madeleine into silence as she could tell that Jack was being very serious. He pointed to one of the leather chairs, "do you mind if we sit over here and talk, I don't like the idea of yelling at you from across the room?"

Madeleine got up from her drafting table, picked up her tea cup and walked over and sat down behind her glass desk facing Jack. *This should prove to be good*, she thought.

Seeing that Madeleine was rather presumptuous of him, he knew that he had to tread waters very carefully with her or he would lose her, for good this time. He made his mind up that he was not leaving Canada without her.

And so Jack began his story; "the day you were standing out on the balcony while the police officers were chasing me."

"It was not because I had done something wrong, actually, I have not done anything that would bring my parents to shame!"

Jack made sure that Madeleine heard every word he said to her, "Let me know if I am speaking too fast or if you don't catch every word I say, will you?"

Madeleine only nodded her head to him, she was curious to hear what he had to say for himself.

"Yes Madeleine, you were right about the police chasing and taking shots at me, but not for the reasons you were thinking of."

"You see Madeleine; I wasn't telling any lies when I told your father that I was the owner of one coffee shop, a vineyard and negotiating for the second vineyard."

"I had planned on getting into growing and marketing my own brand of Champagne, the first vineyard had produced a good quality and it won the award for the best Champagne of the year."

"How admirable," she nodded to Jack.

"Thank you."

"After a long hard negotiating, I now own my second Vineyard, this one I called "Holts Vineyard 2""

"This vineyard number two has produced both red and white wines. And it is really good quality, I might add."

"You see Madeleine; I hope to someday to hand it all down to my children before I am gone."

While Jack told his story, Madeleine couldn't help but wonder where all this information was going, and what did the police have to do with all? Madeleine took this opportunity to study Jack while he told his story; she noticed that he was more handsome in the bright office lights.

His skin was an evenly tanned coloring, a little on the dark side but with his black hair he looked good. It must have been from working out in his vineyards with all that fresh and sunshine. She could smell the woodsy cologne that he was still wearing, while sipping on her tea, she didn't mean to but, she quickly glances at his hands and noticed that he wore no rings, *he is not yet married,* she thought. She listens to him with intensity, waiting for him to spill out the beans on his gangster activities and then be on his way. That did not happen!

"The policemen you saw chasing me were not the real policemen."

Now, here we go, time for truth or dare thought Madeleine.

"I know you will find it hard to believe but, they are hitmen who work for an antique collector by the name of Professor Perrier Burnet, it was his men that came after me, I was their target because I have something he wanted and I am not about to give it up anytime soon."

"Remember when I told your parents that I bought out my first Vineland?"

"Well, one day, my worker and I were digging holes to plant a special breed of grape roots when my shovel hit something hard. I dug up this big clump of hard dirt, we washed it down in the bucket of water and it turned out to be a gold medallion of some sort. It's about the size of a large apple; there was some sort of ancient markings all over it that none of us recognize."

Jack studied her face to see if there were any signs of her believing him, there were none so far.

He knew that he had to try harder, he was not going to let her get away with it till he plead his case, not after the hell he had been through of having just met and losing her both at the same time.

He continued on with his story, "my mistake was that I took the gold piece to Professor Perrier Burnet at the Paris University and after inspection, he told me that it was not real gold but fool's gold. You can imagine how disappointed I was."

"The professor even suggests that he keep it for his class to study it and I told him, thanks but I'll have to think about it."

"My instincts just told me that he was lying about it and I brought it back with me to my condo and made a few phone calls to Paris Ministry, they gave me the number and address of mineral resources."

"I took it there and sure enough, it was real gold and not the fool's gold that the Professor claims it to be."

For the first time, Madeleine spoke up, "well I certainly hope you reported him to the police!"

"Oh I did and his lawyer went to bat for him, who claims there was no real concrete proof that I even came to see him regarding any such item."

"I put in a complaint and it came up before the University's tribunal board and he lost his tenure contract for two whole years, apparently, this is the third time he has been in trouble."

"When I left the boards office, we crossed each other out in the hall, he told me not to sleep too tight, I thought that was rather harsh of him threatening my life."

"So what did you do with the medallion?"

"Don't worry, it's in a safe place for now, I don't know who to trust anymore."

"But, what about the policemen who were chasing you, what became of them?"

"Again there was no real proof, the camera on the corner of your hotel was out of commotion that day," said, Jack shrugging his shoulders.

"And I don't believe they will ever catch them."

At that moment, Madeleine's eye caught her staff passing by her office.

"My staff is coming in to work and I have a full day today, I'm meeting with a couple of new clients," hoping he clue in that it was time for him to take his leave.

On hearing her staff's voices, Jack got up and closed her office door and returned to his seat.

"Madeleine, I am aware of this tall adventure story of mine, none of it seems real but I assure you, that I am telling you the truth. Why don't I give you my lawyer's phone number if you need more proof," handing her the business card.?

"Thanks, she said, for some reason, she took his card and tossed it into the small basket that she keeps on the corner of her desk for odds and ends.

She stood up and in her small voice, "I must really get ready for my client now, if you don't mind, Jack?"

Jack stood up and offered his hand and Madeleine hesitated for that one second then she took his hand and shook it gently this time.

"Does this mean that I am forgiving?"

"It doesn't mean anything but goodbye," she politely said.

"Look Madeleine, I'm in town for a week, can we have dinner sometime, and I'd like us to start this off on the right foot this time?"

He study her face, hoping she would say, yes but instead she said,

"I have a very tight week this week."

"Well how about we meet somewhere after work for a quick drink or would you rather we go for coffee sometime this week?"

Wow, is he always this persistence with women, she wondered.

"Your sister mentioned that you are staying with her, well, when I find time, I'll text you if you will give me your cell phone number."

Jack laughed out loud, "Thank God for texting uh." Jack jumped to her offer.

"I agree with you."

"I afraid I'm not very good when it comes to answering cell phones, for some reason or other, cellphones have a lot of interferences with my hearing aid, something to do with microwaves, so I am set up with texting my family and friends."

"Speaking of family, how are your parents doing?" hoping to keep the conversation with her going.

"They are both fine, thank you for asking."

"Ok, well then, I'll leave you to your work and I'll be waiting for your text, have a good day Madeleine."

After Madeleine and Jack exchanged phone numbers and gave each other cell phone a quick test to be sure the numbers were installed and working correctly. He turned to leave her office and she called out to him, "Jack, you didn't say why you are here in the city?"

Jack felt there might be hope yet for them and responded to her question.

"Because Madeleine, I have a couple of meetings with your city's liquor board and private buyers, I'm hoping to become one of their major suppliers for my wines and Champagnes."

"You may as well know now, I plan to buy a condo apartment here in this city, after all, my only sister lives here."

Jack saw her surprised look.

"And I kind of like having my own place, now that I'll travel back and forth between countries."

Jack said his goodbye to Madeleine and went back to Rachel's office to pick up the house keys, "we will chat tonight," he told her, in his serious voice and he took his leave. Rachel walked with her brother out to the front hallway, out to the small front lobby of the building.

She couldn't help but notice noticed all the staff ladies were staring at this tall, good-looking gentleman. At the door she gave Jack a quick hug and peck on his cheek, "see you tonight Jack."

And on her way back to her office, she whispered to the gawking ladies, "retract your claws ladies, he has been spoken for," pointing to Madeleine's office door.

She heard their groans as chuckled quietly to herself.

Madeleine saw Rachel later in the afternoon while preparing a pot of tea to take back to her office and asked if she had anymore siblings that she should know about.

"Nope, Jack and I are the only two children that our parents had."

"What about cousins, nieces or nephews?" trying not to seem interested in Jack.

But, Rachel clued in decided to give her the information anyway.

"Our parents were orphans themselves, and due to a car bomb explosion in front of their grocery store, which left Jack and I orphan as well, how ironic is that?"

"How awful, what happened?"

"They were both outside in front of their store restocking up their fruits and vegetables on the stands for the day. A car that was parked out in front blew up; they didn't stand a chance in hell. According to the investigator, they think it was a terrorist bomb attack that went off."

"It happened while I was away at an English College and Jack was just in his early pre-school days at that time."

"I was there studying for Major English and taking Business courses when I got the call to come down into the dean's office, they let me take the phone call from my parent's young Butler Wilbert, on hearing the news, I passed out."

"I quite University, came back home to look after Jack, because he still needed a woman figure in his young life and wasn't old enough to care for himself. I continued with our parent's grocery chain business of two stores until Jack, finished his with all his schoolings and later struck out on his own."

"When I sold the chain, I offered Jack one-half of what rightfully belongs to him, Jack would not accept it. I applied for Canadian citizenship and was accepted."

"And when I came to Canada, I worked for a small brokerage company, which is how I met your father, he offered me this position and quite frankly, it's the best offer I have accepted."

"Well Rachel, I am glad you took this position," Madeleine told her after listening to the story.

"By the way Madeleine, I should have clued in with the same last names you both have, it's like there are many Windsor's living in Canada and yet, we are all are not related to one another, is Holts a popular name in France?"

"Now that you mentioned, it is not very popular."

"I didn't mean to listen to yours and Jack's conversation earlier, but, please let me tell you Madeleine, that Jack is telling you the truth about his misgivings."

Madeleine only smiled at Rachel, "I kind of felt he was telling the truth, but let's just see how this plays out shall we, and besides, I don't have time for a relationship," giving Rachel a quick wink.

CHAPTER 4

Madeleine was at home in her condo, curled on her sofa patting Ginger who was glad to see her master. She was enjoying the attention she was receiving. In the last two hours that she had been home, she checked her cell phone a couple of times to see if Jack left her any messages. There was a couple of text messages for her parents who were away on a Mexico retreat, *no doubt soaking up all that sun and drinking pina colada's*, she smiled.

Donna Wilson and Greg Walter married just Christmas past and Madeleine had designed her wedding gown. The wedding was a fairy tale comes true which made the local news. It was a unique wedding with all the Christmas trimmings; they even had a ten-foot-tall Christmas tree decorated with small token gifts for each of their guest. Each guest had to collect them from Santa to take home with them!

Before Donna married, as promised, she sold half of the condo to Madeleine at market value. Since Ginger had taking more liking towards Madeleine, she decided to keep the cat as Donna would be traveling more so than ever. Again she looked at her cell one last time before turning in for the night. There was a text message from Jack.

Madeleine,
Thanks for letting me tell you my side of the story and I hope that we can have dinner together some time soon. I like to tell you more about my vineyard. Sleep tight.
Jack

Madeleine decided not to respond back; instead she plugged her cell phone into the charger and turned out her bedroom lamp, took out her hearing aid placing it in a small container and went off into a deep sleep.

Suddenly, she jumped wide awake with a sudden startle and pounding heart; she had dreamt that she was in some kind of tunnel with the police officers chasing behind her.

Oh just a crazy dream, no doubt it was about Paris and Jack, then whispered to Ginger who was lazily staring back at her from the foot of her bed.

She glances at her alarm clock, 5:30 a.m. it was time for her to get ready for work, another full day with clients and wedding gowns fittings.

After Donna's wedding, Madeleine had contacted the hearing society to see what she could buy to help wake her at the designed time just in case she should sleep through, missing early appointments.

The society came to her condo and did a demonstration on a couple of things she could try, one of them, was a vibrating pad. Plugging it into a specially designed alarm clock to be placed under her pillow; when the specific time on the alarm clock sounded, the pad would gently shake, waking the sleeper up instantly.

The other item was the strobe lighting to be replaced her bedroom ceiling light. At the alarm set time, the strobe lights would flash a bright red light penetrating her eyelids. She worried what harm it might do to Ginger.

She had chosen the first option, the vibrating pad which worked very well for her. It even came with backup batteries for the sudden power failures. The best thing about this one, she could take it with her while traveling. Most of the time her internal clock woke her out of a sound sleep.

The only problem she ran into was, Ginger. Every now and then, if Ginger slept too close to Madeleine's pillow, with the vibrating she would quickly jump up off the bed and run out of the bedroom.

Next, she purchases from the society a new telephone system that came with a louder voice volume control dial and it also rang at a higher pitch tone. She could hear the phone ringing from any room she might be in. It was usually Donna or her mother that often called her just to chit chat, their voice was much easier to hear clearly than her father's whose voice was deeper. If she didn't recognize the number on the call display, she didn't bother to answer it, *no doubt spam callers.*

Business and things had been going really well for Madeleine until Jack came back into her life! *Dam him again*, she thought.

Morning came and Madeleine still did not answer Jack's last night's text, she decided to ignore him for the time being. Wanting some time to think things thoroughly, *after all he is born an Irishman raised in France and there was no way in hell that she would leave her beloved country, Canada.*

And she thought of calling his lawyer to confirm his story but felt that it was a waste of time now that Rachel confirmed the truth.

It was a long dragged-out day and she was glad when her day had ended, the staff and Rachel had already left for home. It was just after seven-thirty p.m. when Jack knocked on her opened office door, he was standing there holding a plastic shopping bag and a flat carton sporting two large coffee cups.

"I don't know about you, but I am starving! I hope you like Chinese food," holding up the bag for her to see while walking over and setting everything down on her desk. He sat himself down on the leather chair opposite her.

"I thought to myself, it's not likely that I would be hearing back from you, and I sure as hell don't plan on leaving Canada without spending some time, getting to know you," he told her in his no-nonsense voice.

"How in the hell did you get in?" she question this brazen man.

"I mean Rachel was the last one out and she always locks the door behind her."

"Uhmm, she did and I asked if she would leave the door unlocked for me."

"Oh really, pray, tell me how did you know what time she was leaving, Rachel leaves here at various times?"

"Because, I asked her to call me twenty minutes before she was leaving, so I could get us some dinner, seeing how I have not heard back from you at all!"

"Now, where are your plates and napkins?"

"In the back kitchenette, at the end of the hallway" she told him drily.

"And by the way Jack, how do you know if I like Chinese foods or not?"

Jack smiled back at her, "because, I called and asked Rachael and she told me where you lovely ladies do your ordering, then I called ahead to have it ready for pick up, and here I am."

Madeleine had to admit that she too was starving, and the Chinese food smelts really appealing to her. She hasn't had any Chinese food in a long time.

By the time she got home from work late at night; it was easier to toss in a frozen dinner tray into her microwave.

Since Donna had moved out, Madeleine was beginning to get tired of eating alone every night; she was thankful for Ginger's company, but Ginger could not talk.

Jack was back from the kitchenette with the paper plates, napkins the cutlery.

He noticed that Madeleine had cleared the papers off her desk, making room for their food. *An improvement, he smiled.*

Together they dished out the foods and began eating with small talk of the difference between Canada's and Parisians taxes and their weather patterns. He asked her questions about her business and who her major suppliers were and about the type of clientele she handles. He was keen on getting to know her now that they have linked up. He told her stories of his vineyards and the pros and cons of how he kept his ship running smoothly. They even talked about each of their employees and how they deal with problems and the public in general.

After they cleared away the food she suggested that she give him a grand tour of her shop and he greedily accept the offer. He followed her as she explained all the working of the City of Lights, "and how did you come across this company's name," he asked her.

"Oh that was easy, it was in Paris when my parents told me that they had bought out my place of work from my old boss "Hugo.""

"Ahh, the City of Lights, yes, I can see why you gave it that name, after all, Paris is the city of thousands of lights because she never sleeps!"

At that moment while she turned the corner of one of the many sewing machine desks, the electrical cord that was still plugged in had caught her foot sending her tripping. Jack, with his quick reflexes shot out his arm, grabbed a hold of her arm, drawing her closer to his chest.

They looked deeply into each other's eyes and Jack had wanted to kiss her from the first moment he had laid eyes on this beautiful woman. Now he had his chance, he leaned forwards and let his lips brushed hers, testing the waters to see if she would respond back to him.

As much as he wanted to kiss her hard and long to show her what he felt for her. At that moment he heard her give a quick little gasp and Thanked God that he didn't give her one of his full forced kisses.

All his instinct told him she was not like the other women that he was used to kissing; she didn't melt into his arms even though she fitted into them perfectly. He slowly retracted back from her clumsy fall.

Madeleine was suddenly forced up against Jacks firm chest, felt his lips brushed against hers, leaving her feeling a little different. She felt sudden warm flashing rising to her chest after she got whiffed of his woodsy aftershave cologne and without thinking; she pushed herself gently away from Jack.

"Thank you," she said breathlessly.

She continued to talk about the different machinery while walking at a slower pace, trying to regroup herself. She did notice that Jack was walking even more closely behind her and a serious look on about him, his eyes looked hooded. He reminded her of an animal on the prowl.

When they got to the material department, Jack took ahold of Madeleine's shoulders and slowly turned her around to face him. He could see and feel her shyness.

In his low husky voice, "Maddie darling, you have no idea how hurt I was when you left Paris, I have never felt this way about any-one before, you've done something to me, I nearly went out of my mind, I even tried to locate you but, the dam hotel clerks wouldn't give me no information on your address."

I even called your Canadian operator and learned there are thou-sands of Windsor's families."

"How did you know my nick name was Maddie, only my friends call me by that name?"

"Because my silly girl, you drove me mad when you left Paris, hence came the name, Maddie, it suited you."

They stared into each other's eyes for a few seconds more, again, Jack leaned down to kiss her, only gently this time with a little more pressure.

Her lips felt warm and he could taste the coffee she finished off earlier.

He broke away from the kiss, again looking deeply into her eyes trying to read her.

She looked puzzled and breathless almost wanting more, he couldn't be sure which.

"Will you have a proper dinner date with me tomorrow night, Maddie?"

A little confused, she pulled away to recollected herself, "I'm afraid I must decline," in an almost whisper, while at the same time trying to catch her breath.

"And may I ask why, you must decline?" in his low husky voice.

"Because I am picking up my parents at the airport and drive back to their house after we have dinner out."

"Then please let me come with you," not wanting to let her out of his sights again.

"Thanks, but I think it's best that I go alone."

"Well, at least let me meet you and your parents somewhere for dinner, my treat again this time."

Madeleine couldn't help but chuckle, "oh, you are a glutton for punishment, Jackie?" giving him a nickname too.

"Now hold on a minute here, let's get something straight, I have always hated that name 'Jackie' please do not call me by that childish name," he said, snapping suddenly out of the mood. She noticed how quickly he had turned cool towards her when she called him 'Jackie' and wondered why it bothered him so. She made a mental note to ask Rachel later about it sometime.

She wanted some time alone with her parents to tell them all about Jack, and then take it from there.

Madeleine felt trapped, she was not used to this new dating thing and wasn't sure how to handle the situation.

"Tell you what; let me have time with them tomorrow night and I promise you, I will go out to dinner with you on the next night."

Jack thought about what she had said and agreed to her terms.

"All right, we will do dinner the next night, now darling, are you ready to go home or do you have more work to do?"

"No I don't, I am tried and think I'll head on home." *Did he just call me darling?* She quietly thought to herself.

Jack helped Madeleine close up shop for the night and walked with her over to her car. Before she got in, she turned to face him, stood up on her tippy toes and gave him a light kiss on his lips, surprising him, "good night Jack and thanks for the dinner, if truth be told, I was famished" she whispered.

"I'll be looking forwards to your texts," he told her, brushing away a strand of hair from her face.

He stood back and watched her drive away, and then he got into his rented car and drove back to Rachel's house.

Rachel was still up waiting for him when he came in.
"Was your surprised dinner date ok, did you tell Madeleine the truth about the medallion?"

Jack flopped down the high wing chair beside her, "yes I brought the dinner to her office and I convinced her to eat with me and to tell you the truth, she sure can eat for a skinny girl like her," he chuckled.

"She doesn't trust men very much, does she, sis?"

"Don't know about trust, I think it's more that she never had the time or found anyone who will understand her hearing impairment."

"In any case, I believe she has mellowed a bit towards me, I'll know more the day after tomorrow, we are going out on our first real date, finally!" throwing his hands up in the air.

"What is wrong with tomorrow night?"

"Because, my dear sister, after she collects her folks from the airport, they are having dinner out somewhere, later she is driving them home by then hopefully she will have to mention me."
"Oh that is right, she did mention the other day that her parents are coming back from Mexico, but, Jack, you are going back home is a couple of days."

"I know, I know, I have been thinking of staying on for another week if you can handle my being here?"

"Of course my silly brother, you are welcome to stay for as long you behave yourself!"

"Well then, in the morning I will make a few phone calls to the guys at the vineyards and at the coffee house, letting them know of the plan."

"And by the way, Rachel, are there any condos for sale around these parts?"

"There are always condos going up in this city, I'll put you in touch with a good sales agent," smiling at him, it was good to see Jack come alive again.

They chatted for a while longer and he asked her more questions about Madeleine.

Madeleine had fed Ginger, changed the litter box, made herself some tea and went to the living room window and looked out over the city lights while she thought about Jack and his kisses.

His story of the gold medallion ran through her mind. *It must have been awful for him to deal with it and running a couple of businesses at the same time, but was he being honest with her?* While thinking to herself.

Before Madeleine turn all the lights off and went into her bedroom and she glanced at her cell phone and decided to leave a message for Jack.

Jack,
Thanks again for the surprise dinner that you brought for us; it was great, looking forwards to our real dinner date. Maddie

She then plugged the phone into its charger and prepares herself for bed. She tossed and turned, sleep would not come to her. She got up and went into the kitchen and made herself some warm milk, add a little honey.

Watching the city lights below, Madeleine wonder what Jack was doing at that moment, *was he sleeping or was he reading.* And she thought about everything that Jack told her, she thought it most preposterous tale that she has ever heard of in her entire life, then again, she has heard stories of other people's adventures. She would have never dreamt that she herself one day would one day come even close to an adventure of her own.

Before she climbed into the bed, she checked her cell phone one more time only to see a message from Jack.

Maddie,
I'm glad we talked, and yes dinner was great, I like to meet your folks and by the way, I plan to stay in Lansing for another week, Rachel says it's ok. Sleep tight till the day after.
Jack.

Madeleine's heart gave away to pounding while she read Jack's text over again, *he is staying another week,* and she suddenly felt flushed on remembering his gentle kiss. She put her fingers to her lips and gently brushes along the bottom lip, feeling Jacks lip sent a warm tingling sensation over her once more. She knew that she was inexperienced and that Jack was far more experienced than she was. In Paris she had seen the ladies all turning their heads to him at the Opera house and at the dinner club as well. Madeleine finally fell into a deep slumber sleep at last.

The next day Madeleine left her office a bit earlier than normal, she wanted to beat the rush hour. Right on time she met her parents at the airport; they had collected their luggage and now having a private dinner at her parent's favorite restaurant. She barely listened to their tales of Mexico, they both sounded like a couple of lovebirds in love all over again! In some small way she envies them.

And in between the details of their Mexican dinners, she tried to think of a way to tell them about Jack. After all, back in Paris she had crucified him, turning her parents against him. Now she had to untie and repair the damage she had done or does she really want too?

Do I really want a relationship with Jack or not, is there room in my hectic life right now, she mused to herself. She decided to let it all play out and bravely took the first step.

"Mom and dad, there is something you need to know, Jack Holt is back in town."

"What, why, what the hell is he doing over here in these parts, did he get kicked out of France already?' perked up Fred.

And Courtney looked at her daughter wide-eyed, "Oh really?"

Madeleine groaned quietly and realized *this is going to take some work to unravel it all, he better be worth it, here goes or nothing!*

"Dad, it was all a misunderstanding, it wasn't the police who were chasing him it was a Professor Perrier Burnet from the Paris University School who had his hitmen go after Jack. You see, they were ordered to bring him in," not sure if her parents believed her or not. *Oh my God is my daughter that gullible* thought Courtney who was listening to her.

Madeline could see where this was going and decided to start from the very beginning.

She told them about the gold medallion that Jack had found while digging in his vineyard and how Professor Perrier Burnet had lied about it not being real gold. How he wanted to keep it for himself, "I quote for his student training" and how Jack had taking medallion to be verified with the mineral ministry department.

"So, Jack found out the medallion was real gold after all, and where is it now, did he cash it in?"

"No, he didn't cash in the gold and no he didn't tell me where he is keeping it at the moment, just said that it was in a safe place for now."

"And what are his plans for it?"

"He didn't say." shrugging her shoulders.

"Well, I did like Jack and I knew he was a smart man." smiled Fred.

"And not to mention, handsome too," smiled Courtney

Madeleine's face suddenly turned red at the last remark.

Both Fred and Courtney looked at each other and smiled, *it this going somewhere*, sending ESP signals.

Madeleine told them the details of how he came to her office, and that he had invited her out for dinner. Unsure how they would react now they heard the truth, she decided to take the chances.

"Also, Jack would like to take us out for dinner before he returns back home to Paris." She almost hoped they would say, no.

"Well in one sense of way, I think we do owe him an apology for our shameful behavior, ok, so when and where would he like to have dinner with us?"

"Tomorrow evening if possible, that is, if you both are free," Again, hoping they would say no.

"I'll send you a text once I get the full details and by the way dad, he did buy his second vineyard."

"Huh, so he is moving up the corporate ladder," said Fred by now whose wheels were beginning to spin, once again.

Madeleine had driven her parents back home, said her good nights and went on home herself. As tired as she was, she checked her cell phone to see another message from Jack.

Maddie,

Hope your parents arrived safe and sound and trusting your dinner was to your satisfaction. Have they agreed to dinner together tomorrow night?
Jack

She decided to respond back this one time.

Jack,
Yes, my parents arrived safely and thank you for asking, and yes our dinner was likable. My parents agree to the dinner plans tomorrow night, just name the time and place; by the way, we will meet you there. Good night, Maddie

She was in her PJ's when she picked up her cell phone, another message from Jack.

Maddie,
Remember I'm new in town, you name the time and place, agreeable to meeting you there. I do believe my rented car is equipped with GPS.
Jack.

Thank God for cell phones, thought Madeleine, without it she may not have been as independent as she is now. She immediately responded back to him.

Jack,
My parents have always enjoyed going to the Starlight Restaurant, they serve the best lobster and steak in town and it's down on the harbor front, fallow the signs, meet you there say, seven-thirty?
Maddie.

She waited for a few seconds and saw the flag showing up on the corner of her cell phone.

Maddie,
See you there, do me a favor, and wear blue. Until tomorrow night,
Yours, Jack.

Madeleine couldn't believe her eyes when she saw that already Jack was telling her what to wear and 'YOURS' *I don't think so!* She quickly sent him a text.

Jack,
Sorry, but I wear what I like to wear, and goodnight!
Maddie.

Next, she sent her father a quick text telling him the place and time of their dinner arrangements, then turning off her cell phone for the night. Picking up the brush, she began to softly brush Ginger's coat while she was purring away and listened to her master complaining.

"Don't know about you Ginger girl, but I can't see myself with him, I mean, he is a bit bossy and I have to admit he is good looking, another thing, he isn't afraid of hard work. Umm, both mom and dad seem to like him, and he seems to understand hearing impairment and that, dear Ginger is a bonus for me!"

And she quickly rubbing the top of Ginger's head, "what do you say girl, should I take the chances with him?"

The next morning, Madeleine put in a full day's work, as much as she tried not to think of Jack, he kept popping into her thoughts especially when she walked by the same sewing machine where she had tripped. Where Jack caught her, she blushed at the thought of Jack's lips touching hers.

Rachel happened to be near Madeleine and she noticed her distraction, she asked "Is everything alright?"

"Uhmm, why yes, I was just thinking of the next summer's clothing line," she clucked.

"We do have the appointment date for the textile company, they want to show us the new materials they are bringing in from India."

"Oh right, did you book us a flight to Paris and made the hotel arrangements?"

"It's all set, we leaving on April the fifteenth, I knew you enjoy seeing Paris in the springtime, not quite so busy as it is in the summer, right?"

"You are so right Rachel and thanks."

Earlier back at home, Rachel had told Jack of their plans to be in Paris on the fifteenth of April. He was ecstatic and mentally began making plans for her and asked,

"How many days she booked for and is she coming alone or are her parents tagging along too?"

Hoping they were not, he wanted Madeleine to himself this time. Rachel detected his disproval of Madeleine's parent tagging.

"Don't worry bother, I booked two extra days at the hotel, which should give you enough time to show her around Paris and no, her parents and not coming along this time, but I am."

"After all, someone has to keep you in line and make sure you treat her with the proper respect!"

"Rachel dear, do I look like an animal deflowering all young virgins to you, grrrrrr?"

She laughed out loud after reading his words, "I know all about you and your ladies!"

"Now tell me dear sister, what would you know anything about me?"

"You be surprised, brother."

Then a thought struck him, "Have you been keeping in touch with Wilbert," he questioned her.

"Now and then, I did, he kept me informed on your colorful ladies and you're where- bouts, after all, someone needed to keep tabs on you."

Suddenly feeling embarrassed that his only sister caught him in the act of being a playboy.

"Remind me to have a private chat with that butler of mine uh?"

"And by the way, cancel the hotel, you two are staying with me, and I won't take no for an answer!"

Rachel took the opportunity to ask her brother just what his intentions were with Madeleine, after all, she did promise Fred and Courtney that she would watch out for their hearing impairment daughter and she knew Jack was in fact, no saint.

"I am head overheal with her, sis and I would never hurt her, if she will have me, I plan to someday make her my wife!"

"Whoa, brother, that is coming on a little strong, don't you think, I mean, I knew you had a thing or two for her, but not to this extreme? Besides, I am having a hard time pantomime you being married!"

"Sis, from the first moment I laid eyes on her, I knew immediately she was the one I wanted in my life and I will make it my personal mission to have her!"

"Wow, such confidence, well, in that case, take it slow with her; after all, I do want to keep my job here!"

"Have you ever thought of opening your own business sis, I'm mean I can set you up with one, hell I have the money to do it, especially after the way you looked out for me?"

"Thanks, Jack, but at my age, it would be too much."

"If you change your mind let me know, I'm here for you and if you come back to France, I have a perfect position for you!"

"Really, and what position would that be jack?"

"How about you look after your nieces and nephews while Maddie and I travel around the world?"

"Dream on brother, dream on! Hey, you better get a move on or you are going to be late for your first date!"

Jack said goodbye to Rachel, got into his rental car, turned on his GPS and made his way down to the harbor front, he did as Madeleine had instructed him, but wanted to see if the Canadian GPS was any different than the French one was. He found the Starlight Restaurant and was surprised to see that Madeleine and her parents were already there waiting for him.

"Good evening folks, sorry I got held up in the traffic jam," after he was escorted to their table.

After the acknowledgements around the table, Jack check out Starlight's wine menu and suggested one of the newer wines, one that he has never heard of before.

Looking over at Madeleine and smiled, he saw that she was wearing a black lace evening cocktail dress; it was a cut a bit low to the front with the three-quart sleeves. It suited her perfectly, especially with her dark hair swept upwards. And noticed that, unlike other women, wore very little makeup, *heck she was beautiful, she didn't need to wear makeup anyway.*

Fred and Courtney apologized for their sudden cancelations on the picnic lunch, all was forgiving and placed in their steak and lobster orders, Fred had asked Jack about his treasure findings that Madeleine mentioned. Jack then told the story of coming into the gold medallion and he told them about his vineyards and contracts that he picked up while here in Lansing.

Madeleine paid attention to the details just in case Jack slipped up, he didn't. *Maybe he really is telling the truth,* she thought.

"Did the mineral company give you a proper quote on what the gold medallion was worth today?"

"Yes, they did Fred, according to them in terms of Canadian dollars, the gold alone is worth a lot more than a million dollars, but, get this, to ancient archeology history dealer, with the markings, it could be worth four or six million."

"First, it would have to be carbon tested to see just how old the medallion really was and what the language it's written in, so far the language is unrecognizable."

"Wow, I do hope you are keeping it in a safekeeping place." He told Jack.

In his almost whisper, "in case you need it in a more secured place, at our bank, we have a good lockdown system. Its alarm system goes directly into our city's main police headquarters, should it get set off."

"Thanks, Fred; I do have it in a safe place."

During the entire meal, Jack had a hard time keeping his eyes off Madeleine who, most of the time, was talking back and forth with her mother while he talked vineyard business with her father. Fred could see that Jack was very interested in his daughter and for that he was happy. After their dinner bill was taking care of by Jack, Fred and Courtney said their goodbyes, they left to go home in their own car, and once out of sight, Jack suggested to Madeleine, they walk along the docks to work off their heavy meal. To his surprise, she instantly agreed.

They walked for twenty minutes and she felt a sudden chill in the air and shuddered. Jack put his arm around her back waist, bringing her closer to him.

Madeleine looked up into his hazel eyes and recognized that hooded look once again. Jack leaned down to her face, with one finger he tilted her chin up, facing him and whispering

"Maddie darling, I've missed being with you like crazy, it's women like you that drive us men mad," gently placed his lips on hers. She responded back to his kiss. She felt comfortable and secure being alone with him.

Together they walked along the docks taking in the sights and sounds of Lansing, and then out of the blue, Madeleine asked him how often he would be coming back to Lansing.

Jack told her about buying a three-bedroom condo; he would have his own place when in the city dealing with his wine sales.

"And besides Madeleine, you are giving me a very good reason to come here more often." He chuckled.

"Oh, I thought Rachel was a good enough reason?" teasing him, once more allowing him to kiss her.

Together they walked arm in arm, "Maddie, mind if I ask you a question, how did you lose your hearing," not sure if he should touch on this subject and not sure how she would react.

"No, I don't mind, as a child I had far too many ear infections and it caused severe nerve damage."

"Is there an operation of some sort that can make you hear again?"

"No Jack, my parents have taken me to the hearing specialists and they all said the same thing, nothing they can do, the damage is permanent."

Jack felt her disappointment, "who knows, maybe one day they will come up with a new surgery."

"I did notice you only wear one hearing aid in the one ear, what about the other ear, can you hear out of that one?"

"I have ninety percent hearing loss in my left ear and eight-five percent loss in my right, which is where I wear the hearing aid. It gives me almost one hundred percent clear hearing but, there are still certain things I don't hear very clearly, like men's deep voices and radios. I pick up the higher frequencies and not the lower frequencies whereas some hearing-impaired people might pick up the opposite to my condition."

Looking at Madeleine and whistled, "That is a major hearing loss, and I'm surprised at how well you do."

"I take it you know all about hearing impairments."

"I do Maddie, my father was mildly hearing impaired himself. Something must have happened when he was younger, thanks to my mother, when they both married they ran a small grocery store in Ireland. I was a toddler when they packed us all up moving to France, again opening another grocery store, later on, with the extra income, they opened a couple more stores."

Madeleine was surprised that Jack was beginning to open up with his life story.

"So you were not born in France." She questioned him with interest.

"No Maddie, we were not, my family is originally from Tipperary, Ireland. You see, they both were orphans themselves, they practically grew up together in the same home for the orphans, which, back then were run by the Catholic nuns."

How sad that he did not know of his grandparents she thought to herself.

"Yes, Rachel did tell me about the bomb that killed both your parents and about her having to leave University to come back home to look out for you."

"That's right Maddie, she did come back, dealt with the insurance companies and rebuilt the storefront. She basically gave up her own life and career and for that, I am in debt to her."
"And personally, that is one of the reasons why I like to own a condo here in Lansing; I would like to spend some quality time with Rachel."

Jack then took advantage of this opportunity, "if it's ok with you, I would like to spend some time and get to know you better, if you will let me, Maddie!"

After hearing about Jack's life and known that is not a real true Frenchman, but an Irishman making her feels relieved. She was beginning to feel even more comfortable with him.

Without hesitation, "I would like to get to know you and yes, spend some time with you too, Jack."

"Really Maddie why, this is the best news I've heard all week."

Surprising her, he suddenly picked her up off the ground, and swung her around in circles, setting her down gently while he kissed her hard on her lips.

When Madeleine finally caught her breath, "hey wait a minute here, I thought your wine contracts were the best news all week," she chuckled at him.

"Hey, I can pick up contracts anywhere around the world, but I can't get a beautiful woman like you, you are a rare flower, my lovely Maddie," teasing her.

Together they walked arm in arm back to their parked cars, said their good nights. He made her promise that she would send him a quick text message to let him know she has indeed, arrived safely home. And so she did.

The final week that Jack spent in Lansing was hectic, with the signing of the condo deal and with furnishing buying. It was a good thing that he had the key that Saturday morning.

Madeleine asked Hugo if he would mind taking her place for the week so she could help Jack get settled, he gracefully accepted, claiming he was tired of retirement life and was pining for some excitement. She gave him all the instructions, as did Rachel, *"have fun and don't bankrupt City of Lights"* she teased him.

The furniture arrived on Monday as promised; Rachel and Madeleine kept busy with unboxing and washing up all his kitchen wares, beddings and towels and putting them all away.

Both women brought in enough groceries to get Jack through for a couple more days, and Jack went to the liquor store buying up his favorites his liquors and stocks his cabinet so he could offer his guest drinks.

He was glad that Rachel and Madeleine got along well. The atmosphere was cheery full of energy. Fred and Courtney invited all three back to their condo for dinners, "to give them a break," as Courtney put it. She wanted to get to know more about this Jack, now, that her daughter was interested in seeing him, as did Fred.

That final day at the airport, he surprised both Rachel and Madeleine each with a set of keys to his condo, "just so either of you can check in on it once in a while."

He hugged and kissed Rachel goodbye, and whispered into her ear, "look after Maddie for me Rach, I love her."

Then he turned to face Madeleine, taking her in his arms, not wanting to let her go, "I'll be back soon and if and when you do come into Paris, I want to show you around, ok."

"Jack, we'll keep in touch every day through texting!"

He looked into her eyes, *God, I miss her already* and he gave her a long and passionate kiss, hoping she would never forget him.

Tears came to her eyes as she watched him walk away from her. She stayed till she spotted him on the out on the tamarack, when she saw that he spotted them, she wave franticly to him. He blew her a kiss and she laughed out loud, remembering that day in Paris while out on the hotel's front balcony, her wild dashing Frenchman was once again flirting with her, only now, is wild an Irishman instead.

Rachel finally understood that her brother was truly in love with Madeleine and she will now keep her promise watch out for her, after all, someday, she will be her new sister-in-law!

Once Jack settled himself on the plane; he checked his cell phone for messages and saw a message from Madeleine.

Jack my love,
I miss you already! LUV...Maddie.

And Jack didn't hesitate and replied,

My dear Madeleine,
I'm glad things worked out they did, thanks again for all the help you've been, will you keep an eye out for Rachel, she is the only one I have besides you. I miss too you, I'll see you in April, there are so many places in Paris that I want to take you too. Love you too.
Yours Jack.

Madeleine read and re-read his message and this time, she was happy than she has been for years, for she has found someone she was in love with.

CHAPTER 5

Wilbert was relieved to see Jack back home; things had been kind of quiet and boring since he left to go to Canada. Once his master settled in, Wilbert gave Jack all his mail and phone messages, mostly messages from women that Jack had dated, all missing their playboy toy.

Jack told Wilbert to toss them into the garbage and do not accept any more messages or phone calls from women other than, Rachel and Madeleine Windsor.

"Sir, are you telling me that you finally found Miss Madeleine?" raising his eyebrows to Jack.

"That my dear man, I did find her by accident and she is coming here in April. I like to have a couple of guest rooms' ready for Rachel and Maddie, but not for long for I intend to marry her... and please make sure to include a daily vase of fresh flowers for both ladies, I don't care if you have to order them every day!"

Jack turned to go into his office to make some phone calls leaving his butler standing in the middle of the hallway with his mouth opened.

Over the course of months, **City of Lights** became so successful that Madeleine decided to buy a larger building that had plenty of parking spaces for her all employees. She was now an employer with fifty-five some odd employees and she needed the extra space. The building itself was only two years new and the previous business occupants went bankrupt. The new building was just four blocks over from her small old building.

The exterior outside of the newer building was painted with all the same coloring scheme of 'City of Lights' lettering, gold with black backgrounds.

Once the word had gotten out on Madeleine's talent, small shop owners were coming from different parts of Canada to place in their orders for their store's own clienteles.

Hugo was asked if he likes to come back to work full time, according to his own hours, he eagerly accepted his title position of head foreman along with his own well lite up office. The company hired both male and female Jr. designers and seamstresses; the atmosphere came alive and business was bustling.

The City of Lights reputation was well known for its high fashions, placing Lansing on the map. Rachel, who's titled, was now, director/head assistance and her new office was much bigger with more expensively decorated more to her style, and she treated Madeleine like a sister she that never had, as did Madeleine too. Her office was twice the size of her previous one, only, a little classier. She had pictures of the Eifel Towers as well as supermodels from both France and Italy hanging up on the walls of her office. Her major suppliers were located in Paris and Italy.

The last couple of months have been hard on everyone especially with the moving and transferring of some of their equipment and materials. The setting up consisted of more modernized sewing-computerized equipment and it took time to train her staff how to use it.

Madeleine, with missing Jack, wasn't sure at first if the relationships long-distance route was what she really wanted. She kept in daily touch with Jack who kept her up to date with all his activities as much as she too kept him updated on her business. He even asked how Rachel was doing, *brotherly love* she would smile.

Once the women on Jack's dating scene had gotten wind that he was no longer available forcing things to quiet down for him. Jack kept himself busy with his coffee/chocolate shop, along with both vineyards; his employees all enjoyed working as Jack showed them respect - equally. He didn't beat about the bushes when it came too late-night calls on the damaged vines or if one of the winery stills sprung a leak, he was always beside them, working till the problems were all solved.

April the fifteenth quickly came around and both ladies were on their early-afternoon flight to Paris. Madeline had texted Jack to let them know their airport arrival time. She was excited and could hardly wait to see Jack again.

Rachel told Madeleine about their new arrangements of staying with Jack instead of the hotel, at first she was a bit upset and got over it quickly when she spotted Jack at the gates waving franticly to her. Jack met and gave both ladies a large bouquet of mixed wildflowers all hand cut from his property gardens. He gave Rachel a bear hug and peck on her cheeks, then he took Madeleine into his arms, looked into her eyes, he could see that she missed him and gave her a long tenderly kiss that he so carefully, planned and dreamed of.

With the ladies in each of his arms, they collected their luggage and walk them out to his waiting Mercedes Benz car. Madeleine sat in the front with Rachel sitting behind Jack. All three were chatting about everything that happened in the last few months till suddenly, a car came up to the driver-side of Jack's car. The unknown car was trying to force him off the road. Jack quickly glanced out of car his window; he didn't recognize the other driver. He hung onto his steering wheel with both hands as hard as he could, he turned his car sharply towards the other car; he pushed harder on the gas pedal and quickly sped past the strangers car causing the other car to run amok upwards a small hillside forcing it to miss hitting a large standing rock. The car suddenly revered and was back on the road catching up to Jack's car leaving behind a trail of dust.

Jack didn't look at or hear the ladies screaming, begging him to slow down. The noise from both car engines roaring against each other was deafening.

The other car quickly caught up behind Jack's car, bumping hard against his trunk's end, forcing Jack, again to speed up. Just up ahead, Jack made a sudden wide sharp left turn, just narrowly missing the guard rails on the right side of edge a steep cliff.

Madeleine could hear the car tires screeching and hung tighter to the door handles with both eyes tightly closed. *Dear God, don't tell me Jack has a death wish too,* was all she could think of.

The other driver was once again gaining on Jack, as he made the sharp turn; his car suddenly gave way hitting the guard rails, sending the driver barreling down the cliffs side. On impact, the car suddenly exploded sending smoke and fireball up into the air.

When Jack saw the fireball exploding through his rearview mirror, he pulled over and all three got out of Jack's car and ran back to the broken guard rail. He told Rachel to contact the police while he made his way down the hillside. He had hoped to see the man alive; he had fifty questions for him. Madelaine stood in shock.

As he scrambled down to the bottom, the car was engulfed in flames and the heat kept him back from trying to find the car's driver. Too late, *he probably incinerated with the explosion*, thought Jack. And he turned away from the hot and searing flames to make his way back up the rough hillside. He suddenly stopped when he heard groaning; he quickly scanned around the grounds and spotted the driver curled up into a fetal position by a trunk of an old tree. Running over and knelt down on one knee shouting at him, "who the hell are you, why were you trying to force me off the road, answer me, dam it."

The man gave a low groan, in a barely audible broken English voice, "he wants your gold medallion," pointing his finger at Jack and suddenly dropping his arm down by his side, lifeless.

"Who wants my medallion, dam it, tell me, who wants it?"

Then Jack heard the drivers last breath suddenly faded out. Jack checked for his pulse just under the man's jawline. No pulse, the man was dead. *Shit*, thought Jack.

By the time Jack reached the top, police cruisers, fire trucks and ambulances all had arrived. Some of the men were already making their way down, Jack pointed to where the body was lying.

"He didn't make it."

One of the officers, who reached Jack first, asked him, his French-language if there are any more people to search for and Jack shook his head, 'no, there was only one driver in the car!'

Once he made sure that both his sister and Madeleine who was still shaking were not hurt, he gave the police officer his statement of the car chase and being forced off the road, leaving out the details on the gold medallion. Jack had an idea who it was that wanted his medallion but, where to find Professor Perrier Burnet who lost his University tenure, was another question. He planned to contact his lawyer and have Professor located and then pay him a nice little visit, after all, he put both his loved one's lives in jeopardy today.

Jack took Madeleine and Rachel to his country home estate. They made their way through the massive iron gates, driving down the long narrow driveway and Madeleine was expecting to see an old farmhouse and was shocked at the sight of the castle.

Rachel gasped out loud, "Why Jack, you didn't' tell me that you bought a castle, you always referred it to your country home," she chuckled.

Jack laughed, "Ladies, I hope you brought along your fishing rods, there is a small stocked lake just around the corner!"

Wilbert was standing outside the massive double oat doors waiting for their arrival and immediately noticed the marks on Jack's car.

Getting out of the car, Rachel walked up the front steps and gave Wilbert a gentle hug, "been a long time old friend and it is sooo good to see you again, has my brother been getting into any kind of trouble lately?"

"It is good to see you too and no Rachel, he has been a perfect model citizen."

"Good, I'll need a grand tour of this palace!" She told Wilbert while her eyes were looking all around.

"Wilbert, I like you to meet, Madeleine Windsor from Canada, they both will be staying with us for a time."

Madeleine extended out her hand to him while looking at lips, unsure if she would be able to hear or understand every word he would say to her but, she planned to concentrate on hearing him.

He carefully shook her hand, "Welcome to Holt's Castle," politely, in his slow and even tone of voice and she heard every word.

Jack is correct in his description of Madeleine, thought Wilbert. He could see why Jack fell in love with her so quickly.

On hearing the name of her brother's castle, "why, what was the name of this castle before?"

"Ok, let's get these ladies inside and settled, no doubt they are starving and while we eat, we will answer their fifty trillion questions and tell them everything they want to know about the castle, shall we!" Glancing to Wilbert.

Madeleine agreed with Jack, she was famished and tired from all the flying and the driving scare they had earlier.

While Wilbert took Rachel's luggage and showed her to her room, Jack took Madeleine to her room. Once inside her room he set down her luggage just inside the doorway and took Madeleine by her hand, 'are you alright my dear?'

Madeleine nodded her head that she was.

'Then come, I want to show you something,' taking her hand and walking her over to the double glass French doors.

'You have the best guest room in the entire castle; now tell me what you think of this view darling,' he opened both the French glass doors exposing the lakefront.

Madeleine stepped out onto the balcony and saw the lake, in her small voice, "why Jack, this is stunning, this is even better than my lakefront condo!"

Jack turned her around to face him, with both his arms around her small waist and whispered softly, "Maddie, I have missed you so much," he carefully kissed her, very tenderly; Madeleine once again, returned his long waited kisses, for she too had missed him.

Together they stepped back into her bedroom, she notices that her bed was a king-size and with many plump pillows; she looked into Jack's eyes with a slight frown and questions of her own. And Jack could see that Madeleine was worried.

"Don't worry your pretty head off, Maddie, until we are ready, my room is the second door down the hall," assuring her.

Blushing and embarrassed about being caught thinking the worst, "umm thanks Jack."

"And where is Rachel's room?"

"Her room is in between us as she demanded" he said, chuckling out loud," I think your parents would even approve of that!"

Madeleine only smiled shyly at his remark.

"Now, if you like to freshen up, we will have dinner in about thirty-five minutes. "

"And how am I supposed to find the kitchen in this massive place?"

Jack laughed out loud, he was going to enjoy every minute with her.

"That is easy, follow the hallway down to the main floor, the dining room is the second door, just so you know, we eat all our meals in the dining room."

He kissed her one more time and took his leave; he wanted to make sure the cook and staff had everything ready for his guests that were a long time in coming.

Madeleine closed up the French doors and inspected her room. She found the door leading into a large walk-in closet with built-in dressers and shoe racks that could hold up to fifty pairs of shoes. Next, she put away her clothing. She opens the door to the bathroom, reached in and turned on the lights, she could see that it was massive and very impressive, she barely heard soft music filling the bathroom; she glanced around and saw speakers on the ceiling. The room had a rather large gold-footed tub, a separate shower stall that was big enough to shower four people, double sinks with gold taps along with a bidet and toilet.

The bathroom wallpaper was decorated with a very expensive texture. She knew Jack would in extra touches into her guest room. Not only were their fresh flowers but also in her bathroom as well. Both vases of flowers were of matching colors.

On the double sink stood two crystal cut bottles of French perfumes of different fragrances. She opened one and recognized them to be expensive perfumes; she knew that he had bared no expenses on her.

She saw, on the tub wide edges were many colored bottles of bubble bath to try out and wondered if Jack did this for every one of his female guests. She quickly brushed the thoughts out of her mind and proceed to get herself freshen up for dinner.

Walking over to look out the large picture window beside her French door and was surprised to see the entire lake. With it being mid-spring, already the lawn and tree colours looked vibrant. Along the water's edge were park benches and one canoe. *No doubt, that is how Jack does his fishing*, she thought with a soft smile.

When Madeleine came out to the hallway and saw Jack waiting for her at the foot of the massive stairs. He smiled up at her, held out his hand for her to come down towards him. He watched her make her way, gracefully down the steps and time stood still, imprinting his memory, to him; she looked like an Angel floating down. He did recognize the same blue dress from that spring day out on the balcony, the memories made him smile up at her.

When he saw that she was looking at his lips, "Maddie, you look stunning as ever," he told her.

"I guess you recognized this dress, when I got back to Canada, I had it dry cleaned and never wore it again, and now, it is a bit lose on me," she smiled shyly up at him.

"Yes, I would say it is, you have lost some weight, but that goes with owning your own business, long hours and no play, eh!"

"You should know, with your business, did you have time for playing." teasing him back.

"The only time I had, I spent it thinking of you and wishing you were in my arms and not halfway across the world and thanks the God for internet and cell phone texting, uh! Now come, let's go to the dining room, shall we?" Offering her his arm and Madeleine slipped her arm through his.

The size of the dining room took away Madeleine's breath when she noticed a massive sparkling crystal chandelier hanging over the long dark mahogany dining room table. She counted a total of fourteen high back chairs, with two more at each end of the table, sixteen altogether.

Windows from top to bottom lined one side of the wall and a long dark mahogany buffet lined against the other side solid wall. A large wide glass curio cabinet stood against the end wall. She couldn't help but noticed that it was empty, puzzling her. The table was set for a service of three, sliver, crystal glasses, the very best fine bone china dishes were all waiting to greet them. Two serving staff members were standing neat and tall, waiting by the buffet.

She saw that Rachel was already seated when they both arrived. Jack quickly pulled out Madeleine's chair for her and Wilbert pulled out Jack's chair for him. She was sitting closer to his left-hand side while Rachel sat next to him on his right side. *After all, she should, she is his family*, thinking Madeleine.

He knew that Madeleine's hearing aid was in her right ear and wanted to make sure she heard every word he said especially tonight.

Once their dinner was served, Wilbert and the staff left them alone; Jack in between bites spoke up. "Now I will tell you all about this castle."

And so Jack told them the story, " Before I purchased the entire package, it used to be called the Dumont's Castle, built for a Count Dumont and his wife Annabelle, who died giving birth to their first child. After losing his wife, he neglected the grounds till one day the town had enough and decided to buy out and take it over. The castle was updated. All was well, till WW1 came along and the Germans came in and took over and made it into their office headquarters. Now, when the war was over, the town reclaimed it back using it for a museum. Because of the expenses of the up keeping, they no longer wanted the headache and put it up for sale."

"A family by the name of Blythmen had it for seventy-five years, he passed away and his wife put the entire estate up for sale and that is when I stepped in and bought it."

"You would not believe the condition this place was in, I hired contractors left and right to update this place, put in new copper pluming's and electrical wirings."

"The lake had to be drained, cleaned out and restocked. We have pictures of before and after the renovations."

"Jack, how long ago did you buy this palace?" asked Rachel.

"I bought it five years ago; my first vineyard is just over beyond the lake side."

"I do hope to see it before we leave, if we have time."

"By the way Maddie, in case you don't hear the music in the bathroom, I had the electrician mount a new volume control on the wall by the light switches; you can adjust it to make the music louder while soaking in the tub." Giving her a wink, having said that, he noticed she blushed.

"Why yes, I did notice the dial, I wasn't sure what it's propose was for, so I left it alone, and thank you for the gesture!

"And by the way, how have your vineyards been doing?" wanting to change the subject.

"Thanks for asking, we have had a good fiscal year, so far."

Jack could sense that Madeleine was enjoying herself so far. He wanted to spend as much time as possible with her. He told his winery staff that he would be unavailable for a short time and if any problems should arise to take it up with their warehouse supervisors.

"So ladies, what are your plans for these next few days?" looking at each of the ladies.

"Well, Madeleine and I have an appointment early in the morning to check out the new materials that just came in from India. Next, we have another appointment to meet up with another fashion designer regarding, the copyrights of their summer clothing designs."

"Umm...all in a day's work, any plans for tomorrow night?" asked Jack.

"No, not at the moment, why do you ask?"

"Because Rach, I like to take you both out to dinner."

Glancing over to see Madeleine who was sipping her wine, what do you think Maddie, would you like to go out for dinner tomorrow night or would you be too tired from your trip?"

She set down her wine glass, "No, I'm fine and yes, dinner sounds good."

"Then it's set, we will drive into Paris and have dinner by the Seine River and afterward, we can all walk along the boardwalks."

"By the way Jack, did you contact your lawyer and reported what happen to us on the way here?" studying her brother.

"Yes I did, while you were getting settled upstairs, I took the liberty and placed in an emergency call, I gave them the driver's license numbers. I hope to hear back something soon."

Madeleine was shocked to hear that he managed to memorize the plate numbers through their game of smash-up derby.

With dinner over, the three of them took the coffees into the living room, the conversation was casual, and they talked of events that were happing around the world. Jack inquired about his condo, Rachel ensured her brother, all was taken care of, no worries there. After good food, good conversations, Madeleine being so relaxed yawned out loud without realizing just how tired she was. Jack quickly clued that his guest was tired, and before they all retired for the night, he gave Madeleine a gentle kiss while standing in front of her bedroom doorway.

As much as Jack hated to say good night to Madeleine, he wanted to show her respect.

"Sleep tight darling, I'll see you in the a.m."

Madeleine said her goodnights to both Rachel and Jack. After closing the door behind her, she sent her parents a quick text message stating that she safely arrived in Paris and all is well. She did not tell them that she was staying at Jack's castle nor did she tell them about their harrowing driving experience. The less they know, the less they worry.

She plugged in her cell phone and got herself ready for bed. Once under the covers, sleep came easily for her, exhausted, she was down and out for the night.

Jack went into his own bedroom and got ready for bed and realized with anticipation of Madeleine's visit, he was not yet tired. Instead, he went over and sat down on the chair by the large window, and mentally went over the day's events, still very upset of the fact that today; they all could have been killed. *What, am I going to do, if it should happen again,* he thought?

He had thought about unloading the gold medallion, *if it was going to cause trouble, he didn't want it. Who would he sell it to, and what do the markings mean,* were his next series of questions.

An hour passed on by, Jack had just gotten out of bed when he heard Madeleine's blood-curdling screams coming from her bedroom. Without hesitating, he was up and running down the hallway, almost knocking over Rachel coming out of her bedroom.

"What happens, what's hell is going on?" quickly questioning her.

"I've no idea!" she yelled at him as she quickly opened Madeleine's bedroom door.

Jack ran ahead of Rachel and was at her bedside, he could barely see her form of a body sitting straight up, screaming and pointing to the French doors at the same time.

Rachel found the light switch flipping it on.

"Maddie, what is wrong, what's happening," while he grabbed ahold of her shoulders and wrapping his arms protectively around her.

Rachel came quickly over and was sitting on her bedside trying to smooth down her hair.

"What is it Madeleine, were you dreaming?" nervously asking her.

Madeleine came to her senses when she realized that both of them were in her room trying to calm her down, leaving her feeling utterly embarrassed. She pointed her finger towards the French doors.

"A man, he was standing in front of the French doorway, both doors were open."

Jack immediately jumped off the bed and ran to the doors, swings them both wide open, he notice the doors were not locked and he quickly stepped out to look around, with the full moon's light, he barely spotted a tall figure running through towards the tree lines along the lake's edges.

He ran back in and shouted to Rachel," Stay with her." And he then ran down the stairs two at a time.

Wilbert heard screams earlier and was already out in the hallway. He saw Jack, and said, "Here" tossing him the long barrow rifle just as he quickly made his way out the front door.

Jack blindly ran into the night, running around the back of the castle towards the lake shouting out, "Stop or I'll shoot you on sight!"

Jack could no longer see the man who skillfully disappeared into the dark woods. Wilbert, out of breath, caught up to Jack.

"Here Jack, take this flashlight, I have already informed the cook to call the police, they should be here soon!"

With flashlight in one hand and shotgun in the other, Jack ran as fast as his bare feet would allow him to rum. With the flashlight, he scanned the direction the man ran, no use, he was long gone. He scouted the grounds for footprints and saw a couple of them. Just then, he heard the sirens coming closer towards the castle and decided to make his way back. He wanted to make sure that Madeleine was ok, *dam, her first night at this castle and no doubt, she'll want to stay at the hotel,* he grumbled to himself.

By the time he got back to the castle, Wilbert had already given the officer the information and Inspector Dupert ordered his officers to search over the grounds.

Jack introduced himself as the owner of the castle; he asked if there had been any reports of trespassing on other owner's property. The answer was none at the moment.

"It looks as though you were targeted, perhaps you should check to see if any of your valuables are missing."

"I think we better talk to my guest, Madeleine Windsor and my sister, Rachel Holt."

"Just so you understand Inspector Dupert, Miss Windsor is from Canada."

The two went inside to find Madeleine and Rachel sitting together on the sofa.

Jack saw that Madeleine was still visibly upset and Rachel had her arm around her shoulders, consoling her.

The moment Jack and the Inspector walked in, Rachel was on her feet, "Jack, what is going on?"

"We think he may have tried to break and that is when Madeleine saw him coming through the balcony doors."

Walking over and knelt down beside her on his knees and asked Madeleine if she was alright. She nodded her head and was unsure what to do at that moment, feeling rather embarrassed, she only wished that she had stayed at the hotel instead.

"Madeleine dear, I like you to meet Inspector Dupert, he is investigating the break-in and if you are up for it, can you tell him what you actually heard or saw?"

She took a moment to recover and looked up at the Inspector.

"I was feeling a little jet-lagged from my flight, the chaos from being chased by around by another car on our way over here this afternoon, it was extremely tiring. We all had dinner and I came into my room, showered and got myself ready for bed. I was so tired, that I had forgotten to remove my hearing aid. I thought I heard what sounded like a scuffling sound, and first I thought I was dreaming. Then I opened my eyes, I looked over to the French doors and there he was. He just standing there and I noticed only one door was open. The other door was still closed, and when I screamed out loud and he took off out the door. That is when Jack and Rachel came into my room."

The Inspector cleared his throat, and in broken English, did you happen to notice what the burglar was wearing, Miss Windsor?"

"No I don't think so, it was too dark, but I did notice he had a cap of some sort on his head and I saw the outline of his dark trench coat if that is any help?"

"Every little bit helps, madam."

"Now think carefully, was the man was coming inside or was he on his way out through the doorway?"

"Madeline thought for a few seconds, "No, I honestly can't tell what he was doing, all I know was that he was standing there staring at me. He gave me the shivers.""

Wilbert came up to both Jack and the Inspector, "Sir, I don't see anything missing from Miss Windsor's bedroom."

"Well in that case, I would say that it was a premeditated burglary and on hearing Miss Windsor's screams, he took off."

Jack looked at the Inspector and over and question Wilbert, "Is this the first time something like this has happened around these parts?"

"That is correct sir, for as long as I have been here, this is the first time someone has attempted to break in."

"Is anything missing off the property?"

"No sir, not that I am aware of."

Jack scratched his head, "I think there is something else you should know Inspector, what Miss Windsor didn't mention was earlier an unknown car chasing us while I was driving us back home from the airport. A car came up beside me, and he was trying to force us over the cliffside."

"Yes, I did read the reports on our way over here."

"What is going to happen now, Inspector?"

"Well, I already ordered my men to see if they could collect fingerprints off the balcony, after that, we will take them back to our office and run them through our computer system to see what it can come up with. Till then, I suggest you beef up your security system here."

"We have a security system but not out on any of the balconies, I'll call my security team's office first thing in the morning."

Jack asked Rachel if she could stay with Madeleine. He then thanked and walked everyone outside.

"Mr. Holt, mind if I ask you a question?" studying his face for any signs of keeping information from him.

"Not at all Inspector, ask away."

"Why is Miss Windsor here, what is her purpose in France?"

"I understand your concerns; Miss Windsor is here on meetings with a textile company in downtown Paris in the morning. She is Canada's well-known fashion designer and she owns her company called; City Of Lights, it's on the internet."

"Any idea how long will she be staying?"

"She just landed this late this afternoon and they both are here for the week."

"Well then, if I was you, I would keep a closer eye on them, you just never know, maybe the trouble is following them here to France!"

"What? Now, who would be after sister or Madeleine Windsor?"

"For now, till the evidence tells us something or and until we get to the bottom of all this, ok? In his broken English as detectives or police inspectors must master their English language due to immigrants and visitors alike.

The inspector thanked Jack for his cooperation and walked out to his car, got in and closed the door, about to put up the window when Jack quickly caught up and walked over, he leaned into his window, spoke up, "if you don't mind, I like a report on who this man was and what was he after?"

The inspector understood and nodded his head to him and handed him one of his business cards. Jack took it.

While Jack stepped back and watch all the cars take their leave through the opened gates, he began to wonder if the burglar was really after Madeleine or was looking for his gold medallion. *What the hell is so special about this dam thing, other than its money value, what am I going to do about it, maybe I should sell the dam thing before somebody gets hurt?*

Right now he wanted to get back to Madeleine.

Wilbert who was still in his housecoat, was pouring tea for both ladies when, Jack walked in. "if you don't mind Wilbert, I'll have a cup too."

With his cup, Jack went over and sat beside Madeleine, slowly sipping his sweet tea, unsure what she was thinking or going to tell him.

"Maddie, you have had a hectic day today, I suppose you rather sign in at the hotel tomorrow after your morning's meeting?" said Jack, in his disappointed voice.

As much as she wanted, to be safe at the hotel, but she wanted to be with Jack too.

"No, if this is just only one little incident, I'm sure he won't be returning."

"But, I would like the French doors locked down, tightly, if that is possible?"

Oh thank the French God or is he Irish? Thought Jack to himself.

I'm taking care of it at first sunrise, for now, I rather you sleep in the other guest room; there are no French doors, only a large window. I know you will feel much safer there."

And Madeleine agreed to his terms but asked, "And where is this guest room?"

Jack gave her one of his famous mischievous grins, "across the hall from my room."

Oh this is just great, across from my playboy brother and I promised to keep her safe, now, and how the hell am I supposed to do this, wonder Rachel.

Jack turned to Wilbert, "is the guest bed made up for Maddie?"

"Yes, sir, I ordered the cook to take care of moving some of Miss Windsor's belongings after the Inspectors men were finished with her room."

"That's my good man, always onestep ahead of me!"

When they finished their tea, said their goodnights once more, Madeleine was standing in the middle of her new guest room watching Jack checking her windows, making sure it was locked. Satisfied, he turned and looked at Madeleine; she looked so helpless that he wanted to take her into his arms, hold her tight to keep her forever safe.

Instead, he walked over, taking her into his arms and gently placing his lips on her lips; he could taste the sweet tea she had drank earlier. He slowly and skillfully searched, found her tongue and began to give it a soft little tease; he felt her bottom lip quivering.

Madeleine didn't know what to do, but gave way to his tongue, it felt hot. Suddenly she felt a rush of heat racing through her young body, almost melting herself deeper into his arms. Wanting more, inexperienced as she was, she was willing to let him take her there and then. Instead, he pulled away and looked into her soft violet eyes and recognized the flushing look that he often saw with other women. All his instincts told him, that was her first time being French kissed, making him want her even more.

"Maddie, darling, it's late and you have an appointment in a few short hours, maybe you should try and get some rest?"

"And besides we have all our lives to experience our love for each other," whispering softly to her.

She didn't say anything to him, for the first time she felt helpless. And like a small child being put to bed, she let him walk her over to the edge of the bed, pulled back the covers and carefully took off her housecoat, laying it over the back of the chair turned to look at her once more.

The silhouette of her body through the sheer statins full-length gown took away his breath. He was having a hard time controlling himself; he felt the urge to take her now.

But, instead he helped her onto the bed, she look questionably into his hazel eyes. Jack kissed her lips once more, gently forcing her head slowly down onto her pillow, at the same time drawing up the covers up around on her bare shoulders.

Reliantly, he pulled himself away from her, "Good night my sweet Maddie, I'll see you at breakfast and gave her one last kiss, on her forehead, turned and walked out closing the door behind him. She didn't see his tears that quietly spilled down his cheeks, for the first time Jack was truly in love, true love and not phantom love and he was already worried for her safety.

Rachel left her bedroom slightly jarred and quietly laid awake on her bed till she heard Jack closed Madeleine's bedroom door, she knew that tonight for the first time, Jack was a perfect gentleman. And for that, she was thankful; she knew that Madeleine was the right woman for Jack – *at long last!*

Madeleine reached up and turned off her lamp. She was still feeling his kisses when she fell off into a deep sleep, dreaming of Jack paddling them both in his canoe around his lake, and she was lying on her back against the soft pillow and watching his every move, exposing his strong muscular arms and chest that rippled through his tight, thin t-shirt, giving her one of his famous smiles. How she wanted to take him right there in the canoe on that lake.

CHAPTER 6

Against their protest Jack had Wilbert driven both ladies around the city in one of his many cars while they attended their morning meetings and any shopping they had in mind.

Meanwhile Jack talked with his security team who arrived at his first call. As per Jacks instruction, they came well equipped and were already installing security alarms on all the doors and all French doors in the castle. He ordered motion sensor detectors to be put everywhere, even the attic and basement as well as top-of-the-line security cameras everywhere. He wasn't taking any chances of losing the love of his life.

On the final hook up to the local monitoring station, and after the testing was done, Jack felt relieved, known that Madeleine was now going to be safe. *No harm will come to her or his sister!*

He wanted to make sure that the alarm was up and running, he entered all the correct code numbers into the keypad, the signal reached the monitoring station and the police were immediately dispatched. It was a matter of minutes when they were buzzing at the front gates and Jack answered through the gates intercom system. He understood for the first time what it was like to be truly in love with somebody. *Maddie is my whole world and my life and I don't want anything to happen to her,* quietly thinking to himself.

Madeleine and Rachel's meeting was over for the day, they decided to have a late light lunch and do some shopping while still in Paris.

Wilbert busied himself with his own errands, "ladies, I have my cell phone with me, if and when you wish to return to the castle, just call me," he told them in his usual polite voice.

After a light lunch, they decided to go for a walk and have coffee at one of the outdoor famous Café Bristol coffee shops that Madeleine was pointing out to her, "let's go over to that one and try it out, shall we?"

Madeleine had just stepped one foot off the curbside and was about to place the other foot down to cross the street, when a speeding dark car crossed in her pathway, narrowly knocking her over. She felt her clothing being brushed aside from the draft. Rachel, out of the corner of her eyes saw a sudden blur speeding too closely to Madeleine, screamed to her, "Watch out," and intuitionally reached out grabbing the back of her soft leather jacket, forcing her to fall backwards.

With a handful of leather she yanks her backward falling down to the sidewalk causing her back heel to hit the curbside, sending her immediately tumbled down on down her backside. Their shopping bags were scattered into different directions, spilling its contents.

"Oh my God Rachel, was he trying to kill me?" in a barely audible breath when she felt the wind being knocked out of her on Rachel's having suddenly pulled her backward.

She quickly stood up while she checked to see if your hands were bleeding from the concretes impact. She was ok and turned giving Rachel a quick hug, "thanks for saving my life, again."

"That's ok, by the way, we have to stop hanging out this way uh?" hoping to cheer her up, but at the same time, concern for her safety. Little did she know, Rachel was seething and knew that Jack must hear about it immediately, she was sure there was going to be hell to pay when they got back to the castle?

A visiting young couple who witness the whole incident came and asked in brief English if they were ok? Rachel could only nod her head, smile and say "Merci" to them as the ladies gathered up their bags.

Rachel immediately contacted Wilbert, he didn't take long in arriving and picking them up once Rachel told him what happened and Madeleine was already beginning to have second thoughts of staying any longer in Paris.

"Rachel, what is happening to us, since we arrived in Paris, someone is after someone."

"I honestly don't know, but we need to be more alert, and I think I will have a word with Jack when we get back."

Jack was anxiously waiting for them to get safely back inside the gates, more so, after Wilbert made the call on his way to pick up the ladies. Telling Jack that a car intentionally just missed hitting Madeleine and if it wasn't for Rachel, Madeleine could have been killed. On hearing that, Jack was furious; marched into his office and took out the business card from the drawer where he had placed it the night before, he immediately called Inspector Dupert to report what happened.

The Inspector told him that, they had other cases that were more urgent and that Jack needed to be patient.

Jack yelled into the phone, "this is the third unprovoked attack on my family and I want to know what in the hell you are going to do about this?"

The Inspector only sighed and promised to get right on to it and investigate the case more thoroughly. Next, he called his lawyer and instructed him to hire Madeleine a personal bodyguard, "one of the very best," for the duration of her visit. "Make sure he's a good marksman, and I want him to start immediately!"

His lawyer protested the cost of her body guard for the rest of her duration, it's not worth the time and funds, telling Jack.

"Well, I don't care what it cost, just get it done!" he told him.

Jack manages to recollect himself. "One more thing, check around and get me a phone number of an ancient artifact investigator who can put me in touch with the right people. And I would prefer them outside of France. Yes, dam it; I'm going to sell it."

While he was waiting for Wilbert to bring them both back home safely, Professor Perrier Burnet ran through his mind. *Is he the one responsible road incident, what about last night's breakin, and today's car nearly hitting Madeleine??*

So many things going through his mind, *God, if her father knew what was going on with his daughter, he would have his neck.*

Jack stood outside and watch Wilbert's car pulling up towards the front doors. When Madeleine got out of the car, she rushed into Jack's opened arms, he held her tight, and he questionably glared at Rachel. He did not want to let them out of his sight again. After he listened to their story of the near-miss; he checked Madeleine's hands, he turned them over, kissing them on the palm side up.

"How about you, Rach, are you ok?" She smile at his concern for her and said that she was.

Once inside and settled down, Jack told them that he reported the incident to the Inspector who promise to further investigate the incident more thoroughly. He told them that he had a general idea of what was happening and how he had contacted his lawyer and asked to find him the phone numbers of an ancient archeology investigator, outside of France.

"Why outside of France?"

"Because sis, at this moment with everything that has happened so far, I don't trust anyone for that matter, also it is not a good idea for them to think I still have it on my premises, better for them to think it's in the bank vault in another country, just in case we have more troubles on our hands. I am going to sell the Golden Medallion."

"It's obvious, that someone is after my Gold Medallion" he told them.

Madeleine's face lit up, "Oh my God, that is right, it's not me they are after, it's your Medallion they want! Do you remember Jack; you told my father that the Medallion was worth millions of dollars!"

"I believe you are right Maddie; it could be worth more than millions, first thing first, it would depend on what language it was written in and how far back in time the writing goes."

"I hope you still have it in a safe place, right?"

"That, I do, my darling!"

Jack did not tell her about hiring a personal body guard just for her, not just yet. He was a little thankful for a reason to continue her stay in Paris, now that she was more relieved that it wasn't her but, Jack's Gold Medallion they wanted.

Wilbert came in carrying their numerous bags, setting them down on the bottom of the stairs, he shook his head, "I don't know whose bags are whose, but they are all there. It always amazes me, how much shopping a woman could do in a short span of time," quipped, Wilbert.

After Jack gave her a quick kiss on her cheek, he nuzzled and whispered into her ear.

"I hope you bought something very sexy and I'll even help you carry the bags to your bedroom."

"Ummm, no I bought some small tokens to take back to Canada with me."

Madeleine looked at him with a slight smile, she recognized this mischief side of him, and she knew that he wanted some time alone with her. Remember last night, and she too wanted more time with him!

After they entered into her bedroom they set the shopping bags down by the chair and Jack took Madeleine into his arms and softly kissed her. He looked deeply into her violet eyes.

"Maddie darling, today's incident too close for comfort, right?"

Catching her breath from his kiss, "I agree with you and I thought that I should return to Canada."

Jack felt his insides suddenly tighten up, "I don't want you to leave just yet Maddie, and besides, there are so many more places I like to show you."

He walked over to the bed and sat down and patted the bed.

"Come Maddie; sit down on the bed with me for a second, will you?"

She looked questionably at him, unsure if she was ready to be taken there and then, it was not what she had on her mind. And when Jack saw that she was hesitating and he spoke up "cross my heart, I promised to be a perfect gentleman, ok?"
She still hesitated.
He laughed out loud, "hell Maddie, look around, there is only one chair in this whole bedroom and if you don't mind, I have something I wanted to discuss with you!"
She felt a little more relaxed and made her way over towards Jack
"Remind me to ask Wilbert to have another chair brought into, ok?"
Curiosity got the better of her and she sat down by him.

"Please listen to me carefully to what I am going to tell you, then we can discuss this, ok?"
He was thankful that she agreed and he noticed that she began to watch his lips intensely and it melted his heart at the sights of her eyes watching his mouth. Dear *God how he wanted her.*
"Giving light to what's been happening in the last couple of days, I think it would be wise to have a bodyguard with you for the time being."
"What, are you kidding me Jack?" taken aback by his suggestion.
And so Jack told her that he already hired her personal body that will be starting in the morning.
"Actually, it was the inspector's idea and I for once, fully agreed with him."

"Don't be so absurd Jack; I don't need to have a man following me around, one man alone is enough." began teasing him coyly.

"Listen Maddie, for as long as you and Rachel are in France, I don't want to take the chances, you can't stay locked up in this castle till your flight, although, if I had my way, you would be." chuckling out loud, hoping to lighten her concerns.

"Look, I have made the arrangement for him to stay near you but, only when you leave the grounds. His car will follow you into town or the city and I promise, you won't even notice him."

"And where will he sleep and have his meals?"

"He will be eating with the Wilbert and the cook, as for his sleeping; there is a complete guest suite up in the attic area with a small kitchenette."

"Then, I guess I can't say no, if I want to stay, can I?"

"No, it's a firm deal!"

"Fine, but you better tell him of my hearing impairment. I don't want him to think that I'm being rude if he should ask me a question!"

"I will tell him, darling." Gently picking up her right hand and placing it over his heart, then leaned forward and softly kissed her lips. She accepted his kiss willingly.

He pulled back and gently kissed each of the tips of her fingers and in his husky voice,

"Let's get out of here before something else happens, I like to show you around the grounds and you can tell me all about how your meetings went today, shall we?"

The pair, with his arm around her waist, walked around the grounds. She told him about her meetings and Jack answered all her questions about the ground keepings. When they walked around the back, she noticed the oldstyle greenhouse that was attached to the castle and beside the greenhouse was a large in-ground heated pool equipped with a diving board and a change room.

"Let's go and sit by the lake shall we?
Madeleine agreed.

On arriving, Jack walked her over to the large gazebo, helped her up the steps facing the pond. He couldn't resist her any longer and stood behind her wrapping both his arms around her tiny waist. Together they stood admiring the lake.

"So beautiful and peaceful here, I know now, why you bought this property, I'm in love with it myself." smiling up at him.
     She asked if he swam in the lake, to her surprise he has not. He told her that he only likes to take hikes around the lake and through the forest when he has a lot on his mind.
"What about the canoe, do you ever use it?"
"No, I've had no reason to, but now that you are in my life, I will canoe you around the lake if you would like me to."
"Can you swim Jack?"
"Yes, I can, why?"
"Well just in case you get us tripped into the lake," she teased him.
Jack laughed out loud at the prospect of them both being spilled into the lake.
"And what about you my dear, can you swim?"
Madeleine sneered in her own teasing way, "have you ever heard of a Canadian, with all our lakes in our country that can't swim? Why is unheard of!"
Jack tilted his head back and let out another roaring laughter.
"Yes, you Canadians have the best lakes in the whole wide world," teasing her.

"Remind me, the next time you come over, to show you all my swimmers badges and trophies!"

"Aha, so now, you are bragging, are you looking for a swimming challenge?" and began to tickle her waist. She shriek in delight and began to run away from him. Jack raced to catch up to her and when he did; with his whole body he pressed her against the willow tree, kissing her hard, taking away her breath. He could tell she wanted more of him.

When they parted and he saw that she was looking at his lips, "my God Maddie, I'm so in love with you."

Still starring at his lips, she whispers, "And I with you, Jack," returning his kiss.

As their lips parted, "Just promised me one more thing, don't ever walk away from me again, Maddie"

At that moment he didn't care, if they were from different countries or of different cultures or not. All that matters was the moment they were in.

Rachel had been standing by her bedroom window, watching the pair of lovers. She was happy that Jack had someone in his life but, unsure how it will all play out. She knew that Madeline would never leave her beloved country or her parents for that matter. She wonders if Jack was willing to give up everything he worked so hard, from building up his wineries or giving up his castle. She decided not to spend time worrying about it but, to let love play itself out. Perhaps now she can get on with her life and pick up where she had left off.

Back at the castle, the next couple hours were quiet and Madeleine was coming down for dinner when she saw Jack and Rachel talking by the dining room doorway.

"Is everything alright?" She questions them both.

And Jack quickly turned around to face her with a wide grin.

"Yes, Maddie, I just taught Rachel how to turn on and off the alarm system."

"But, isn't that Wilbert's job?"

"It is, I want the system on at night, not just when we all go out."

"Jack was teaching me how to turn on and off the system in case I happened to come down in the middle of the night, we don't want to trip it nor do we want the police rushing over here."

Jack offered Madeleine his arm, "shall we go and eat, I asked our cook to cook up something very Frenchie just for you," he chuckled.

When they turned their backs to Rachel, Madeleine walking ahead of Jack, didn't hear the last sentence that Rachel said to Jack, "Remember what I told you Jack, and be careful with her!"

Jack only wink at his sister and whispered, "With my life."

Dinner was good and the conversations were light and pleasant. Jack suggested Wilbert bring out the coffee tray to the greenhouse instead of the living room.

Rachel said that she was tired and plan to retire early to bed and needed to catch up on her reading. They all said their good-nights and Rachel left the two alone, but not without first giving Jack another stern warning look. *I'm watching brother.*

In the greenhouse and after he poured some coffee in both their cups from a small set up buffet, Jack led Madeleine over to one of the thick cushiony wicker chairs and set down their coffee cups on the round center glass table between the chairs. Madeleine looked around her; she noticed the lite up wax candles scattered about, giving the green house soft glowing effects, very romantic indeed. The lush greenery vines and small trees all around reminded her of the trip she took with her parents to the Caribbean Islands.

From somewhere, soft piano music was sounding throughout the greenhouse. When Jack saw that she was looking to see where the music was coming from, he pointed up towards the ceiling and immediately the round ceiling mounted speakers. Jack also pointed to the large fake rocks scattered about the trees.

"I had the installers place the speakers in and around the greenhouse; they are built inside fake rocks, a new landscaping fashion. Would you like me to turn it up a bit more?"

"No, this is fine, what music is this I'm hearing?"

"You don't recognize this?"

"Uhmm, no, my hearing does not pick up mechanical sounds very well, unless I am familiar with it."

"Ok, it's Mozart's Waltz."

"It sounds very pretty."

Curiosity got the better of him.

"What about singers, can you understand the words they sing, I mean without lip reading, can you make out the words."

"Again, only if I am familiar with the song itself, otherwise it's all mumble-jumble."

"Maddie, can I ask you a very personal question?"

"Sure." Unsure what he was going to ask.

"Is your hearing impairment hereditary?"

"According to the numerous hearing specialists that my parents took me too, no, it is not hereditary."

"So your future children will not be hearing impaired?"

"Not if I can help it, I plan to have every hearing specialist lined up when they are born and have their hearing tested annually." She smiled and sipping on her coffee. "Does it matter?"

Jack was relieved to hear this piece of news.

"No Maddie, it does not."

"I'm guessing that you did not spend much time with the opposite sex, am I correct?" He did not want to say, experience, he knew it would offend her.

Maddie, blushed, "No, my life was too busy for them." Rather than tell him the truth, they were all afraid of her hearing impairment.

He could see that she was slightly embarrassed, getting up from his chair, "why don't I show you the rest of the greenhouse?" Changing the subject to stop further, embarrassing her.

During their walk, Jack held onto her hand and every now and then, he gave her hand a little squeeze. He pointed out the little creek with goldfishes swimming by the lily pads, as well as pointing out the many beautiful flowers. He proudly told her the names of each of the plants and low trees. Explaining how sometimes when it was raining outside that he would hang out in the greenhouse. "I love the sounds of rain pelting against the glass windows."

"I want you to hear something ok?" Madeleine only nodded her head.

Out of curiosity, she watched his tall slender body make its way over to one of the tall supporting pillars. Having found what he was looking for, he pushed some buttons. Then turning to face her and watched her reaction.

Suddenly, the music stopped playing and Madeleine heard the sounds of tropical birds singing and shrieking. She suddenly recognized the sounds from the Amazon jungles. Her eyes opened bigger indicating to Jack, who clued in that she indeed heard it. Next he pushed another button releasing the storms of heavy thunder with loud crashes of lightening, while the greenhouse lights began to flickering, keeping in sync with the lightning sounds. She could hear the rainpouring down.

Walking over to where Jack was standing, "that is the most fascinating sound that I have ever heard in my life, thank you darling."

"Which ones do you like?"

"All of them."

"Then let's, leave on Mozart's Waltz, shall we?"

And so Jack switch back to Mozart's music, then he held out his hand, "may I have this dance, my lady," with a gentleman bowing.

Madeleine blushed; she was not used to dancing with men.

"I'm afraid; I don't know how to dance to this one."

"Then let me teach you darling and I promised not to step on your toes, if you don't step on mine," he said with a slight smirk.

He took her into his arms and carefully guided her around the small area of the floor. She fitted perfectly against his body and together they danced. He nuzzled his head against her long dark perfumed hair, *God, how much more this a man can handle,* he wondered.

She pulled back, looked up into his eyes and Jack leaned downwards and kissed her gently, this time he played the part of a perfect gentleman, releasing her.

"Come darling; let's finish our coffee, shall we?"

After he freshen their cups with more coffees, he took her over to the park-like bench, sitting side by side, and listening to the little creek running and softly splashing against the small rocks while Mozart played another tune.

Out of the blue, Jack said, "I could live here in this room forever, it's my favorite room."

"By the way Jack, I have been meaning to ask you something, I heard you tell my father that you live in a condo?"

"I do Maddie, its home away from home but, this is my real home."

"Then how do you divide the time between your two homes?"

Madeleine didn't know, but she hit a raw nerve and he wasn't going to tell the truth about his ladies of the evenings, he wanted to forget they even came into his life, now that he has finally met the woman of his dreams.

"Well, I use the condo if and when I am staying in Paris for any length of time regarding business or if there is a bad storm and can't get home here, besides, I am thinking of selling the condo soon."

"Now that you told me, it's always nice to have a second home away from home, have you thought of renting it out."

"Ummm, there is a thought, perhaps, I could and make some extra cash, couldn't I?"

Jack gave her a hug and long tender kisses and she looked deeply into his eyes, "what are our plans for tomorrow?"

He chuckled out loud; he understood what she was up to. Her breathlessness gave her away; she wasn't ready to be taken.

"I was thinking of taking you on a grand tour of the Louvre Pyramid, or have you already been there?"

"No and yes, I would love to see it."

"What about the Effie Tower?"

"No, unfortunately, both my parents are more into museums and art galleries."

"Then it's settled, we will spend the entire day together. I'll be your tour guide and teach you all there is to know about Paris. Paris is resistible, and with one taste, you'll be back for more! And, I like to take you to some of my favorite dining spots and introduce you to my favorite people."

"I'm game for all that," she said, smiling at him, she wanted to know all there was about this man she has falling in love with.

With his usual waning smile, hooded eyes and leaning a little closer to her," Mmm, bring along your sexiest dress, we are going to Paris most famous club and dance under the stars!!" Hoping that he did not insulate her feelings.

Madeleine could only smile with a slightly scolded look and cleared her throat, "and just where do you propose I'll change?"

"Well, you could always change in the backseat of my car," he said teasingly.

She laughed out loud at the vision of herself trying to change with Jack driving.

"And will Rachel be joining us as well?"

"I invited her but; she plans to meet some of her friends for shopping expedition and a lunch date. She hasn't made connections with them in a long while."

"Don't forget, she has been in Paris a long time, she saw about all there is to see and to be perfectly honest, it's me that is begging to spend some time alone with you."

She fell for his charms and with a heavy sigh, "then I'm all yours!"

"Wow, hold on there, lady, I think you should rephrase that my darling, I just might take advantage of you," whispering in his slightly husky voice.

"Ok, then, I'm all yours but, with my clothes on," surprising Jack.

The two broke out in a fit of laughter, taking her hands and suddenly pulled her up on her feet coming face to face with him. He wrapped his arms around her as she did with him and in his husky voice, "Maddie darling, I am so in love with you and I hope you feel the same way with me."

She nodded her head and in her shy voice, "I'm falling in love with you more every day that we spend together, please Jack let's take it slow."

Jack couldn't believe his luck that he has finally found the woman that he wanted to spend the rest of his life with but, a small voice in the back of his head told him otherwise. Giving the circumstances of their countries' immigration rules, *I'll deal with that later; right now I want to learn everything about her*, thinking to myself. And of all the beautiful women that he's dated in his life, he has fallen unexpectedly hard for this hearing-impaired woman from Canada.

Would she be willing to leave her country for him or would he be willing to leave his country for her?? Only time will tell.

Just as Mozart's music was about to reach its height, they kissed and Madeleine felt her heart soar amongst the stars, feeling altogether different from her own, overly protective world that she was so used to.

Madeleine looked into Jack's eyes, "promised me something Jack?"

"Anything your precious heart desires, just name it darling."

She smiled up at him, "don't ever question my ability to handle myself, my parents spent years teaching me how to become independent, in other words, I look after my own myself."

Jack looked questionably at her, "meaning?"

"It means, if I fall, don't come running to pick me up, if I make hearing mistakes don't speak up for me, and don't try to judge me."

"I'm glad you told me, I have been watching Rachel with you and I have learned a lot."

"What about you Jack, is there something about you that I should know?"

"Other than calling me Jackie, I'm flexible."

Madeline remembers the reaction when she called him by the nickname she gave him.

"Care to tell me why you don't like being called 'Jackie'?"

And so, he told her the story that one spring day, how for weeks he was tormented by an older boy named Gregory in the same school they both attended. Gregory would taunt him by saying, 'come here Jackie boy' and begin to slap him around if he didn't bring any money or treats to him. Jack as young as he was, tried to stand up for himself as all boys do at the tender age of ten. Then one day he had enough, he began to fight back and most time he would come home with black eyes or occasionally a split lip.

Each time, Jack's angry sister would go to the school with a stern warning and finally the last straw came when Jack suffered a mild concussion to his head. She immediately transferred him to another school. On his way out through the schoolyard on his last day, he spotted Gregory and grabbed him by the neck and backhanded him hard across his face, knocking out his two front teeth.

Jack's sister later somehow, learned that Gregory in fact, was the son of a mobster who placed his son in the school, under an assumed identity name to protect his son from retaliation from other mobsters who tried to take over their territories. It wasn't till years later that Jack found out who was responsible for his parents death as well as other small business keeper's deaths because they would not comply with the mobster's money requests, "protection money" they would call it. The case of his parent's murder was still unsolved at that time.

It happened one night while studying for his final exam, he answered the phone to, "Hey Jackie Boy, guess who blew up the car?" the caller quickly hung up the phone. He knew then that was Gregory's father who was responsible for his parent's death. After contacting the authorities with the new information, the father and son were finally captured. At that time Gregory was a wanted teenager. The son spent nine months locked up and his father received a hard life sentence in prison for his crimes. And Jack never heard from them again, at least not yet.

When Jack finished telling his story, Madeleine wiped a small tear that dribbled down her cheek, and she whisper, "I promise never to call you by that nickname!"

"Look darling, we both know that we have a lot to learn about each other, from this point on, let's enjoy ourselves and take it one day time at a time, as you suggested. Meantime, let's always be open and honest to one another, ok?"

Maddie fully agreed with Jack and they seal it with an unforgettable kiss, for now, he wanted to embrace her beauty and her innocence.

CHAPTER 7

After parking his car, the pair spent the entire day walking around in Paris. Jack took her up the elevator to the top of the Eiffel Tower and explained to her, how it took two years to construct the Tower and with the grand opening day on March 31 in 1889.

People from all over the world witnessed the grand opening. He also told the height of the tower to be one thousand and fifty feet tall, along with nine elevators. He also told her that the Eiffel Tower had its first fire in 1956; it damaged only the first floor.

From the tower's top floor they spent most of the morning looking all around Paris, Jack pointed out many interests to her, stating that whenever she was over on a business trip that he planned to show her all of the points of interest.

Their lunch was enjoyable and she met some of the restaurant people that Jack knew. Some of them were telling her stories of Jack, making her laugh. She was surprised at how many Parisian people knew how to speak English and made her a mental note to study more French language.

Madeleine learned that Jack was an easy-going, fun type of man and each day that she was with him, she was feeling more secure in his presents. Together they walked arm in arm through a small park till they came to a group of artists who was painting tourists. Jack recognized one of the painters he went to University with and against her protest, he introduce Madeleine and ask if he would paint a portrait of her, the painter agreed.

It took him all of two and half hours to paint her portrait and Madeleine would shift her body every now and then till she caught Jack's stern look, '*sit still*,' but with his teasing smile. And Madeleine would stick out her tongue at him, making him chuckled out loud.

Jack was enjoying every minute of watching and studying every angle of her beauty, and her small facial gestures. He did notice that people of all ages would stare at her beauty, drawing a lot of attention around her made Jack even more prouder of her, she was all his.

When the painting was finished, Jack studied the portrait, her black hair brushed back away from her face and flowing softly over her shoulder, she looked very serious and loving at the same time, it warmed Jack's heart.

Madeleine stretched herself out and finally got to see the painting and out of curiosity and she asked, "Jack, what are your plans for the portrait."

He chuckled, "I'm going to hang it in my bedroom!" teasing her and heard her sudden gasped, flushing with embarrassment with another male hearing what Jack had said.

"No darling, I'm not, I'll hang it in the greenhouse if that is all right with you?"

She remembers their tender moments, blushing she agreed. Jack paid the painter cash with a very generous tip to have the painting delivered to his home. The painter didn't hesitate to take the cash and promised the painting would be delivered later that evening.

Shortly after, they walked over to visit the Louvre Pyramid. Again Jack explained the building of it in the early 1980's when the

French President Mitterrand had commissioned the new addition attached to the historic museum that was first built in the twelfth century, and with the new addition which housed the Mona Lisa and Venus de Milo. He told her that it was built with a shopping mall inside and cafes.

"Did you read the book "The Da Vinci Code?"

"Why yes I did, I think half the world's population did, why do you ask?"

"Because my love, the movie plot and book was all about this Louvre Pyramid and by the way, not many people know this, but it is true, there are miles and miles of underground tunnels leading throughout Paris. I have heard stories that if you get stuck in the tunnel, you have no chance in hell in finding your way back out, alive."

Madeleine looked at Jack, "remind me to never to entire into one!"

Jack laughed out loud, "no, my dear, I won't even let you have a peek inside one."

And so he took her inside through the glass entrees of great Louvre Pyrmaid, Madeleine found it breathless to see such wonders of glass and lights, next they went on into the museum gallery. He pointed out some of the best paintings and artwork; he was surprised that Madeleine knew about arts.

They found their way down and walked along the shopping mall's level. Madeleine was in awe of everything and wished that Donna was there to share it all with her. *Maybe one day we can come back to Paris while I'm dealing with business,* she thought to herself.

Looking at Madeleine, he did notice that when she got into his car that morning, she was wearing her black dress slacks and tucked-in rose-colored blouse with her cream sweater jacket. Her purse was a beige envelope clutch style, not big enough to store a sexy dress and she wore flat shoes.

"Come darling. There is one more store I want you to see," he told her.

She was about to protest that her feet were already killing her, it fell on deaf ears as Jack started to run with her. They finally stopped in front of the high fashion store that she knew but, didn't get a chance to visit. After catching her breath she asked "why the rush?"

"Because my lady, they close in an hour, now come on, let's go inside!"

Great, now he wants to shop, she thought.

Once inside, a smartly dressed blonde saleslady greeted them and Jack spoke a string of French sentences to her. She smiled at him and nodded her head in understanding what he wanted her to do for him.

The saleslady quickly eyed her body size and motioned for her Madeleine to follow her through a doorway, she turned to see if Jack was behind her, instead, he had settled into a large comfortable arm-chair. He smiled and winked at her and motioned her to follow the saleslady.

Shortly, Madeleine was standing in front of a tall three-way mir-ror looking over her profile when the saleslady came and handed her two short black cocktail dresses, in different styles. She pointed to the cubicle to take the dresses and try them on, Madeleine obliged.

She studied the detailed designs and the material texture to bring back to her office. She understood that Jack wanted her to model them and she was gamed.   After putting on the first one, she walked out to where Jack was sitting and when Jack saw her, he whis-tled loud and clear, embarrassing and her causing her to blush.

He shook his head, indicating, no, that is not the one for her. She returned to the cubical and changed into the next dress and again, she came out. Again, Jack shook his head 'no.'

Then an idea struck her, "Wait one minute, I'll be right out!" telling him in her firm tone and Jack chuckled wondering what she was up to and he was enjoying every minute.

Back inside the dressing room, she looked to one side of the room and looked over the racks and racks of dresses in every shape, size and colour till she found the one she wanted. After checking for her correct size, she removed the dress from the rack; she went into the cubical, changed out of the dress and carefully put the chosen one on.

After admiring herself in front of the three-way mirror, made a small minor adjustment and looked to the saleslady for her approval, she gave Madeline thumbs up and put her finger up to indicate, 'wait one minute' and went into another room she came out with a pair of black sling back high silhouette shoes.

Madeleine put on the silhouette with spiked high heels, it fitted her perfectly, and next she took out from her purse, lipstick and a small comb. After adjusting her lipstick and quickly combed her hair, with one side was swept up away from her face, the other side flowed over her shoulder, she was satisfied with her looks.

The sales lady handed her a small bottle of perfume, Madeleine barely recognized the label, with the cap opened, and she took a small sniff and instantly recognized that it was Channel No. 5. With a light dab of perfume here and there, the saleslady handed her a glittery barrette to hold her swept-sided hair up. Madeleine was ready to present herself to Jack.

After thanking the saleslady, she decided to walk out towards Jack, like a model only in a seductive manner, who was patiently waiting for her to walk out with anticipation.

When Jack saw Madeleine walking towards him, it was as though time had stood frozen, he slowly stood up, and letting the newspaper that he was reading slipped down on the floor. The closer she got to him, the more she took away his breath and when she walked even closer to him, in her low seductive voice, "Does this one meet your approval, sir?"

She had chosen a sleeveless, deep royal blue tight cocktail dress, cut just above her knees, and cut dangerously low, exposing her young cleavage.

She watched his eyes fall lower as he scanned her from her hair to her shoes, and she knew she was pleasing to him.

Jack could not believe who stood before him, she looked like the Goddess that he dreamt one day to be with. She was stunning, the color of the dress not only did her justice, it showed off her narrow waist and it brought out her violet eyes more so, violet.

He gave a long and slow whistle; she could see that his eyes were beginning to hood over when she heard him say. "You are playing a very dangerous game lady, shall I call for your bodyguard now or later?" he said teasing her.

And Madeleine only smiled at him, "No, I trust you will be a perfect gentleman tonight, am I correct?"

"All I can say is, I'll try, as long as we stay out in public, you will be safe with me, my dearie" he teased her back.

Before they left the store, Jack asked the sales lady for a light jacket to match with her dress, she brought one over for Madeleine to try on and it fitted her perfectly. Against Madeleine's wishes, Jack paid for the entire purchase and he left a large tip for the saleslady who smiled and handed Jack a shopping bag with Madeleine's street clothes and the brand new bottle of Channel No 5 perfume.

Jack knew that it was a long walk back to his car and with Madeleine in silhouette heels; he didn't think she would enjoy the walk, he politely asked the saleslady to call a cab for them.

When the cab arrived at the dress shop, he held out his arm and looked Madeleine with pride, "shall we go out on the town tonight, darling?"

Madeleine only laughed out softly, "I'm ready when you are."

They took the taxi to where Jack had last parked his car, with the traffic being heavy; it was a good ten-minute drive. During the drive, Jack held onto her hand, and brushing his fingertips back and forth along her knuckles, as excited as she was, it helped to calm her.

They arrived at Jack's car and put away the bags into the trunk, and he helped her into the car and drove through central Paris and made a sharp turn onto a narrow dark street. He parked his car, like a perfect gentleman, he held open the car door for Madeleine. He noticed that she didn't have any problems walking in her silhouette heels, like some of the other women he has dated.

While they walked towards the front door of the club, Madeleine asked "why it is so dark along the alley and where is the restaurant sign?"
Jack understood her concerns.

"This is one of the last private elite dinner/dance clubs around, it's only for the selected few, and the owner of this establishment wants to keep that way."

"May I ask for whatever reason?"
" So the younger generation doesn't turn it into a heavy rock night-club for themselves, God, knows there are enough of them around already!"

"I know what you mean; it's like that in Canada too, kind of sad."

They arrived at the door and Jack gave two loud knocks and two short taps, the small door at face height quickly slid back, exposing a burl-looking face, he grunted a sentence. Jack said his name and gave a group of serial numbers. The man nodded his head and opened the door to allow them in.

Jack ushered Madeleine briskly inside with the door closing quickly behind her, almost, not wanting to let the room's light escape.

Madeleine felt as though she was ushered into an illegal establishment of some sort and gave a little shiver, she wasn't sure if this she had in mind for a dinner dance club or if she would be able to relax at all.

Jack gave his name to the waiting maître and followed him to their table.

He helped Madeleine remove her jacket and gave **to** the waiter and Jack pulled back the chair for her, but not before, planting a soft kiss on her cheek. "Welcome to La Charriere"'s Hideaway," he told her with his reassuring smile.

While seating, Jack gave orders for a bottle of Champagne and Madeleine glanced around, she saw that it was all adults around their own ages, some were older and a couple of the women were much younger than their male partners. Then, the ladies noticed, wore fashionable high-class clothing and most of them were drinking Champagne or cocktails.

The clubs lighting was low and the music was a low-keyed soft jazz, on the small stage, a single female singer crooning softly into the microphone, a French song that she did not recognize.

The club's interior was modern but with more expensive tastes, the tables were far apart and fitted with starched white linen table cloth, with a lone candle burning in its candle holder, sterling silver cutlery on both sides of the fine bone china plates, along with tall crystal wine glasses. She couldn't help but notice around the club walls, hung portraits of Jazz singers from the last forty to sixty years or so.

Jack noticed that Madeleine was absorbing everything around her, her beauty outshone the other ladies in the club tonight; he even noticed that she made other men's heads turn to stare as they walked towards their table, waiting for them against the sidewall. Jack knew which table he wanted and had it on reserve for their arrival. The table being against the center wall, the stage and dance floor viewing was very good. He had made the call while Madeleine was changing at the dress shop. His timing was perfect.

"So darling, tell me, what do you think of this place?"

"Well it really does remind me of an Al Capone's jazz club."

On hearing this, Jack broke out laughing, "I never thought of it like that, but, I must admit you are quite right, it does have that gangster look, let's hope there are none here tonight." He chuckled.

Their Champagne arrived and the maître showed Jack the bottle before opening it, Jack nodded his head in approval. The maître quietly popped the cork; poured a bit of chilled Champagne into Jack's tall fluted glass, Jack took a small sip, savored it and gave his approval.

He topped up Jack's glass and proceeded to pour some into Madeleine's glass, then carefully placing the bottle into the tall Champagne bucket, filled with ice, sitting within easy reach by their tableside.

Jack picked up his glass to toast to her, "For our new beginnings and may the night stay forever young."

Madeleine could only smile shyly at him, *he is well experienced in these matters,* thinking to herself as she toasted along with him.

The bubbly liquid at first taste, stun her tongue for a couple of seconds while it went down her throat. Jack set down his glass and picked up the bottle from the ice bucket, brought it forwards and showed it to her.

"Maddie, tell me what the label reads?"

At first glance she read out loud, "It says, Chalons-en-Champaign, Holt's Winery!"

She suddenly looked up at him, "Oh My God, Jack is this is your Champaign?" looking at him with her questionable wide shocking eyes.

"That, it is, my darling," with his usual wide grin.

"It's from my vineyard and for your info, most of the restaurants and clubs around here now carry it as well as my wines, they are aboard in USA and you will find them in Canada as well."

"That is so wonderful, then, you are doing good business, I'm so happy for you."

He leaned forwards and gently kissed her on the lips, and she did not feel the least bit of embarrassment this time and he returned the bottle back into its bucket.

"Let's order dinner, shall we, I'm starved and you must be too?"

The maître brought over two menus; Madeleine could not make heads or tails, she closed it up and asked Jack to order for her.

"What would you like to order, beef, chicken, fish or shell fish?"

"Mmmm, I would like chicken tonight if you don't mind."

After Jack ordered their meal in French, she asked him what he ordered for her, "and please tell me in plain English."

"At your command my lady," teasing her.

"I ordered you roasted chicken with Parisian potatoes and a light salad as for dessert, I ordered us, my favorite Carmel Crème Brule."

"Ummm sounds all good to me, what did you order?"

"I ordered myself a med-rare steak, a baked potatoe along with mixed veggies. Oh yes, a couple of bottles of a red and white wine, by the way, both are from my vineyards."

"Why Jack, I believe you are trying to get me drunk?"

He laughed out loud, "No, we will take a little sip of it, we will make the bottles last all night long."

"And how do you propose we do that?"

"Easy, in-between dances, we'll slowly enjoy our wines," he said chuckling quietly to her. "I'm not so sure about this," eyeing him.

"Have you forgotten, I do have a condo just up the street, we could leave the car and walk there?"

This last remark shocked her, she didn't anticipate staying at Jack's condo, and alone for that matter, "I would prefer if we went back to the castle that is if you are able to drive."

"Ummm, we shall see, I'll let you do the drinking tonight and this will be my last glass, ok?"

He sensed her nervousness when he mentioned the condo; he didn't want to put her in any position where she would feel trapped. He respected her and he made up his mind that he was going to marry her, he wanted her first night to be a special one but, how and when, was the big question.

They ate their dinner quietly and he noticed that she had barely touched her white wine; he knew then, she was nervous when he earlier mentioned the condo to her. She was like a delicate flower; he would be more careful what he would say to her in the future. *No more testing her out*, he thought.

With dinner cleared away, Jack stood up and asked her for a dance, at first she declined. He reached down, gently taking her hand, and with his boyish grin "come darling have this dance with me, I promised not to step on your toes."

Madeleine couldn't help but giggled and gave in to his charming. He brought her close to his body and they danced a slow number to the singer's melody. Even though the song was in French, she enjoyed the music and kept in tune while they danced. Jack could feel all eyes were on them.

And Jack was amazed for a hearing-impaired lady; she could sway with the music's rhythm.

Finally, Jack brought her body closer to his, there was no room between them and Madeleine began to feel like he was carrying her around the dance floor.

She felt herself flushing up as her knees began to feel weaker, something deep down was beginning to stir, a feeling that has been hidden away till now. She looked up to say that she would like to return to their table but, instead, Jack leaned forward and kissed her long and deeply, leaving her, for wanting more. The kiss blocked out everything, she didn't notice people were starring and smiling at the couple in love, all she felt was Jack and herself, she didn't want it to end.

And the feeling was mutual with Jack as well. When their bodies parted and they returned to their table, Jack took her hand while searching her into her sparkling eyes.

"Darling, I know we have only known each other for a short while, but it seems that I've known you all my life, perhaps, in our past lifetime that we did. I'm going to ask, if you will marry me and share my good fortune with me?"

This shocked Madeleine, "what did you just ask me, Jack?' hoping it was the champagne tricking her hearing.

"I'm asking you to be my wife, Maddie."

She wasn't prepared to hear Jack's sudden proposal.

"I, I, don't know Jack, I, I mean, as you said, we have only known each other a short time, I do love you, but there is so much between us with our business, our countries and all."

"Ok, slow down and let me talk, will you, please?" still holding onto her hand.

"Firstly, we could apply for your French citizenship and have the wedding at the castle, as for your business, with the money that my winery is making; we could open your very own fashion shop here in France.

My sweet Maddie, I'm already a millionaire ten times over so you see, money is no object and we can continue to live our lives at the castle."

Madeleine was beginning to understand that all Frenchmen were a like; they all fall hard for their women.

"Jack, I don't know about this, at least, can I think about it, I mean I don't plan to leave my country?"

Jack knew the country separation was going to be hard on them both; still, he wanted her to be his wife and bear his children.

He smiled, "yes, you can think about it, as for you leaving your country, no, you don't have to, and did you know that you can have dual citizenship. You would be free to spend as much time as you would like in each country, your parents can come over anytime they want."

"Come darling, let's have another dance, let's just enjoy the rest of the evening and we will talk tomorrow."

And so the pair danced the evening away while, as much as she was in love with Jack, Madeleine's thoughts of premature marriage ran through her mind, could she live between their two countries or not. And what about their children, will they be Canadian born or French-born, so much for her to think about.

As promised, Jack stayed sober and the drive back to the castle was quiet. Jack feared that he made the proposal far too early began to worry if Madeleine wanted to go home in the morning.

When they arrived back at the castle, and on the bottom of the stairs, Madeleine was about to say her goodnights to Jack, the out of the blue saying,

"Wait darling; let's go into the greenhouse shall we?"

They stood quietly by the small trickling creek; Jack took her into his arms and looked sincerely at her.

"I'm sorry Maddie, if I came on too strong tonight with my marriage proposal, you have to understand that I am deeply in love with you, and I hope you are with me. I want to spend the rest of my life with you and I want our children to be as beautiful as you are!"

Madeleine laid her head on his shoulder, "I do love you and want you, but, there is so much to think and do."

With his hand rubbing softly at the back of her head, "darling, while driving home, I came up with a solution, we could ask Rachel to move back home with us, she would be able to help with your new shop and while I'm out of the country, and when you can't come with me, at least she will be here for you. We could hire you more staff to help you out."

"It all sounds like a fairy tale coming true too fast, Jack."

"Then let's make our own fairy tale to tell our children!" he chuckled.

He lifted up her chin with one finger, forcing her to look at him, "say that, you will marry me Miss Madeleine Windsor?"

Irresistible and charming as he was, she gave in and braved for the worst to come, "yes, I'll marry you Mr. Jack Holt!"

Jack couldn't believe what she had just said, "Really, you will marry me?"

Madeleine laughed out loud, "Unless you changed your mind already?"

"Hell no, if I had my way, I'll marry you right here and right now!"

Jack held her in his arms and kissed her soft lips, she was going to be his, now and forever, a beautiful wife. He finally found the woman he truly loved; it was a matter of getting her the correct citizenship, getting married and moving in with him, his playboy days were finally over.

Picking her up and swung her around, "the lady said, YES," he screamed out loud, again kissing her.

Carefully setting her feet back down on the floor and looked into her eyes and whispered to her, "I knew from the first moment that I laid eyes on you that we are both kindred old souls, now, come darling, let's tell Rachel the good news," he commanded.

"Wait Jack, it's late, she is probably sleeping, let's tell her in the morning."

With his wide grin, "Darling, I've waited all my life for this moment."

No stopping him now, she thought to herself and together they ran out of the greenhouse into the front hallway and Jack flipped on all of the Castel's inside and outside lights and he began to shout out loud.

"Wake up everybody," while they both laughed and hugged each other in excitement.

Rachel jumped up from her bed with startled thinking that something bad had happened to Madeleine and she quickly got up, put on her housecoat and running down the stairs. Wilbert, a light sleeper raced out from his main floor mini-apartment at the same time to see what all the commotion was all about.

They all gathered around, "Are you two drunk?" demanded Rachel while glancing at both her brother and Madeleine.

"No my dear sweet sister, we are not drunk!"

"Then please tell me what the meaning of all this ruckus is about, will you?"

Jack cleared his throat, "Rachel and Wilbert, I like you to meet the future Mrs. Jack Holt." he said with a wide grin and looked lovingly to Madeleine who was shyly smiling at the sounds of her future new name, soon about to be.

"Oh my God, what have you two been up to, you have only known each other for a short time?" said the now worried Rachel.

Wilbert was beaming at Jack; he knew that it would be a matter of time before Jack would ask for Madeleine's hand.

"Congratulations sir," offering out his hand and Jack grabbed it and shook it hard, "Thank you, Wilbert, now; we have our work cut out for us."

And Wilbert offered his congratulations to Madeleine, he has liked her from the first moment she stepped into the castle, there was something very pleasant about her, she did not try to put on the airs as some of Jack's lady friends did and he was thankful that Jack's playboy days were permanently now over.

Rachel wrapped both her arms around Madeleine, and whispered, "You know, I always thought of you as my sister, and now, you are going to be my sister-in-law, I couldn't be happier, congratulations Maddie and let's hope your parents feel the same way as I do."

For the first time, Rachel used her nickname and she did not mind it at all.

"Thank you both, now I have to deal with my parents, I'll call them in the morning, I need to figure out how to break the news to them, don't forget, I am their only child."

Jack understood her, "Darling, we will put them on the speaker-phone and we will tell them together."

Rachel groaned out loud, she knew she was going to be the one who will be facing the brunt of it all from Madeleine's parents.

Wilbert had quietly slipped away only to return back holding a silver tray.

"Sir, I have kept back your first bottle of Champagne from your first harvesting, I saved it for this special day coming, and shall I remove the cork?"

"By all means, yes, please remove the cork and let the celebration begin. You know Wilbert, you never ceased to amazing me, pour yourself one and join us," he told him.

And so after the Champagne celebration and say their good-nights, Rachel made sure her brother was in his own bedroom and she in hers. Rachel wondered what was going to happen to her now; she was sure that the Windsor's was going to have a few harsh words with her and perhaps even fired.

And Madeleine wonder if she did the right thing by accepting Jack's proposal too soon, even though, her love for him was getting stronger each day they spent together. She knew that he was a real charmer, with certain charisma about him, at the same time; he was his own man, fiercely independent, strong and firm. She wondered why he wasn't already married by now or had he been, another thing she didn't know about him?

And Wilbert was happy for Jack and knew there was going to be a lot of commotion in the next few months; he only hoped that her parents would accept their marriage.

And Jack, in all his glory, was finally going to be somebody's husband; he only wished that his parents were still alive to meet his beautiful bride and knew there was a lot of planning ahead of them, first thing in the morning; he planned to contact his lawyer regarding her citizenship. As for her parents, he was unsure how they were going to react or how to deal with them.

The night had been long and exciting, she was grateful to have slept in for once in her lifetime. While Jack laid awake, he was try to think about how he was going to deal with her parents as well as planning the days ahead for them both.

Jack and Rachel had finished their breakfast and were drinking their coffee when Madeleine decided joined them.

Jack got up and gave her a long morning kiss, "Good morning my love, did you get any sleep last night," while searching her face to see if she had any regrets about his marriage proposal.

"Thank you, I did Jack, as a matter of fact I dreamt that you proposed to me last night!" she said in her joking voice.

"Hummm, me, propose to you, why I don't think so," giving her one of his famous grins."

When he saw her surprised look, "Of course you silly lady, I did proposed to you last night and you accepted!"

She smiled showing him that she was relieved, that it wasn't a dream and chuckled out.

Rachel chuckled out loud known that Jack had finally found his match in the ribbing and teasing.

"Tell me Jack, after all that champagne and wine; do you still want to marry me?"

Jack tossed back his head and broke out in his loud laughter's, "as sober as I am now, will you please be my wife, to have, to hold forever?"

Both Madeleine and Rachel couldn't help but smile at his charming ways.

"I will be honored to be your wife, Jack Holt."

"Then, we will call your parents after you have a bite to eat, I want my bride to stay healthy," said, while picking up the coffee pot and pouring her cup.

Rachel was enjoying the happy couple, she could see that their marriage was meant to be and hope that the Windsor's would agree with her as well.

At first Madeleine wasn't sure if she should eat now or later, she worried about the repercussions from her father. She declined breakfast and drank only her coffee and Rachel fully understood why for, she was feeling worried about the phone call.

The three of them were in Jack's office and behind closed doors, after dialing out Windsor's phone number, Jack switched over to the speaker button and turned up the volume higher so Madeleine would be able to hear her parents loud and clear. She didn't really want to hear them; she knew her father would be concerned for her.

The phone rang four times, a scruffy male voice answered, "Hello?"

Feeling excited and at the same time, edgy as she was, "hello father, how are you?"

"Maddie, is everything all right dear?" saying each word slowly.

"Yes, everything is alright father."

"Well, do you have any idea what time it is, it's five-thirty in the morning over here?"

"I know, it's eleven-thirty here, there is something I want to tell you, can you turn on your speakerphone so mother can hear what I have to say?"

They could hear rustling from the bedding and her mother's voice, "Who is it Fred?"

"Mother is me, I like to tell you and father something very important, are you both wide awake?" looking pleadingly at Rachel.

"Yes, we are now, what is it Maddie, what's going on over there?"

Jack leaned down to the phone, "hi Fred, it's me, Jack, sir, I would like your permission to marry your daughter, sir."

All was quiet at both ends of the phone; and Madeleine hearing the silence, thought she was going to vomit and Rachel put her hands over her forehead, just waiting for their reaction to come.

Suddenly, a loud booming voice broke through the phone's speaker, "Have you people lost your dam minds?"

"God Dam it; it must be all the spring air over there?"

They could hear clearly, Fred ordering Courtney to get on her cell phone and order the first flight out to Paris. Feeling perplexed that her parents would treat her in a childish manner, both forgetting just how old she was. Understanding their concerns of her hearing impairment and why they had been a bit over-protected of her. What her parents didn't know was that Madeleine became independent a long time ago; she was just enjoying their extra attentions.

"By the time we land into Paris, I hope the hell you two have come to your good senses!" Command Fred.

"Sir, email me the flight numbers and time of arrival and I'll have Wilbert pick you up at the airport," suggested Jack.

"That I will do Jack, see you all soon!" and so Fred hung up the phone.

Jack seeing Madeleine's surprised look, with his arms around her, "they will calm down and have some time to absorb it all by the time they arrive here and we will deal with it then, for now, let's enjoy our day, shall we?"

Madeleine ate a very light breakfast of fresh fruits and small pieces of cheese, Rachel excused herself by saying that she had some things she needed to take care of. And Jack gave his orders to Wilbert who was still beaming with pride.

Madeleine finished her breakfast, was dressed and getting ready to go for a walk along the lake's edges till Jack came up to her," Darling, I like to show you around my other vineyards, later we will go for a nice drive into town and have late lunch there, if you are up for the drive?"

Madeleine decided that it would be a good time to talk things over, now, that it would be just the two of them alone, but not for much longer.

The short drive and the walking through the vineyard would do her good as well as the fresh air that she needed.

While they walked around together, Jack explained everything about the winery business to her, although, he wasn't sure if she was really paying any attention to the smallest details or not?

From somewhere between the grapevines, a voice was heard. "Jack, how are you?"

Madeleine didn't hear the exact word but, followed Jack's glancing through the vines till she spotted a lean short man with a wide brim hat.

"Richard, come on over here, I want you to meet someone!" he commanded him.

The man in question came around to face them both, "Maddie, I like you to meet my right-hand foreman, 'Richard,' he is in charge of all my vineyards. Maddie extended out her hand and was surprised to feel how rough his hand was.

"Richard, I like you to meet my fiancée, Madeleine," he told him with a wide grin while waiting for his reaction.

At first sight, Richard was taken aback by her beauty, "please to meet you madam," as he shyly bowed his head to her. Then his words hit him...

"You are engaged, why Jack Holt that is fantastic, congratulations to both of you!"

He began shaking Jack's hands up and down, as hard as he could, while wiping away tear drops from his eyes.

"Could I tell the others the good news?"

"Sure, why not!" he laughed out loud.

They chatted a few minutes more and said their goodbyes, the couple walked arm in arm into the winery warehouse; he explained more about the process and bottling of red and white grapes.

"Why not pink, I believe they call that rose color."

"Why, Maddie, you are good, I had in mind to do that in two years but, now would be as good time as any and thank you for the suggestion. When I produce the sparkling rose wine, I will call it, 'Madeleine's Rose'' after you my dear."

"Are you serious, it was only a suggestion?"

"I believe this will be a killer wine, people are always looking for something different to add to their wine lists, and we could suggest to the public, 'an after desert wine."

Madeleine felt a sudden chill in the air and shivered and Jack noticed her. He grabbed a blanket from the nearby testers chair, shook it and wrapped it around her small shoulders, "it does get chilly in here, we need to keep the temperature controlled on the cooler side to help keep the white wines chilled or with the fermenting of the grapes otherwise, they tend to turn into moldy tasting wines, not good for our winemaking reputations."

While he wraps the blanket around her, he couldn't help but noticed that she looked so much younger. He wanted to protect her from anything and everything, and he himself a promise that he was going to. Leaning forwards and kissed her lips, tenderly and she accepted and returned his kiss.

With his hooded eyes, "I think we better clear out of here before I lose control of myself." And Madeleine feeling weak at her knees, agreed.

They walked out arm in arm to his car. "Let's go into town and have lunch."

She was happy for the break and while they drove into town, she asked the question that had been fighting on her mind," Jack, have you ever been married before?"

On hearing her question, Jack almost drove off the road; he slowed down the car, pulled over to the edge of the road and put it in the parking mode.

Turn and looked into her questionable eyes, "whatever processed you to ask me that kind of question, darling?"

"Well, giving the fact that we know so very little of each other, I thought we should start somewhere, and I must admit that with you, being very good looking, I am surprised that you are not married with umpteenth kids by now." She teased him.

Jack tossed his head back and let out a roaring laughter.

When he collected himself, "No Maddie, cross my heart, I have never been married before in my entire life nor did I ever live with a woman and nor do I have any little bunnies running around. Can I say the same for you?'

Jack caught her off guard, "umm, no I have never married, besides, who would want me, with my hearing condition and all?"

This surprised Jack, coming from her, "Well, first off, I do want you as my companion, as my wife and as the mother of our children. As for your hearing, you hear as much as the next person, other than not hearing clearly, hell, even our president is deaf himself, after all, he can't hear what the public is telling him half the time!!"

This made Madeleine feel a bit better about them and she quietly chuckled.

"Darling, I take it, that I have a lot to learn about your hearing, am I right??"

She only nodded her head, "I know sometimes I feel self-conscious about my hearing and yes, I get down about now and then."

"Well, we'll work on that together, ok, now let's get into town!"

Together, the blissful couple drove the rest of the way into town till Jack pulled up in front of the town's main jewelry store. Madeleine tossed him a puzzling look.

"Hey, my fiancée needs a big fat diamond engagement ring before her parents arrive, am I right, and besides, it's time to make our engagement official and I don't want any other man chasing you around with no ring on." He said teasingly and was enjoying himself at the same time.

The idea of going in and choosing her very own rings made her feel embarrassed as she knew all about fashion but, not so much as jewelry or their quality. She did enjoy wearing cosmetic jewelry from time to time. She had not required the taste for gold or silver, only her watch, pearl earrings and a gold necklace with a little heart pendant that her parents had given her for Christmas one year ago.

Once in the store and in his perfect speaking French, Jack introduced Madeleine to the jeweler and he requested to see only the very best diamond rings. Jack knew that all jewelers kept the better-quality diamonds locked up in a safe only for the elite customer who had money they could afford to toss around.

The jeweler, on hearing Jack's name, instantly invited them into his private office; he excused himself and went into his safe room, returning with a large tray of only the finest quality rings for Madeleine to choose from.

She looked at each and every one of them; all inviting her to try them on. She picked out three sets that she liked but, still unsure which one suited her slender hand.

"Would you like to do the honors? She asked Jack, pointing to the three sets.

Jack agreed and he looked them carefully over, he had chosen the largest princess cut diamond with two smaller ones on both sides of the bigger one.

When Jack put the gold engagement ring on her finger, the diamond picked up the light and gave way to many sparkling colors. Next, he placed the wedding ring on her finger beside the engagement ring, together they looked beautiful. The wedding band, a simple band with three smaller diamonds, set was perfectly matched up.

"How about this set, this suits you perfectly."

Madeleine held up her hand and looked them over, she didn't care if it was a simple ring or not, but, the fact that Jack had chosen this set made it more special to her.

Jack translated the jeweler's explanation about the main center diamond, which was a two-carat stone and flawless, the two smaller stones on each side are both half a carat each, and on the wedding band the total of the three diamonds are two carts in total. Thus making it a grand total of five hefty carts wedding ring sets.

Jack spoke a few words in French and the jeweler told him the price, with his acknowledgment he agreed to the price and ordered the set.

Checking over the sizing, she needed one size smaller. He promised the rings will be ready for the next day's pickup.

Madeleine looked over the men's wedding rings and had chosen a simple wide gold band, with his approval. She placed the ring on his finger, it was a perfect fit.

He leaned a little closer to her, "Is the band wide enough to keep all the women away from me," he teased her.

They both laughed quietly and Jack paid for them with his gold credit card with instructions to have the rings delivered by tonight, shocking the jeweler who agreed. The jeweler was going to be a very busy man getting her rings ready and shipping them to Jack's place by a late courier.

The happy couple went out for late lunch and Jack once again, being the perfect gentleman that he was, introduced his new fiancée to the chef of the restaurant.

Along with their ordered meal, the chef sent over a bottle of his finest white wine. Jack read the label to see which vineyard it came from, it pleases him, "my competitor," joking along with her.

After their light lunch, they walked arm in arm, like lovers without a care in the world, they stopped in front of the large winery, and she suddenly recognized the place.

"Isn't this the name of the company where your Champagne was produced, the one we were drinking last night?"

"It is my love," pleased she had caught on quickly.

"You see, I didn't have my wine making warehouse quite finished before the first harvest came in and I had to pay this company to produce it, which is why their name of production was on the bottle."

She continued to look around when suddenly, "Why, Jack, I was here with my parents, it was this time last year, my father brought four cases of their finest Champagne, two for him and two for my office, actually he bought up six cases," she told him excitedly.

"Are you sure it was the Chalons-en-Champagne winery, I mean they all look alike?"

"Why yes, I am positive, look Jack, there is one of the helpers now, the man with the red shirt, he was the one who put the cases into the trunk of our car!"

Jack was stunned to think that his Madeleine was even that close to his home. Was it fate or not that they were meant to be?

"Are you telling me that you had your picnic, the one I planned to take you on, right here, near this town?

"Yes, as a matter of fact, I know the way to the riverside where we ate our lunch. The river itself was wide at one end and it narrowed down at the other end, my mother and I walked along the banks. Father even took pictures of a fox on the other side of the river bank. Come to think of it, she did mention something about a castle, but, I was too absorbed in my new company, 'City Of Lights' to pay attention to her, I wished I had of now. I can tell you that it's just a way down that road, about five kilometers west."

Jack broke out into a fit of laughter; "oh my God, how ironic is that, you had your picnic on my property!" continuing to laugh, then wrapped both arms around her and held her tightly close to him.

"Had I known you were here, I would have come back to the castle and join you for lunch?"

The realization of how close they actually came was beyond her comprehension.

"But, how do you know we were at your river, I mean, I didn't even see the castle. Now that I think about it, my mother mentioned she saw a castle hidden behind the trees!"

Madeleine laughed out loud, "and to think my father thought your castle was a tourist's attraction!!"

"Darling, you are funny, did you know that it's the only river that runs down towards my lake, the river trickles down from the mountains of the Vosges which stretch along the west side of the Rhine valley. And did you know it's that water makes all of the champagne for the town of Chalons-en-Champagne?"

"So, if the river runs into your lake, where does it go from there?"

He could see her wheels churning, "the little creek inside the greenhouse that you like, I had the construction crew dig a narrow canal in the cement flooring to allow the creek flow though. The water comes through the east greenhouse wall and runs out under the west side and down deeper into the ground shafts to continue onwards to my vineyards and towards my other vineyards as well. It also feeds all the other neighboring vineyards, and outside it's all buried underground."

"But, what about the river on other people's property, maybe it was their river we picnicked on?"

"Unless you walked in kilometers miles towards that river, I'd say you climb over my fence and walked, twenty feet to my river, am I correct so far?"

Jack was right on with his description and she gave a low groan, "Ohh, I'm so sorry we were trespassing on your property and by the way I thought you had high walls down on both sides of the gate?"

"No darling, the walls only go so far and it's fenced the rest of the way, it's there to keep trespasser off the front property. Remember, that was how the burglary got away that night, he has probably parked his car on the side of the road and walked in."

"Come to think of it, maybe I should have the contractors to run the short walls all the way to both ends of the property?"

Jack held her close to him while she took it all in and he suggested they both get back to the castle. She agreed.

CHAPTER 8

As promised, the rings were delivered by courier on time and Wilbert brought them inside and handed them to Jack who planned on putting the engagement ring on her finger tonight during dinner sometime; he wanted it to be official before her parents' arrival.

Madeleine freshened herself before the dinner but, not till after she sent Donna a quick text.

Donna, my dearest friend,

Good news, I am engaged to the mobster I was telling you earlier but, please hold a million questions and no I have not lost my mind or did I??

Jack Holt is sensitive and very handsome and we both are extremely happy. He owns his own vineyards. Look his name up on the website. I will tell you more, once I return home to Canada.

Love Maddie

Satisfied that her text went through, and feeling that no doubt Donna will give her a piece of her mind. And before leaving her bedroom, she took one last look into the full-length mirror and was pleased that everything was in its proper place. She had chosen a simple black skirt with small side pockets, and her Ivory long sleeve blouse was neatly tucked in.

Next she went down to the dining room where Jack and his sister were chatting. *No double about our engagement,* she thought.

When Jack saw Madeleine come into the dining room, his eyes lit up, forcing out his usual wide grin. He still could not phantom that she had said, yes, she would marry him. He felt his chest swelling out with pride and his heart bursting with joy, he didn't care about Rachel's warnings; he will deal with her parents later.

Dinner was a variety of mixed shellfish soup cooked in a cream broth along with a large salad and crusty roll. When the deserts fruit tarts came around, Madeleine passed it up, she knew that she would have to watch her waistline, now that she was getting married soon.

Already she had been mentally planning the new design for her wedding gown and her honeymoon outfits.

After dinner the three of them took their coffees and sipped them while they walked through the greenhouse. Already it was dark out and a spring storm had begun to form. It looked like it was about to burst. Jack had pointed out the creek that he mentioned earlier and Madeleine studied its construction.

Setting down his coffee cup on one of the smaller side tables and secretly took out a small green velvet box from his dress pants deep pocket.

On clearing his throat, "Maddie, let's do this right this time, I know my proposal earlier was a bit rushed."

Opening the box, exposing the engagement diamond ring, "Maddie darling, will you do me the honors of becoming my wife and the mistress of Holt's Vineyard?"

Madeleine's tears suddenly spilled on her flushed cheeks, "yes, Jack Holt, I will be honored to be your wife!"

Jack smiled and proceeded to remove the ring from its box and placed it on her left finger, it fitted perfectly, he brought her hand to his lips and kissed the top of her knuckles, "love you forever my love," he whispered softly to her.   Madeleine heard and lipped read every word Jack had said to her, she wanted to remember his words forever and wrapped both her arms around him and whispered into his ear, "love you too and yes, it's forever." They kissed long and sweet.

Rachel standing back watching the scenes began to clap her hands softly and walked over towards the happy couple, wrapped her arms around them both, hugging them while shedding her tears of joy for them both.

Jack had found the love of his life and she was going to be Madeleine's new sister-in-law. They were about to become a family, she only wished that their parents were still alive to witness this special union.

When they broke apart, Rachel kissed Madeleine on her cheeks, "welcome to our family dear, now, what about the wedding date, have you picked a date yet?"

Jack grind, "hell, if I had my way, it would be tomorrow."

"Then mister, I guess it's a good thing you don't always get your own way!" She looked to Madeleine, "and you make sure of that he doesn't or he will have me to answer me!"

Everyone broke into a fit of laughter.

"Darling, how soon would you like to marry?" almost afraid to hear her answer, he wanted to marry her in the next month or two but, he knew deep down in his heart, that most women wanted long engagements lasting a year or so.

"Given the fact of dual citizenship and both our businesses, I'm guessing in a six month time frame, if that is ok with you?"

When Jack heard how soon, he jumped up into the air with joy, shouting, "YES" out loud, he had not anticipated her answer to marry sooner. In any case he planned to stay on his lawyer's case and get him to put a rush on the immigration papers.

Madeleine was going to make her dream come true, she was going to have a Thanksgiving wedding back home in Canada. And Rachel asked her what month did the sixth-month place the date.

"I have always wanted a fall wedding and because the Canadians Thanksgiving usually falls in the month of October, it would still be cool enough not to roast ourselves in the long gowns and warm enough not to snow."

"So, this means the wedding will be taking place in Canada?"

"I would like it to, but only if Jack agrees to marry on Canadian soil?"

"And, may I ask, why Canada?"

"Well, if I'm to become a dual citizen then I like to see Jack has his dual citizenship as well."

"I agree with her, Rachel, it does make sense, we both can travel between countries and tend to our business."

"Then, it's settled, a Thanksgiving wedding, now, let me have a look at your ring; the sparkling has been blinding me!"

After inspecting her engagement ring, "Oh my goodness, Jack you spared no expenses!"

The rest of the evening was spent talking all about the happy couple's upcoming Thanksgiving wedding. Suggestions and idea's began to float around and Jack even suggested that instead of the wedding in Canada, why not have the wedding on the castle's grounds, with the wedding ceremony taking place inside the greenhouse, "why. It's roomy enough," he suggested.

"And we can have the wedding guest dance and the partying inside a large tent down by the lakeside; or would you rather have the dinner inside the castle?"

Madeleine said that she like all the ideas and needed time to think about them, she was more worried about her parent's reaction and what their father would do to Jack.

When they said goodnights, Madeleine back in her own room, had a fitful sleep; she tossed and turned all night long. She got up and grabbed her housecoat and draping it crossed her shoulders, she unlocked and walk out through the French doors. She took a couple of deep breaths while staring at the stars; she recognized the big dipper and decided to make a wish.

Please tell me I'm marrying the right man for all the right reasons and let's hope my parents accept him too.

The lake looked so peaceful and still, on remember the burglary, suddenly feeling chilled she stepped back inside and locked the doors behind her. Climbed back into her bed and crawled under the covers, sleep finally came to her at last.

Come morning, she was exhausted and it showed on her. Next, she checked her cell phone and saw a text message from Donna.

Maddie,

Have you lost your mind? Meeting a mobster and marrying him, all in the same year??

Took your advice and looked him up, wow, great looking man and very successful too, nice catch there girl, but, be careful, these Frenchmen are full of surprises!!"

Luv u/miss u, Donna

Madeleine turned off her cell and placed into her pocket of her dress pants, *I will correct Donna on Jack's nationality, he is Irish and not a true Frenchman,* she thought happily to herself.

Every one greeted everyone at the breakfast table and Jack told her that Wilbert, later in the afternoon was going to pick up both her parents at the airport. Madeleine felt relieved; she was too tired to deal with all that stress.

"I told him to write 'HOLT'S WINERY' on a large card and hold it up in the air for them to find him," I'm sure your father will give him an earful and hopefully he will be out of words, by the time they both arrive here," Jack laughed

Sensing the couple needed to talk; Rachel excused herself from the table, telling them that she was going to take a drive into St. Denis and meet up with a couple of ladies that she hasn't seen in a while, "Don't worry about dinner, I won't be missing this one," she teased Jack.

Jack knew what his sister had done and he nodded his head, thanks, she flashed him a stern warning sign to behave himself in the meantime.

Jack tossed her his famous cocky smile, "I promise, he whispered."

After breakfast, they decided to take another walk around the lake; the pair had a lot to discuss, but first there was something he wanted her to see. Walking arm in arm, he steered her towards the five-car garage, on arrival, he punched in a series of coded numbers. At the same time, all five doors rolled upwards exposing four shiny cars and one large four-wheeler terrain machine. Madeleine saw the cars, she knew they were all newer cars, as studied them all and recognized two of them, and she pointed out the first one and said their names, the Mercedes-Benz Sedan, the Renault Sedan but, the other two she didn't know what they were and looked to Jack for answers and saw that he was smiling at her curiosity.

"The third one is the two-seater, 2012 Peugeot, the one I was driving the first night I met you," teasing her.

Pointing towards the final car, "And the last one I picked it up for a good price, it is a vintage 1969 Veyron, it's built for speed, it can go from zero to sixty kilometers in four second flat," he told her with pride.

And, pointing to the final machine, I'm sure you Canadians recognized the four-wheeler terrain machine."

She turned her head towards him and with a wide grin, "Yes, they are very popular in our country."

"Then what would you say, if I start up the machine and take you for a ride around the property?"

She hesitated for a few seconds and looked down on her watch; she knew that her parents were due in a couple of hours.

"Ok, just a quick and short run, say, around the lake and back?" she chuckled.

Jack was taking back and quickly he opened the key box that hung close, took out the key and started up the machine before she changed her mind.

After he rolled out the machine from the garage, he help her to get on the seat, she sat behind him and placed her arms around his waist and hung on tight. Jack heart swelled with pride and he slowly drove them over to and around the lake; he was enjoying Madeleine hanging onto him tight. He only wished the new feelings of her hanging on tight would last forever.

They pulled up to the park bench, turned off the machine's engine; and carefully helped her getting down off the machine. Arm in arm they walked over and sat down on the bench.

And together they watched the few ducks swimming along the lake's edge. It was at that point, he broke into her concentration.

"Maddie, once we are married and moved in with me, I like to give you the Mercedes-Benz Sedan; it is a much safer drive than the rest of the cars I have. Will you be happy with that or do you have something else in mind?"

She was shocked that he was giving her the car.

"Honey, the Mercedes is fine."

"By the way what type of car was that you driving back home, I have forgotten?"

"I'm driving my 2009 Murano, a Nissan."

"Let me guess, it is blue?" teased Jack.

"Wrong, it a burgundy color," began chuckling at his sense of humor.

They sat back to enjoy the lake view and Jack put his arm around her shoulders.

"Maddie, are you regretting your decision to marry me?"

"No, I am not, I'm more concerned about the reaction from my parents, and after all, they have always been a bit overly protective of me all my life, don't forget Jack, I'm their only child, besides, they may be more concerned about your French laws and rules here. And I am one hundred percent positive they don't want me to live in France, forever."

He took her by her shoulders and slowly turned her around to face him.

"Maddie, look at me for a minute please, as your future husband, it will become my job to protect you, not theirs and I promise you this, here and now, I will do whatever it takes to make your parents proud and as for countries, I know people in high places!"

She smiled up at Jack, sensing the security about him.

"And, what of my parent's tantrums tonight" She questioned him?

"I'm willing to take the fifth degree from your father but, after we are married, it will be only you and me that will matter anymore."

"Don't worry so much darling, your folks will always have a place to stay when they come for visits."

"The next question will be the French citizenship, what if my application gets turned down??

"I guarantee you will NOT be turned down!"

"How can you be so sure?"

"Think about it darling, if they turned you down, they will lose an award-winning winery company, that's right, I will pack up all my secrets, my works and bring them over to Canada's Niagara winery district, I'm sure the welcome mat will be waiting for me and I'll start from scratch all over again."

This surprised her, "Would you really do that for me?" questioning him.

With his grin, "Honey, you have no idea what I would do for you."

"Are there anymore thoughts bothering your pretty head?"

"Yes, do you really think we can get all this done in six months?"

"Well, there is a way we can get it all done and over with!"

"Oh pray, tell me how?" almost afraid to hear his answer.

He looked at her seriously and said one word, "Elope!"

Madeleine quickly sat up and looked shockingly at Jack, "I don't think so, Mr. Holt!"

"Well, it was worth saying out loud, it would solve all our problems," he chuckled out loud to her.

And she couldn't agree with him anymore but, she still planned to have her Thanksgiving wedding come high waters or hell, whichever comes first!

A thought hit Jack, turning to face her, "Darling, what would you say if I suggest we have the wedding here on my, uhh, I meant 'OUR' property?"

"I have thought of that idea too, I mean if I am going to live here in France, wouldn't it be sensible to be married here and perhaps one day our future children can be married here as well?"

That suggestion had sunk in, "I couldn't have agreed with you more, then it's settled, marriage, babies and more weddings right here on Holt's property!"

The rest of the morning was spent around the property learning more every hour by the hour about each other. Together they enjoyed their lunch in the greenhouse and discussing more on the wedding subject such as, where will the priest be standing, then a thought hit him, "umm, I do have a very important question for you Maddie."

She was almost afraid to ask him, "and what would that be?"

Without thinking he blurted out, "what is your religion, I mean what church do you belong to?"

"Why that is an easy question, I'm a Catholic and you?"

He was happy to hear her tell him that, "I am too." *That solves the first problem!*

Both in deep thoughts till again, he broke her concentration, "darling, I like to confess something?"

"Oh-oh what is it Jack?"

"I know you only planned to spend only one week here in France but, when Rachel called to tell me about your flight arrangements, I asked her to change the plan for an extra weeks stay, I hope you don't mind?"

"Oh really, and how did you know that I would stay here for the second week?"

"Hmm it was just a wild guess," he joked with her.

"And what of Rachel, will she stay too?"

"No, Rachel said that she would head back and make sure no one has bankrupted your company!"

"How sweet of her, I could always rely on her." And Madeleine wondered if she was doing the right thing by being alone with Jack in his castle, *I must talk with him before Rachel head home.*

"I think we should be getting back, I like to change and freshen up before my parents arrive."

The rest of the afternoon went fast for the couple; they both checked in on the dinner plans and talked things over with Wilbert regarding her parents. Madeleine had given him some advice on how to deal with her father's predicted ranting's once inside his car.

"Better take along some earplugs Wilbert," teased jack.

Once Wilbert left for the airport, Jack took Madeleine gently into his arms, "don't worry about Wilbert, if he can handle me, then, I am one hundred percent positive, he can handle your folks."

Madeleine was not too sure about that and was thankful; it was Wilbert and not her that went to pick up her parents.

Right on time, Wilbert was at the gates with his place card held high up in the air, waiting for the Windsor family. He didn't know who or what to expect at this point with Jack sudden proposal to their daughter, he just knew that, if he had been in Windsor's shoes he would have been furious himself and drag his daughter, scream and kicking all the way back home. *But, then that is Jack's way,* he thought.

A burly voice shouted out behind Wilbert forcing him to almost jump out of his skin. "Is this Jack Holt's butler?" questioned an angry man and almost embarrassing him in front of the passengers who were mingling around them.

Wilbert quickly turned to face him, "Yes sir, my name is Wilbert and I am Mr. Holt's butler, you must be Mr. and Mrs. Windsor from Canada?"

Fred gave a low growl, "I see that my daughter, Madeleine did not come along with you, not surprising?"

"No sir, she is with Mr. Holt's waiting for your arrival, shall I collect your luggage for you, sir?"

"I have it with me, we only have one bag, don't plan to be here for long, we hoped to catch the next flight out!"

Oh boy Jack is in for one hellva a surprise, thought Wilbert to himself.

"And what about Rachel, I don't suppose she will be there when we get there?"

"No sir, Miss Holt is away for the day, she will be in much later sometime this evening ."

"It figures," growled Fred.

"Darling, you promised to be nice today," spoken the anxious Courtney who was used to her husband's aggression.

The ride back to the castle was quiet, surprising Wilbert; he had expected to hear some fireworks and some foul languages bouncing off the car windows and its interior.

"You speak pretty good English for living in France, Wilbert!"

"Thank you Mr. Windsor, I am originally from England," he told them while continuing his driving.

"Mind if I ask you, how you came about living in France and how you do know the Holts?" questioned, Courtney breaking into the silence before her husband became uncontrollable.

"No, I don't mind Mrs. Windsor; I was born and raised in England until I met the Senior Mr. Holt. It all started one day, while he was there in England regarding business. I was a very young teenager when he hired me to help out at one of his stores, it wasn't till much later when I moved in with the Holt family's home in Ireland and eventually became their butler, and I have been with Jack from the time of his birth. I am sixteen years older than Jack is himself."

"Oh, so I take then, you do know this Jack Holt very well?"

"Yes sir, I do!" Not volunteering out any more information.

Fred planned to pump Wilbert for more information till he recognized the area they were driving through.

"I should know these areas. Wilbert, are we in near the town of Chalons-en-Champagne?"

"Yes sir, The Holt's address is Chalons-en-Champagne, they are on the outskirts of the town."

"Why yes Fred, look, there is the very spot we had our picnic last year!" she said, pointing out the area just beyond that fence.

Before Fred could respond back, Wilbert pulled up to the massive double black iron gates, stopped and he stretched his arm out through the opened car window and entered the five digital codes into the free-standing pedestal.

Both gates slowly swung wide open, he began his slow drive up towards the castle, hoping the Windsor's were taking the landscaping till he heard Courtney's quick gasped on seeing the exposing castle.

"Look Fred, this is the castle I saw through the trees just before we packed up our picnic, remember, I told you about it!"

Fred spoke up to Wilbert, "are you sure this is Jack Holts home and not some dam museum?"

"Yes sir, this is the Holts castle" he said, while beaming with pride.

"Mr. Holt lives here and his vineyards are not far, just beyond the castle.

When they got out of the car, the two solid oak doors suddenly swung open, Madeleine came running out ahead of Jack who followed behind.

"Mom and dad, you are here at last."

Courtney held open her arms and in her teary voice, "My Maddie, my darling girl, what have you gotten yourself into?"

After the tearful hugs and kisses, she brought Madeleine's left hand up for inspection, on seeing the ring with three large and sparkling diamonds, "oh, so it is true, you are engaged?"

Jack who stood a few steps behind Madeleine stole a questionable glance at Wilbert, to see if there were any signs of trouble. Wilbert clued into his looks, only shook his head, 'no.'

But my dear man, you certainly are in for one hell of a ride, though Wilbert to himself.

Relieved that he did not crucify his butler, he walked over and offered out his hand first to Fred, at that point unsure, just what his future father-in-law would do to him, like a man, Jack was willing to take his lumps.

The gentleman that Fred was, he took his future son-in-law's hand, shaking it firmly and yet in his stern voice saying "Hello Jack, are you one of God's fools or what?"

This stunned Jack, "I beg your pardon sir?"

"Why hell, don't think you are out of the woods, just yet, my boy, you and I, we have some serious talking to do."

"Fair enough, sir." *Oh brother, this should be good, well, he is going to find out just what kind of stuff we Holts are made of*, he thought to himself.

As they all went into the Castle, Jack noticed that Wilbert brought in only one bag inside and setting it down by the staircase.

Wilbert, would you mind bringing into my office, tea for the ladies and some brandy for us?"

Wilbert nodded his head, *brandy, yes Jack, you will need not only glass but, the whole bottle.*

"Mr. and Mrs. Windsor, would you care to step into my office and we can discuss our engagement or would you like to be shown to your rooms to freshen up?"

"No thank you we are both fine, I like to tend to this, 'engagement matter,' if you don't mind."

"No problem Mr. Windsor," saying as he stole a glance at Madeleine, he could see that she was nervous.

"Then please allow me to show you the way to my office."

"Very well, come along, Courtney," grumbled Fred while following Jack and Madeleine into his office.

Jack walked around his massive tidy dark oak desk and sat down in his tall leather chair and Madeleine stood beside him with her left hand on his shoulder exposing her engagement ring. Both Fred and Courtney sat across from the young couple. They were looking at each other, almost to the point of daring that who would speak first.

Being the man of the castle, Jack cleared his throat, "sir, as you know, I have asked your daughter to marry me because we are both in love with one another and we are asking for your blessings."

In Fred's grumpy voice, "yeah, well, love is in the spring air and you too caught the love bug!" pointing out his boney finger at them.

Jack chuckled out loud, "True to what they say, when in Paris, love is only in the spring air and lesser in other seasons."

Fred starred hard at Jack, and saying out loud enough for Madeleine to hear,   "First things first, you were labeled a gangster, and of course you have money to be able to live in this castle. Oh yes, your coffee shop, and winery, are they all cover-ups."

"Father," Madeleine shockingly gasped out loud.

When she recouped herself, "Look father, I made a terrible mistake, as I told you before, Jack was not a gangster which was my entire fault. I misunderstood the whole meaning of everything and I take full responsibility for the misunderstandings!"

"Yes, I do remember our discussions at the Starlight restaurant, by the way Jack, did they ever catch the phony policemen?" he question Jack.

"I have not heard anything more, Mr. Windsor."

He intentionally left out the earlier commotions and Inspector Dupert.

Their conversations were interrupted by Wilbert's usual two light taps on Jack's office door as he normally does when he was about to interrupt. Without looking at anyone, he walked in carrying a large silver tray of tea and brandies, he set the tray down on the side table by the door, and he lightly bowed his head to Jack, he turned and walked out, leaving quietly as he came in.

"I'll pour us some tea mother." She said while walking over to the side table. They all waited till she brought them their refreshments.

After pouring the tea into both their cups, she picked one teacup and one brandy glass, walked over and handed them to her parents. Next, she brought over Jack's brandy and her tea; once again, she stood by Jack's side sipping on her hot tea.

Half way through their refreshments, Fred picked up their conversations where they left off, "Well Jack, not only do you have money but, do you really love our daughter or is this one of your fantasy flings?"

Jack could see that Fred's eyes were blazing with fire, and the brandy seemed to have fueled it more, and Jack couldn't blame him one bit. *What if it was him in Fred's shoes, would he be able to let his own daughter marry some love-struck stranger, not on their lives*, he thought.

Setting down his brandy on his desk, began to choose his words carefully and in a calm and rational voice.

"No sir, Maddie is not one of my, so-called flings, I have been in love with her from the first moment I had laid eyes on her standing on the hotel's front balcony and I am going to do right by her. Maddie suggested that we have a traditional Canadian Thanksgiving wedding, I have agreed to her terms, and I suggested that we have it here on our property to which she has agreed. I think it would be a unique wedding to tell our children," looking up at Madeleine with a loving smile, patting the top of her hand, still sitting on his shoulder.

Hearing the word, 'children,' Courtney gasped out loud, "Maddie, are you pregnant, is this why you are rushing into this marriage?"

"Good heavens mother, NO, I am not pregnant!" blushing a crimson red. The thoughts of having sex with Jack left her feeling weak in her knees.

The marriage debate continued for another three hours. The Windsor on seeing how much their daughter was in love with Jack and how strongly he defended his love for their daughter. The lovers reluctantly left them no alternative but to finally agree to the couple's upcoming marriage. It was their understanding that she would have a dual passport and make her life presentably in France along with transferring her company which shocked her parents.

It was also agreeable that Fred and Courtney obtain dual citizenship so that they too would be free to travel back and forth, on a whim, should they desire at any given time to visit with Madeleine and their future children. And Jack also, told her parents that he would give them, when in France, their very own small apartment in one of the wing sections of the castle. This way, they could be near their daughter rather than spare the expenses of staying at a hotel. The discussion and terms were hammered out to the finest detail.

When they finished putting the final nail on the marriage coffin, Jack suggested a very generous offer to the Windsor's, being bankers they were, go halfway in on a purchasing deal of Jack's neighboring vineyard that he was present was looking into. He told them, yes, the vineyard did need some work and that he, along with his crew were willing to get it up and running once again. And surprisingly, on hearing of the partnership, Fred easily agreed to Jack's terms.

Madeleine couldn't wait to ask the question that has been on her mind any longer, "and by the way mother, how is 'Ginger' doing these days?"

Jack look puzzled at her, "and who is Ginger, Maddie?"

"Oh, I am so sorry Jack, she is our cat, she's been with us at the condo since the year Donna and I partnered up together and bought our three-bedroom condo, she was our housewarming gift, from our parents!"

"Let me guess, this 'Ginger' has her own bedroom" he chuckled.

Fred joined in, "By the way Jack, 'Ginger' comes with the package, you marry our daughter, and you get the cat as well."

"I don't mind one bit, as long as she likes me, we will get along just fine, heck , I'll even give her, her very own bedroom," throwing Madeleine one of his famous hooded looks with a side smiled that she so loved.

And Madeleine again blushed at the word, 'bedroom.'

It was all settled; Jack got his woman, the cat and her family, he was now going to officially become a family man.

Wilbert who was sitting patiently waiting outside by the office door, he had thoughts of his own; he was worried about Jack and the Windsor family, now that they were all about becoming one big happy family. Wilbert was happy for Jack and yet he was secretly pouting.

By the time Rachel returned, the engagement celebrations had already begun but, not till Fred had a few words with her. With that behind her, she was able to breathe a sigh of relief. She knew that she had her work cut out for her with the upcoming wedding and moving the company to France, but, she had ideas of her own to present to the happy couple, but, not till Madeleine's parents return back home to Canada.

The Windsor's stay on for another two more days and the ladies all went into Paris to buy extra clothing and toiletries for her parents. The evenings were spent together at Jack's favorite places; he introduced his future family to everyone with-in ear shots of them. With a loving future wife by his side and a family that he and Rachel could call their very own, Jack was in all of his glory, nothing or no one could take that away from him.

What Jack didn't know, that behind their backs that somewhere in Paris's tiny apartment, that, fireworks and planning stages to retrieve the Golden Medallion that Jack had secretly hidden away, were top priorities for Professor Perrier Burnet.   One way or another, the Professor was going to have the Golden Medallion, it was a matter of the right timing, and soon, he will have it in his hands.

CHAPTER 9

After the tears, hugs and kisses they all said their goodbyes at the airport along with promised to keep in touch by emails and texting every day just until Madeleine returned back home to Canada. And Madeleine had decided to spend not only an extra week but, a month with Jack so that they could plan the wedding together and get to know one another a little more.

Rachel went back home to take care of business in the office of 'City Of Lights', but not till she had a long and firm talk with Jack about his behavior towards Madeleine.

"Lock and bolt your bedroom door and take cold showers, do you understand me?"

Jack assured his sister that his intentions were honorable; he planned to do right by Madeleine and her parents.

"And besides, my dear sister, I want our first night to be very special for the both of us!"

She had also, approached them with her ideas for 'City Of Lights,' "why not leave the business where it is and I'll run the Canadian parent company while you open a sister company here in Paris or even from Chalons-en-Champagne?"

After a lengthy discussion, it was agreeable as it made a lot more sense to them, now that she will be living in France and with Jack's promise to help her start up another company, she agreed to Rachel's suggestions.

Once again, with Rachel back in Canada, finally, it was just the two of them alone, for the first time at the dinner table and having a very late dinner of a ham sandwich, soup and fruits.

"Darling, I was thinking, tomorrow morning I like to take you into Paris to see the catacombs and learn of her history. By going early, we can beat the rush hour and get in a full day at the catacombs, would you like that?"

Hearing the catacombs, her eyes lit up as that was one place, that Madeleine had her heart set on seeing before returning back home.

"I would love to see to it, will we be doing the touristy thing or a private showing?"

Jack laughed, "The touristy thing," he questioned her?

"You know what I mean!"

"Anywhere else your heart would desire to visit, my mademoiselle?"

"No monsieur."

"Ahhh, I see you are speaking French."

"Only a few words from my school days."

"And would mademoiselle like to learn more French words?"

"I would like that but, one day at a time, for me, it's very hard to hear each vowel and accents clearly."

"No worries mademoiselle, I am a very good teacher, I'm sure you already know," giving her the hooded eye look that she came to understand its meaning.   Madeleine blushed on remembering her first French kiss. It had heightened her sexuality to the point that she would never have dreamed that it would make her feel the way she did, wanting more.

The rest of the evening was spent in the greenhouse drinking their tea and chatting about the Parisians ladders of government, its rules and regulations on dual citizenship.

Madeleine became quiet, "Jack, mind if I ask you a question?"

"You can ask me anything, darling."

"What will happen if I am turned down for this citizenship?"

Jack look at her seriously, "if you are turned down, as I said before, I will pack up and move to Canada, remember the other day when we had this conversation, I meant every word I said, now, come here!"

When Madeleine went into Jacks opened arms, she felt the security and felt his love, for now, that was all that mattered.

"I promise you darling, that I will move heaven and earth to get you that citizenship."

They sealed his promise with a tender and sweet kiss and Jack sensed that she wanted more. Remembering the promise to his sister, Jack took it upon himself to be a perfect gentleman, as hard as it was, suggested they say their goodnights and get an early start in the morning.

Together they walked arm in arm up the staircase, down the massive hallway and stopped when they reached her bedroom door, as much as he wanted to follow her in, he gave her a goodnight kiss on the top of her forehead, "see you in the a.m. and please, wearing something warm and comfortable on your feet. The catacombs can be cold and cruel!"

With his hooded look, "Sweet dreams, darling" and he quickly made his escape to his own bedroom, closing the door behind himself. With a heavy sigh, he immediately went to have a long cold shower.

Down for the night, with each in their own rooms, they tossed and turned in their beds, both wondering what the other was thinking, till, they fell off into a deep and dreamful sleep.

Morning came fast, and after eaten a hearty and healthful breakfast, they were finally on their way into the city of Paris to visit the catacombs and to learn of her history.

Jack pulled his Mercedes-Benz sedan into the massive and near empty-parking lot, shifting the car's gears into parked, he turns to face Madeleine, "Would you like to drive back to the castle, later?"

This shocked her, "Umm, I don't think so, your French drivers all have death wishes!"

Hearing what she had just said, Jack tossed back his head and howled out loud, "death wishes, did you say, really, my dear?"

"Yes, Jack, on the first day here, I had to keep my eyes closed most of the way to the hotel, I thought for sure we were all going to crash into each other. Why it was like, they were all playing an arcade game of some sort and I mean the taxicab drove like he had no desire to live!"

When Jack finally was calm enough, "Yes, they do drive fast over here but, while I was in Canada, I did notice that your drivers have respect for one another, they drive, the way grannies do," teasing her.

"Hey, you just watch what you are saying about us, Canadian's mister, after all you are marrying one of them," giving him a playful punch on his shoulder.

"Ouch, you punch like a boxer," teasing her and quickly stole a kiss, surprising her.

They gathered their jackets from the back seat of the car and Madeleine put her purse with the long leather strap over her head and across her shoulders, resting on her hips, giving her freedom to hold onto Jack's hand.

Together they walked arm in arm to the Catacombs front entrance. They were right on schedule as the doors and gates had just opened for business, they were the second couple making their way through the gates. Jack paid for their tickets and bought Madeleine booklet on the Catacombs, "this one is in English," he whispered.

She quickly scanned the twenty-page booklet of the story of how it all came about, and notice in the center of the booklet was a full map layout of the inside catacombs, *good she thought, this would be interested to read while I'm on the plane going home next week* and she placed the thick booklet in her purse.

More tourists came and once there was enough to make a small group of them, the gatekeeper after giving them all safety instructions suggested they use the washrooms as there are no washrooms down inside the tunnels. They also told them the temperatures deep down was fourteen Celsius and recommended putting on their sweaters or jackets before they begin going down the narrow steps.

Once everyone listened and took their advice; some did their washroom business and put on their jackets, together, they all began their descent into the catacombs. The small tight group of twenty together walked the one and half kilometers into the lit up tunnels before they were able to see that it split up into two sections; one section for the museum area, which Jack suggested they go into the museum first and check out and learn the stories on the Catacombs. The group agreed.

They spent more than two hours going through the incredible stories of how it all began and he made sure that Madeleine was able to understand everything.

Madeleine shocked to read that at present, there are over six million bodies all buried inside, beginning all the way from somewhere around the ten to the eleventh century and at one time, the tunnels originally were called the stone mines. And how it took two years to transfer many thousands of bones, to be buried out into the cities cemetery and how only the elite people were buried deeper down into the catacombs.

When they finished touring the museum tunnel, they made their way back to where the tunnel split and turned off into the second tunnel. While some of the tourist decided to head back up for some fresh air.

Jack brought Madeleine a closer to him, "you may want to stick closer to me for this last walk, darling."

"Why Jack," she said while looking seriously at him.

"Because, these tunnels lead to the cavern where they buried millions of bodies and the bones are now exposed to the opening for viewing," slowly breaking her into to the drastic news.

"Oh my God, good thing you warned me otherwise I may have screamed blue murder."

After pointing out the walls, he told her that just beyond the caverns, that back in the olden days the bones are carefully arranged as walls to help to hold back the limestone in its place; some were placed in an artistry fashion. He also explained to her the catacomb tunnels runs for many kilometers in every direction leading into and out of the city and that all entrées are tightly locked up.

"It's what I call, Labyrinths of tunnels and corridors and I have heard strange stories that a couple of the houses have actually broken through the limestone flooring and falling into the catacombs, I'm not sure if they fell into the museum part of the burial area but, that was long before my time."

"Tell me something Jack, has anyone ever gotten lost inside these Catacombs?"

"Yes they have, it has been said that it was mostly the gangsters hiding out from the law, they made their homes somewhere down here and during war times many people were hidden and ushered in or out to safety from their enemies.

She was amazed that Jack knew so much about the Catacombs.

"Then, there are some brave souls who thought they knew their way around, later, they have been found dead, some, found curled up in a corner and some were found stretched out on the flooring."

"This is one of the reasons why they recommend that people tour together as small groups, just in case something should go wrong, by the way, they keep count of how many goes in and comes out before the gates are locked down each night."

"And what would happen if one or two didn't come out?"

"After a certain length time goes on by, if they don't show up then a large group of search party will come in and split up into pairs along with their radios, maps of the Catacombs, their backpacks of foods to last a couple of days and fresh drinking water, should they too lose their way, it may take them hours or sometimes it might take a few days to locate them!"

Madeleine shivered to think what could go wrong and she stepped a little closer to Jack who put his arm around her shoulder, he knew she would stick closer to him.

The pair, along with a few couples who dared to brave the burial grounds all stayed closer together as they walked further along the narrow corridors leading into the open caverns, suddenly exposing the thousands of mortared bones and skulls lined lining limestone walls all around them, shocking Madeleine. Behind her, she could hear the others all gasping out loud.

She leaned closer to Jack and whispered, "I would say, this is one massive mausoleum."

"Why are you whispering, they are dead and can't hear you."

"Because we must show respect for the dead, I don't want their ghost following me home."

"Are you that superstitious, my dear?" Jack chuckled.

"When it comes to the dead, I am."

"As long as I am with you, no ghost will follow you anywhere, only me my darling!" he chuckled.

"Come along, I want to show you something," he told her once he saw the others were about to leave the area for viewing the next phase of caverns.

The small group continued to walk further into another narrow corridor way. Jack and Madeleine where the last couple following behind them till Jack spotted art design that he wanted show her, letting go of her hand and he quickly walk over to point out the art design to her, only Madeleine was not there.

A few seconds earlier as Jack walked away from her, Madeleine noticed the lace on one of her sneaker shoes had somehow came undone, bending over to tie it up, when suddenly, she felt from behind a damp cloth being placed over her mouth and nose forcing her to breath in the chemical, she recognized it, was chloroform.

Fighting the urge not to breathe it in, she tried to scream out Jack's name, but the cloth was held tightly over her face, she tried to kick the ground below her to attract his attention to no avail. Jack was talking at the same time while walking and pointing something out. Suddenly Madeleine's loose untied sneaker slipped off, too late she felt herself passing out at the same time and powerful strong arms around her waist began to dragging her across the grounds as she watched a narrow door close in front of them, when suddenly; the darkness sunk her mind further down into the bowels of hell as she disappeared behind the wall.

Jack turned to point out the artwork and dropped his hand down when he saw that Madeleine was not standing there, he had assumed she turned and walked just around the last bend in the corridor where they just came from.

"Madeleine, where are you?" saying as he felt his stomach muscles began to tighten as he proceeded to walk back to see why she left him.

Jack wondered if she went back to go to the washroom, he knew they were more than an hour into the Catacombs and kept calling out her name, she didn't answer him.

He wondered if somehow she walked past him to join up with the other tourists. He turned back and quickly walked towards the group when he stumbled onto something hard, looking down, he recognized Madeleine's sneaker and saw that the laces were undone.

Puzzled, he looked around to see if the matching sneaker was nearby and didn't see it. Taking it with him he ran towards the group just up ahead of him and shouted out in both French, then English if Madeleine was there with them, only to watch them all shaking their heads, no.

"Oh nooo," he said and panicky screamed out her name, "MADDIE," her name bounced off the cavern walls back to where everyone standing still and quietly listening for her response, none came through and again he screamed out her name even more louder. Again everyone stood still, and once more, they heard no responds.

The small group quickly gathered around Jack, and suggested that she may have returned to the gates. And Jack rejected that idea and explained that she is hearing impaired and a little nervous about being alone, especially in the Catacombs. She would let him know if she needed to return and he would have gone back with her.

While the group tried to console Jack, who by now was frantic with fear for her safety, two of the men took it upon themselves and came forwards to suggest they stay where they are while the rest of the group returns to the gates to immediately request a search party. They all agree and left quickly to make their way back to the main gates, given light to what happened they grouped a little closer to one another.

Jack was glad they were speaking English and stayed with the two men who introduced themselves, Roger and Blake Williams, both of whom are brothers from Montana, United States.

And Jack gave his name and told them Madeleine's information as well. Their eyes lit up when he told the pair that she too was from their neighboring country, Canada.

"Where in Canada is she from?" They wanted to know and Jack told them Ontario.

"Well in that case, Jack, we don't leave one of our neighbors behind and I promise you sir, we will find her."

"By the way, Jack, would you know if the Parisians Military has links to these tunnels?"

"To tell you the truth, I really haven't the foggiest notion if they do or not."

And so all three began calling out her name and stood silent to hear a slight sound or movement, disappointed, they heard none.

"What about cell her phone, did she bring hers?" asked Roger.

"Even if she did, we are too far down into the catacombs for any kind of cell phone to work," telling them with a heavy heart.

Both the brothers took out their cell phones and turned them on and checking for the reception. Jack was right, the reception didn't come through. To pass the time while waiting for a search party to show up, the brothers explained their careers to Jack who barely heard a word they said. All he caught were the words, mining and explosives. And Jack as frantic as he was, managed to tell them that he was the owner of vineyards and coffee house and that they were engaged to be married in the fall.

After the hour and a half went swiftly by, the security team of six men and women showed up wearing large backpacks and light-ning equipment joining the three men who were still calling out her name.

Once he spotted the team, Jack quickly walked up to the leader to ask if anyone saw her at the gates, they told him, no, that only the group came out and told the gatekeeper what happened and that no one who fits Madeleine's description came through the gates.

And Jack put his face into his hands and let out a loud cry, "MADDIE."

After a heavy discussion and collecting the facts on her missing person, and Jack even showed them Madeleine's photos on his cell phone that he had taken of her earlier. The team set up portable flood lamps where Jack last saw her standing. Jack even pointed his shaky finger to the area where he picked up one of her sneakers. Due to the cavern's poor lighting, with flashlights the security team in-spected her sneaker for any marks of any kind and studied the rubber treads on the bottom, they placed it into a clear plastic evidence bag.

Next, they concentrated on footprints on the ground, carefully following and marking each shoe prints with different color mini flags to indicate the same person walking on that path. Most were different sizes and went into different directions until they spotted the prints that matched up with her sneaker. The team leader pointed out to Jack that it looked like, she was dragged, but where, the last dragging heel mark stopped at the wall. The leader asked Jack if they were alone or if they were with the group and Jack told them, they were the last ones behind the tourist group. A member of the team began inspecting and push at that wall, giving up on realizing it was indeed a solid wall.

"Was anyone else following behind you or did you hear anything at all coming from behind?" questioning the leader.

Each time, Jack answered with shaking his head, 'no!'

The next question the leader asked him, "Questions that I always ask before bringing in a bigger search party, do you or Miss Windsor have any enemies that you are aware of or has there been any friction of any kind between the two of you?"

Hearing the questions, Jack suddenly remembered the incident that had taken place a few weeks earlier.

"I think you better call in Inspector Dupert, I've had some problems a few weeks back with a break-in, here, I'll give you his business card and I want him in on this search." taking out his wallet and handing him the card.

This puzzled everyone, till Jack had all he could handle and threw up his arms, "Dam it; she didn't disappear into thin air, where the hell is she, we are engaged to be married so there is nothing going on?" He didn't dare tell them they've only known each other a short time.

It was decided that they all go back to the main gates, closing it down for the time being while they make their preparations for a larger search party to come in to look for Madeleine. The leader made the call to Inspector Dupert and explained who it was missing and about the situation at the Catacombs.

Jack looked at his watch, it showed that it was already past six o'clock p.m. and she disappeared around noon. He knew what this meant; it could take hours or even days to find her and he made up his mind that he was going to be part of the search party, himself, one way or another, even if he had to hire the Williams brothers to blow up the tunnels while looking for her. He had been too long without her and now, that she was back in his life; he was going to have her back once again. He took out his cell phone, hoping to see that Madeleine had somehow found her way out and sent him a message; no text came from her.

Next, he saw that it had reception and he decided to get away from the chaos to make a private call. Quickly walked over to where his car was parked, unlocked the door and slid down into his driver's seat. Feeling overwhelmed, he wrapped his arms around and placing his head down on the steering wheel, he began to choke up.

He said a small prayer for her, "Please God, I know I don't deserve Maddie, but I promised to remain forever faithful and if you are there, show her the way out, please give her the strength to get through this and let her hear my voice."

Next call was to Wilbert to give him the details on Madeleine missing and Wilbert told Jack the news was already out. This news made Jack furious and he swore out loud. He gave him instructions for a change of heavier clothing and to pack up a couple of backpacks with flashlights, batteries, foods and water enough for three men and a small first aid kit. Wilbert asked Jack, if the burglary had anything to do with her missing, and he responded back.

"Yes Wilbert, my gut feelings are telling me so, and while I have you on the line, I want you to contact the University and find out what the hell that Professor Burnet has been up to lately."

"Very well sir, I'll make the call and will be there shortly."

Then, he immediately contacted his lawyer and have the media muzzled, but with no such luck. Fearing her parents may have already gotten wind, he called her father's cell phone to give them the bad news of their daughter missing. On hearing Jack's news, the Windsor's told Jack they had already heard the news and were on the plane to Paris in less than two hours away and asked if Wilbert would meet them at the airport, to this Jack said that can be arranged.

After Wilbert picked up the Windsor's and immediately drove to the Catacombs, searching around and manage to locate Jack amongst the thongs of people who were all offering their help. He pulled up as close as he could get to the Catacombs entrees then spotted Jack talking to one of the local inspectors. After a few choice words with Jack and on the Inspectors advice, recommended that the Windsor's go back to the castle to wait and pray for the good news to come.

Jack told Fred what had really happened and as near as the inspector can tell, yes, that Madeleine had been kidnapped while inside the catacombs. After much discussion and debating, the Windsor's agree to wait out at the castle, but not until Jack promises to call them first with the good news. Wilbert then drove them back to the castle.

And so Jack with his backpack on joined the group who began making the preparations for the massive search. The other two backpacks went to Williams's brothers. Together, they began to make their own plans in finding Madeleine when Inspector Dupert's men came cruising in with their sirens blaring. Jack counted four cars, he was hoping Madeleine could hear the sirens, and then a thought came to him and knowing that Wilbert would be on the highway, quickly called Wilbert on his cell phone.

Wilbert, do we still have the cans of Air Horn we used to attract the workers attention when there has been a problem or an accident?"

"Yes sir, the other day we just got in a new order and have two cases, how many cans would you like me to bring?"

"Good, bring both cases with you, we can always order more and Wilbert, please hurry, looks like things are getting underway here."

After turning it off, Jack put his cell phone back into his pocket and walked over to where the Williams brothers were discussing their line of work with the search party leader.

Jack interrupted to explain to everyone in both French and in English about Madeleine's hearing impairment.

"She hears the higher pitch sounds better than the lower tones, like the Air Horns that sports fans used when cheering during the Soccer games, and also whistles or large handheld bells are a higher pitch, I have instructed someone to bring us both cases of Air Horns that I use for my workers, we all could use it to try to attract her, hopefully she could follow where the sounds are coming from."

Everyone had agreed on the new ideas and it was at that point, he heard his name being said out loud, "Jack Holt," causing him to automatically turn around to face Inspector Dupert once again.

"We have to stop meeting like this, now, what the hell is going on here?"

Jack gave the Inspector the complete details of losing Madeleine.

"Oh great, just what we need, a foreigner lost inside our Catacombs, the reporters will have a field day, hell, it's probably already all over the worlds media," tossing up both his hands into the air. Jack cringes on what he else he would say when he hears the news has already reached Canada and that her parents came over to Paris.

"The last time someone got lost inside the tunnels was over four years ago and they found him ten kilometers in past the second cavern area and barely alive and now this?"

Everything, during a couple of hours was beginning to fall into its place; Wilbert arrived as promised with Jack's requested items. He also told Jack that according to the University, the professor had left France for a supposedly long vacation visiting relatives overseas.

With the new Air Horns and Catacomb's special maps were passed along to each of the different search parties; they were divided into smaller groups, waiting for the main signal to begin the long search. Jack and the Williams brothers agreed to stick together, they too were given maps and radios along with further instructions what to do if they should find her and if she was hurt.

The Inspectors, with the ambulance crews had set up a large tented area after they all agreed to wait there for the information on locating Madeleine Windsor.

Jack was amazed at how quickly everyone had gotten together and how things were planned down to the finest details. He was more thankful they allowed the Williams brothers in joining with them, especially, on hearing how qualified they were with the expertise on tunnels due to their mining experiences in USA, and how it would be beneficial to the search.

The team's leaders earlier explained and pointed out on the map, the corridor area the different groups were to follow them. And once there, splitting into different directions. The brothers and Jack understood, agreeing with them, later they would go their own way.

Jack said his goodbyes to Wilbert who went on back to the castle in case, Madeleine should call or show up, Jack knew deep in his heart, otherwise and he was very anxious to get started on the search.

Finally, a loud foghorn was blasted into the air for everyone's attention. All the chattering came to an abrupt halt; the signal again was giving to begin their descending down the steps into the Catacombs of Hell.

CHAPTER 10

Madeline woke up finding herself lying face down on a cot. Feeling a slight headache and softly moaning out loud at the same time feeling nauseous, she rubbed the sides of her temple and taking deep breaths in and out. After a few minutes she could feel the nauseous was beginning to leave her body, she began forcing herself to sit up. Looking around she saw that she was inside a small square and windowless room. Suddenly remembered what had happened to her, a soft cloth of Chloroform was placed over her nose, putting her into a deep sleep sending her into a state of panic, *the bastard, she thought.*

Glancing around the room, in the middle was a small old wooden table with two chairs that looked like it could collapse if she were to sit on it. In one corner was old wide-mouth metal creamery milk can with a lid, it stood two and a half feet high and the room had a single light bulb hanging down on the end of the cord dangling down from the ceiling.

All she had in her room was a table and chairs, a narrow cot with a woolen blanket with a flat pillow, plus the creamery can and nothing else. The air she noticed smelled musky and slightly damp, causing her to shiver when she felt the chill and looked at her watch, it read six-thirty p.m.

She remembered the gatekeepers telling them, the temperature in the Catacombs was around fourteen Celsius and it could go down lower by a few more degrees, depending on the seasons. She tried to breathe in deeply to flush out the rest of the chloroform from inside her lungs till she felt her ribs were sore and suddenly remembered being dragged with something closing shut on them. She stood up and clumsily ran to the bare wooden door and began to pound on the door with both of her fists.

"Let me out of here," she screamed and screamed to deaf ears till she remembered being dragged behind a wall. She was determined to get out of the room. After leaving the door, she quickly placed her hands and began to push hard against it, she worked her way along with all four of the surrounding walls, hoping to find the one that would open up a bit, just enough to let her body through.

Finally she gave up when she realized that it was of no use, she was locked in for a purpose but, why, or who did they do this to her, for what purpose, it didn't make any sense to her??

After twenty minutes of being ignored, the door swung opened with a loud creaking sound and a tall dark-skinned and muscular-looking man stepped into her room, blocking the entrance of the doorway just in case she should make a run for it.

Madeleine noticed that the door itself was at least four inches thick, forcing her to realize the walls must be just as thick or thicker as the door itself, there was no way she would be able to break through the door or wall particularly that thick.

The dark man did not say anything to her but, just stood starring at her, with both arms folded neatly across his chest. She decided to take the first lead and questioned him.

"What am I doing here and who the hell are you," in her lady like voice hoping to entice him into a conversation.

She watched for his lips to move, instead, the dark-skinned man did not so much as flinching a muscle on his stone-cold face and this aggravated her even more. Five minutes of the staring contest, the dark man on hearing foot-prints behind him, moved a side to let the guilty party through.

"Well, well, you are finally awake, good, you must be hungry?" questioned the second man who was carrying in a tray of food for her. He carefully set it down on the old wooden table.

Madeleine not recognizing the man, glanced at the tray and saw a bowl of hot steamy soup, a plate with a thick sandwich of some kind and a tall mug of hot coffee; she turned, looking directly into his eyes.

"I'm not hungry and I want to go home, now!" almost daring him to take away the tray, and then she walked over and sat down on the edge of the cot, with her arms crossed, as any stubborn child would do.

The man looked at her and with a smirk, "Don't worry, you may not be hungry right now, but, I will guarantee you this, you will eat because it is going to be a very, very long cold night and your next meal with being sometime in the morning or in the afternoon and my dear, the next one will be at dinner time sharp, that will be your final meal for the day, now, that, my dear lady, from now on will be your meal routine. You see, the delivery on the odd meal times will help to throw off your timing of the day! Also, the less contact we have of you the better, now, are there any questions before I lock this door behind me?"

After paying attention to his lips and glad that she did, she said, "Yes as a matter of fact, I have something to say, you are delusional if you think you can keep me locked up in your square room, why, Jack is probably looking for me right now!"

He couldn't help but chuckle at her nerviness and the way she was pouting like a small child. There was something about her that he liked and yet, he knew to never trust a pretty woman, especially the one Jack picked and would have to be extra careful.

"*Phew*, we will see," and he began to take his leave, and about to close when suddenly Madeleine felt a panic settling in her, "wait a minute, what about the bathroom business?" she shouted out to him.

Closing the door when the man heard her question and quickly poked his head in the doorway to face her, he pointed towards the creamery can and in his jokingly voice said,

"That is why there is a lid on it, oh, yes, and there is plenty of toilet paper rolls under your cot. Every dinner time, this kind gentleman here, will exchange, the filled can for a cleaner can on a daily basis?"

"And what do I do for drinking water; I don't see any taps here?" tossing around her arms.

"Look under your cot, there are two cases of bottles of water, just enough, say, for four or maybe five days' worth, let us know when it's gone and we will give you another case."

On hearing the number of days, she gasped out loud, "And what the hell am I supposed to do in the meanwhile for the length of time?" said, snapping back at him.

The man, shrugged his shoulders, "whatever you want, dearie, although I do recommend you pray."

"Oh, by the way, there is a, umm, how do you Canadians say, a care package, that is also, under your cot."

"While you are here, we will show you respect, we will bang two times on the door before we open, just so you are aware that we are coming in, you know," pointing towards the creamery can.

"Your knocking won't do me any good!"

"Hmm, may I as why is that?"

"Well if you did your homework properly, I am hearing impaired and wear a hearing aid!" Brushing aside her hair and pointing to her right ear.

"Oh really, you are right, we did not know that, but, you seem to hear me very well."

"That is because you have a loud voice and I am lip-reading your ugly lips!"

"Oh I thought it was because you like the looks of my lips. Well in that case, we will open the door very slowly and if you are busy on that can over there, just holler out and we will stop to give you a moment or so?"

"Whatever, and by the way, just where the hell am I?" trying to put on a brave front.

"Oh that, you see, dearie, you are still underground, you know those smelly old Catacombs of Death," teasing her while pinching his nose.

"Are you telling me that I am to stay locked up in this forsaking place, for whatever for, what did I do wrong?"

"No reason for you my dear, you are locked in here on account of Jack Holt!"

With that last remark, he snapped his finger at the tall dark man, and together they briskly walked out, closing the thick heavy door behind him with a sudden loud bang, making Madeleine jump with such fright. She ran screaming towards the door, began pounding hard with both of her fist, too late, the door was lock and judging by the thickness of the door itself, no one would be able to hear her, no matter how loud she would scream.

She turned and flopped herself down on the cot and cried, till she ran out of tears. She knew that she would have to be strong if she wanted to survive this kidnapping and took it upon herself to do everything to stay alive till someone found her.

She pull herself together and decided to look under her bed to take stock of what was all there, perhaps some implements to help her escape? After reaching under, she pulled out a case of water, took out three bottles, placing the case at the foot of her cot, she place the bottles of water on the table beside the dinner tray. Next she brought out a roll of toilet paper, a place that by the creamery can feeling discussed with the idea of using that for a toilet, *but, it's only temporary.*

Again looking under the cot, she pulled out a fair-sized shallow cardboard box filled with things that she would need during her stay. *How thoughtful of the monster.* Looking everything over, she found a toothbrush still in the package, toothpaste, baby wipes, *probably to sponge bath myself with, the perverts,* she thought.

Next, she picked up a large bottle of hand sanitizer and put it also by the creamery can.

Reaching back into the box she found a couple of fashion magazines and quickly flipped through them, *great all in French language,* tossing them over onto the cot, next she found a small thick writing pad with a couple of pens, *at least they are thinking right,* then she found a brand new hairbrush still in its packaging, a package of color ribbons to help keep her hair tied back, a box of snack of healthy bars, a deck of cards. *All things to keep her mind off, but, off 'WHAT?'* she wondered as she put the things back into the box and set it next to her cot.

Her full bladder reminded her that she was about to soon, burst. She quickly looked over every square inch of the walls to be sure there were no peepholes or hidden cameras, she even stood carefully upon the wooden chair and checked out the light bulb's socket. Satisfied there were none and proceeded to use the can. When she had finished she put the lid on tightly and open the bottle of hand sanitizer and cleaned both her hands.

Her growling stomach reminded her that her last meal and fluids were at breakfast time and decided she may as well eat to keep up her strength for Jack.

"Jack, I know you would want me to keep my strength up to get out of here," she whispered softly." She pulled out the chair and carefully sat down; pulling the tray forwards and began to inspect her meal. By the time she tasted the soup, it had already cooled down, she recognized the soup to be a heavy vegetable – tomato soup mixture in a ceramic bowl, looking over the tray and found the plastic cutlery was wrapped inside a paper napkin. *Smart, no steel to work with.*

She lifted up the top slice of the thick bread to inspect, ham and cheese with no butter or condiments; *at least they knew how to make a sandwich!* She took a small sip of coffee, which contained sugar and milk, *probably has sleeping pills in it,* setting down the tin cup back on the table. She ate her entire meal except for her coffee while she scanned over her room at the same time, *I would have to be a strong survivor to survive this hell hole,* she thought again.

When Madeleine finished her meal, she got up and walked the entire room, inspecting every square inch by inch from top to bottom; she knew the ceiling and the four walls were made of limestone and tried to knock on it; it hurt her knuckles and made no sound.

Next she went over to the single door, she noticed the door hinges were facing the outside into the hallway, and there are no key locks for her to try and pry open, no a doorknob of any kind, *it must all be on the outside, they had this well planned down to the finest details, the bastards!*

Discouraged, she cracked open a bottle of water and drank the entire bottle down while she walked over to her cot and picked up her purse searching for her cell phone, hoping, just maybe the cell would have some reception of some sort. At first glance, she was disappointed, no bars showed up on the cell, *useless piece of junk*, she thought.

She turned off the cell and tossed it back into her purse, *may as well conserve the power for when I escape*, thinking to herself. She continued looking to see what items that might be useful and found only a tube of lipstick, comb, and a pamphlet, a package of tissue, some cash and a pack of hearing aid batteries with only one battery left. The other full package was in her luggage back at the castle. Closing up her purse and putting it into the box. *Jack will find me soon; in fact he's probably already searching for me*, she thought. And pulled out the writing pad from the box, opened and began to write out a list.

When she finished writing out her list, she folded the paper and placed it on the tray beside the bowl. Feeling agitated she got up and walked around her small room, she measured her room by placing one foot in front of the other, her room measured only twelve by twelve, a perfect square. She noticed the flooring was hard limestone dirt and must remember not to kick up any dust.

Time went quickly by, feeling bored and restless; she picked up one of the fashion magazines from her cot and looked at the new clothing lines till she spotted a figure of a male model resembling Jack, forcing her, once more to break out into tears.

What does Jack have to do with any of this, does he know that I was kidnapped or does he think I wandered away and got lost, and why I am here? The man said something about Jack, but why, what did he do, the gold medallion, that's it, they are after the medallion?

So many questions were racing through her mind. *Oh my God, my parents, oh my God, this is just great, one more notch on my father's black belt for Jack!!*

She shuddered to think what her father would do to him if she did not make it out of here alive.

Madeleine felt totally exhausted, she was about to lie her head down on her flat pillow till she noticed the light bulb, looking around; she didn't see the light switch to turn off the light. *Perhaps, it's better to sleep in the light instead of the darkness* thinking out loud while reaching for and pulling up the woolen blanket around her shoulders; she closed her eyes to block out the light and tried to get some sleep just until someone came to her rescue.

Exhausted as she was, with nourishment in her belly, she quickly drifted off in to a sleep, whispering.

"Jack, if you can hear me, look for my shoe, I'm hidden behind a wall, in a little room, I miss you."

The sharp echo sound inside her heart startle her wide awake. Panicking and breathing hard at the same time, she quickly glancing around. She thought she heard Jack's voice till she realized where she was, still in the cold square windowless room.

She got up to use the can and disinfected her hands; she notice the door was beginning to slowly open.

"Don't worry; I'm not on the can." And looked down at her watch, it said, eight-fifteen in the morning and she walked back over and sat down on the edge of her cot. She couldn't believe she slept that long, must have been the chloroform that tired her out.

The tall dark man, again stepped into her room, again not speaking, again he stepped aside letting the man through who carrying, another tray of foods setting it down on the table. He pointed to her tray, "Your breakfast!"

He looked over at the dinner tray and smiled at her, "I see you ate your dinner and that is good."

Picking up the dinner tray he handed to the tall dark man and noticed there was a folded white paper tucked under the bowl, barely peeking out. He removed the note and turned to face her, "What is this, a note for Jack, do you think that I would give it to him?"

"No, it's not for Jack, it's for you, I wrote out a list of things I will need if I am going to be here for a while, you may as well make your guest comfortable." She said and returned his smirk.

"I will look at it later," he turned to walk away.

"Hey wait a minute here, I don't know your name and besides, can you at least tell me if you had any contacts with Jack?"

The man looked at her for a couple of minutes and she looked harmless, "fair enough, you may call me Steve and as for your 'Jack' our associates will be making contact with him soon enough, that is all I'm going to tell you!" leaving her alone about to close the door.

"Wait, aren't you forgetting something?"

"What am I forgetting?'

"That can," pointing towards it.

Steve snapped his finger and the tall dark man on cue stepped out and brought forth another can, replacing the old can.

Both men stepped out, closing the door hard behind them once again.

Madeleine looked over her breakfast, two fried eggs, with two strips of bacon and one slice of whole-wheat toast cut in half. Again, coffee along with a glass of orange juice and on her tray was a fresh banana and a green apple.

She ate her breakfast in silence, all except for the apple and wondered if she was going to be getting the same breakfast every morning. She began to pace back and forth from wall to door, twelve steps each way while trying to think how she could escape, it was no use, the kidnappers had everything packed down to the very detail of her staying there. The rest of her morning, she spent going through the magazines, playing with cards while planning her escape. To her, there was only one way to escape and that was through the door she came in through.

She thought about Jack and his flamboyant ways and knew that she loved him but today of all days, she really missed him. She wondered if he was with the search party and what connections did he have with the kidnappers. She couldn't think of anything except buying up the vineyards, *that must be it*, she thought, *maybe he crossed someone during a deal of some sort, yes, that would be it. No it has to be that dam golden medallion!*

She was lying down on her cot when the door began to slowly swing open, this time she didn't say a word but, she did watch to see how long it took to fully open. She counted seven full seconds to fully swing wide open before the tall dark man walk into her room. Again standing like a soldier, arms crossed in front of his chest.

Steve carried in the lunch tray and set it down on the table, he turned to walk out, and Madeleine was about to protest till Steve stepped out and bent down forward to retrieve a large box from the hallway and stepped back into her room, setting the box down on the floor by the table, under the dark man's keen watchful eyes.

"You ask for a lot of things, lady and I had to go to bat for you and I hope you appreciate it!"

"Well, that's what happens when you kidnap someone!"

"My associate told me to tell you, this is all you are going to get, besides your meals!"

"Now, when I return with your dinner tonight, I want you to put the can by the door and he will exchange it with a clean can."

"YES SIR!" saluting, like she was a solider to him.

Steve only shook his head and picked up the breakfast tray and walked back out, closing the door behind them. She noticed her lunch consisted of the same as the day before, the same kind of soup, sandwich and instead of coffee; she was given tea and sugar as requested on her note. Pleased with herself that she was able to make them bend and wondered just how far she could go with them.

She made a mental note to write out her menu, she knew she was pushing her luck and made up her mind for as long as they kept her, she was going to give them a hard time.

With her lunch eaten, she placed the tray beside the door and proceeds to inspect the box that Steve brought in. She began to mentally check off her list that she left under the bowl from the day before. Feeling rather pleased with herself, she took out an extra woolen blanket, two tall tapered candles along with a brass candle holder and matchbox, just *in case the power should go out*, she wrote down on the list, and she open to see only five match sticks inside.

Next, she brought out a couple of new pairs of socks still in its package, pair of opened back black slippers so that both her feet would feel warm at the same and not one being warm while the other feeling cold. Putting them on, a bit big, but it fitted for the time being. Back into the box, she pulled out a small basin, a bar of lightly scented soap, washcloth, old looking bath towel, a box of chocolate chip cookies and a pack of hearing aid batteries, inspected the model numbered six seventy-five, *at least they even got the right model number, I can't believe it,* she thought. She was even more surprised that they put the requested small battery-operated radio inside the box, *but will it work down here, I'll check that out later?* She whispered.

The box had all the right things she wrote down on the list except for one item that she didn't ask for. A folded-up newspaper; she quickly grabbed it up only to see that it was all printed in French language. *Dam them.* When she had put away her things in order, she fully spread opened the newspaper on her table and saw the picture of Jack standing next to Inspector Dupert and she recognized the front gates of the Catacomb entrees and saw a scene of police cars in the background on the front page, *they know I'm missing and they are looking for my, YES JACK, oh thank God, it's you, Jack, you are looking for me but what does it say?*

She noticed that he looked like he had aged ten years older and that he was still wearing the same clothing he has worn that morning going into the tunnels with her, only he had on a jacket.

She managed to pick out a few words that she learned while still in school, but, not enough to tell her want she needed to know and quickly scanned the rest of the newspaper for any more pictures, turning page after page, disappointed there was no further information. She folded up the newspaper in such a way to have Jack's picture facing her, with a heavy heart, she left the paper on the table and opened a bottle of water and poured it into the washbasin and gave her body a quick sponge bath. When she finished she dumped the bathwater into the can and set the basin down on the spare chair and placed the towel and washcloth over the back of the chair to dry out.

She took out one of the candles from the box putting one of them into its brass holder placing it next to the matchbox in the middle of the table, *just in case the power goes out or if I should get out of here, whichever comes first!*

She took out her writing pad and wrote down, *how can, I turn out the light, I can't sleep with it on,* once again, placing the note under the soup bowl on the tray.

Turning on the radio to see if it works, *not surprising it didn't work, then why did they bother bringing it to me;* she wondered to herself, *this just proves how crazy they must be,* while turning it off and placing it back into the box.

Picking up the newspaper, she went and lay down on her cot and studied Jack's photo while saying a little prayer that he would find her before she lost her mind while trying to remain calm for the duration of her stay. Patience had been her best allies since she was younger, especially, with her hearing impairment.

During her earlier years of lip-reading training, she was taught to have patience and now, she was thankful as the long hard training was beginning to pay off. She studied the picture of Jack and Inspector Dupert who along with a small group of men had their heads over the hood of the police car. *They look like they are studying what looks to be a map of some kind, perhaps it's the maps of the catacombs,* she thought.

Then a thought struck her, she quickly bounced up off the cot and grabbed her purse from the box, and rummaged through, pulling out the pamphlet on the Catacombs that the gate people had giving them the day before. She took it to the table and sat down and fully opened the pamphlet and began to study it. *"Good thing this one is in English,"* she whispered.

The pamphlet told the story of the Catacombs from the very beginning to currently, and while flipping through, she saw the small map of the tunnels, corridors and the few caverns. She grabbed the pen and began to traced the pathway of the tunnels, starting from the main gate entrées to the second cavern where she and Jack had just left to go into the corridor, where they had stopped and she remembers hearing him saying, "there it is" and from the corner of her eyes, she saw him running towards whatever it was that the wanted her to see, till she smell the Chloroform and felt herself being dragged behind the wall. Who knows just how long she had been unconscious for or even where and how far into the carven the men may have taking her or even if they are telling her the real truth if she is, in fact, even in the Catacombs, she could be anywhere in Paris, giving her a glimmer of hope.

She circled and began to study the area; it didn't show a square room or an opened wall of any kind and decided that she was somewhere behind the area where she left her one sneaker. Surely, *Jack would have seen and picked up her sneaker and wonder where she went.*

The rest of the afternoon was spent scanning the newspaper and magazine, page after page. She played solitaire with the cards, later took a light afternoon nap till she heard a male's strong voice, "Oh very good, I see you are following orders," startling Madeleine wide awake from her nap.

She bolted straight up on hearing Steve's voice.

"I figured I may as well be a model prisoner since there is nothing else to do here!"

"Any word on finding me?" she looked to him for answers.

But, he only smiled as he set down the dinner tray, "no dearie, no word yet, as I said, it may take a few days and then you will be set free."

At that point, she had enough, "Ok, so why not tell me what is really going on here?"

"What do you mean by, ''what is going on?"

"That is an easy answer, sir, why the hell, am I here in the first place?"

"Oh that, very well, smirked, Steve, you are our bargaining chip, Jack can have you returned in exchanged for the Golden Medallion, now do you understand?"

"The Medallion that he found while digging, is this what, this is all about?" she said, with a deep frown.

According to my associates, yes, they are waiting for Jack to give them the Golden Medallion, in exchange, they will return you back to Jack, I hear, it's a matter of where, when and how the exchange will take place?"

Meanwhile the tall dark man had quickly and quietly exchanged her creamery can, setting the other out in the hallway, while the two were exchanging words. What they didn't know was that Madeleine was paying close attention during the process, at the same time asking Steve questions.

"Now, enjoy your dinner, Mademoiselle," turning quickly and walked out, leaving her alone, once again, in the small square room.

Her dinner was different than last night, this time it was a chunky chicken soup along with a roast beef sandwich, later; she drank her tea while it was still hot and it somewhat helped to calm down her nerves.

"At least I know they have a personal chef, it can't be Steve that is making my meals, hum…I wonder if 'HE' himself is the associate that he often has referred to?" talking to herself. "Or maybe the tall dark man is the only associate that Steve has?"

While the fifty questions ran through her mind, she ate her dinner, only, more slowly this time, savoring every bite. It would be a long time till breakfast.

After she finished her meal, she set down the tray on the floor by the door, as instructed. Next, she lit up one of the two candles hoping to add a little warmth to her cold room and for something to do with her time. She sat down on the chair and watched the flame flickered and danced while it burned. She could not help but noticed something different about the movements of the flame. Carefully she studied the flickering, and began to wonder why the flame was always leaning towards that one wall; it made her curious as to why it did that.

The air, OF COURSE, where is the air coming from and she quickly looked around the room.

It didn't dawn on her that the air she was breathing in and out, had to come from somewhere, but, where? There are no windows and the door opens two to three times daily. She thought about it for a minute or so and realized that the opening of the door was just enough air to sustain her for the duration of the night till the next meal time. *So, where is this air coming from?*

Again watching the candle; she picked up the candle holder and slowly began to walk all around the room, holding up the candle holder higher. She stopped when she saw where the flame was being called towards the wall, and then noticed the flame was drawing downwards; she leaned towards the floor and set it down the hard ground. The candle wick, watching the flame as it continued to be pulled towards the floor, out of curiosity she and ran her finger across the joints between the wall and the flooring, brushing away the loose dirt, she saw that the flame was becoming larger towards the draft.

She suddenly moved back the candlestick and with her finger, she felt a small hole and decided to push her finger through, it worked, next she forcing the hole making it bigger. Then she realized the flame itself was being forced down by the downward draft; she quickly moved the candle holder further back away from her body and so that it didn't get blown out by the draft. Then she laid her body on the hard cold flooring.

Perfect, this is just what I need, a hole, oh please, let there is no one on the other side and please let it lead directly outside.

Kneeling closer to the hole and with one eye closed, she peeked through and saw that it was dark, she couldn't see anything. Then she placed her nose against the hole and took in a deep sniff, almost gagging and choking from the loose dust. *Well, this certainly is not fresh air, so it can't be the outside wall or could it be?*

She glanced at her watch, it show six thirty p.m. *the men should be long gone by now.* She stood up and looked around the room to see if she could use something to help her make the hole bigger, just enough to let her climb through. She will deal with whatever is in the next room beside her or *was it another cavern,* she wondered?

Madeleine knew she had no stainless steel cutlery only the plastic ones and they were of no use. Looking inside the box and at her cot, nothing she would use in there and she sat down on the chair to think things more thoroughly, then it dawned on her. She got up and turned the chair upside down, gave each wooden rung a shake, one rung instantly fell out of its hole. Picking it up, she noticed it was a bit heavy and each end had slight narrow tips, *good this should help me with the digging,* she thought.

Without thinking, she knew that she had at least twelve hours head start before her morning meal came in and with the wooden rung she began to break open the hole.

She made up her mind that she was getting out of there, she grabbed the pamphlet and shoved it into her sweater jacket, bottle of water, matches and the other spare candles all went into her two side pockets, next she place her jacket by the hole.

Two hours of hard work forced her to take a short break in between. While resting and drinking more water, she tried to send Jack a telepathic message to let him knew that she was breaking her way out, whether it worked or not, she just knew that she had to try.

Stepping back, and observing her handiwork and feeling proud that she was making progress; the hole was almost now six inches bigger.

After her rest and back up on her knees, she reached in to feel what was out there and she felt how thick the wall was, to her surprise it was one less than an inch and a half thick. But, how can that be? Remembering the door was four inches thick! She suddenly recognized it as *A DELUSIONAL TRICK*!

She picked up the fallen pieces of limestone to inspect it and she was surprised to that it was drywall with stucco plaster on top of it, giving it a look of the limestone effect.

Looking around her room, and wondering if all four walls were designed that way or not. She got back up on her feet and knocked on the wall in front of her, and walked over towards the door was and knocked on the wall beside it. Until, she immediately noticed a major difference in the knocking with her knuckles. One was a softer knock while the other was a harder knock that really hurt her knuckles.

It's only this one wall that is an artificial wall. She went back to the opened hole, again kneeling back down on both her knees, looking through, still nothing but pitch black air, next she took the lite candle and placed it inside the foot and half-opened hole, hoping to see what was up ahead, still too dark to see anything but, she did notice the flickering of the flame was still being drawing outwards towards something but, what?

Discouraged, she brought the candlestick back inside and set it back down. Madeleine stood up and with both hands on the lower edge of the stucco drywall, with a sudden and hard pull; a larger chunk gave away inwards, falling apart in two larger chunks, but, still not big enough to let her whole body get through it.

Feeling proud of herself and had decided to break up more drywall, this time with both her hands, she drew in a deep breath and with all her strength that she could mustard up, she pulled inwards causing a larger section of the wall to give away, landing both her and the drywall chunks crashing down onto the floor. All she saw were the two-by-four studs that were eighteen inches apart that had been holding the plaster in its place.

Madeleine jumped back up on her feet and strained her ears to listen, she was afraid that a guard might have been outside her door and heard the crashing noise, so she quickly grabbed the lit candle and she grabbed her sweater jacket. With only a pair of slippers on her feet, she managed to squeeze her slender body sideways through the eighteen-inch opening of the studs: it was a tight fit between the studs, but she was able to side her body through.

Once on the outside, she held up the candle high to make sure no one was around, satisfied. She inspected and saw the soft glow against the walls of a small cavern, one that she did not recognize.

Stepping further back away from her room to look behind her and saw her room was designed in a square with its own ceiling; there was plenty of open space just above and all around it. And instantly knew then, that her room had been constructed to hold someone. To think that they went out of their way to build a room to hold someone inside was beyond her comprehension.

She knew that she had to move quickly before anyone found her gone but, didn't know which direction to turn into. A few seconds went by and she decided on going forwards into the unknown, away from the square room. She placed her cupped hand behind the candle flame to stop the flame from being blown out, with only four matches left in the box; she dare not take any chances.

After an hour of quietly and quickly moving out of the cavern area and going wall to wall, corridor to corridor, she sat down and took a break. Feeling chilly, she put on her sweater jacket and drank half a bottle of water. Taking out the pamphlet and with little candlelight, she tried to study where she was, nothing made sense to her racing mind, and she couldn't concentrate at the moment and closed it up. She knew deep down in her heart that she was lost and quietly let out a soft choking cry while she said a small pray for an Angel to come and help her find her way out of the Catacombs of Hell.

For the first time in her life, she felt terrified and alone and she began to tremble all over. *Come on girl, you get up and move, Jack is looking for you.* After she got back up and steading herself, again, going from one corridor into another. The smell of the muskiness was sickening and she began to lose all track of time. Between taking small breaks and drinking the last of the bottled water and trying to run while cupping the candle through corridors, she was exhausted but, still forced herself to keep moving. She didn't want to be caught.

At last she stopped in a corner, holding the candle up higher, she saw a full-sized skeleton hanging by its neck, forcing her to let out a loud and piercing scream, dropping the candle, falling backward and hitting her head against a wall and passing out unconscious from the knock or shock.

Madeleine woke to the smell of the musky air, reminding her that she was still inside the catacombs, it was pitch-black; she began to panic, and forced herself to reach out groping around on the flooring, searching for the dropped candlestick and couldn't find it. She pulled out the box of matches from her pocket, open and removed one of the sticks, with shaky hands; she struck hard on the rough side of the matchbox. It sparked and quickly lit up. The glowing of the flame had softly cast a light showing her where the shiny brass candlestick was lying, it was just off to the right side of her, she quickly grabbed it and replaced the falling wax candle back into its socket and lit its wick, this time, casting a larger glow.

Once again she saw the hanging skeleton. She quickly forced her hand across her mouth keeping herself from screaming out loud again. Rubbing the back of her head with her other hand she felt a small bump, *thank God I didn't cut my head open*, she thinking to herself.

Standing herself upwards and quickly ran as fast as she could while at the same time, cupping the candle to protect the flame from going out. Finally she slowed down; she was in another *dam corridor* and noticed that, she was missing her slippers. *Oh my God, my feet must have been so cold, I didn't feel them falling off my feet when I passed out,* she thought.

She brought her arm up to see the time on her watch, with the soft glow of the candle, it showed that it was just after eight a.m., *Oh nooo, Steve and his dark man must be going crazy trying to find me,*

I've got to keep moving, she began to run into one corridor after another. From one muddy room into another she ran.

She felt a sudden dry thirst that was beginning to hurt her throat and stopped, she reached into her pocket for the water bottle, it too was missing, and she groaned out loud till she suddenly heard a noise, in a panic and with eyes wide opened, she glanced around, *oh nooo, they found me, I have to keep running,* telling herself and once again she was on the run. Each time she would stop and tried to strain her ears to hear if anyone was coming, no use, her hearing aid was only picking up her own heavy breathing and the internal sounds of her heart rapidly beating. As much as she tried to slow down her breathing, it was of no use, with cold feet she kept shivering, breathing fast and hard, making herself thirstier without realizing what she was doing.

A couple more hours passed by, her candle finally burned itself down till it went completely out, causing her to once again panic. She quickly sat down on the cold damp ground and reached into her pocket, pulled out the spare candle and with the third match she lit it up. She knew that she has only two matches left. With her back against a large rock, she looked around her and quietly whispered, *that is odd, it no longer looks like the limestone walls.* She reached over and ran her hand across the wall next to the rock; she recognized that it was hard caked mud wall. She noticed the ceiling was lower than normal. *Oh gosh, what can this mean,* she wondered.

Remembered what Jack had told her at the time, how people going in and losing their way, only later to be found dead in the Catacombs, *a cruel and harsh death, ohhh nooo, I don't want to die in here, please Jack, find me, I need you, oh dear God, please show me the way out,* letting out a stifling cry. She was bone-weary tired, cold from the dampness, hungry, and thirsty all in that order. And all she could think was that she had to keep going before she was caught by her kidnappers. She began to have visions of herself, lying somewhere dead and no one would find her for years or even centuries. With those thoughts and sheer willpower, she knew that she needed to keep moving while at the same time, straining both her ears for any sounds to help her to identify.

Once more, with shaky legs she managed to get herself up and began to run, again and again stumbling along till she finally dropped. Her body was sore all over and ached everywhere. No bone in her body was shielded from the biting numbness and cold dampness that had taken over her tired body. With strong determination and true grit, she would fall down and get right back up, always looking behind her each time. The only sound she heard, again, was her own hard breathing and her heart pounding on her eardrums, they felt like they were about to explode, till finally, her hearing aid battery began to die itself out.

Oh great, another obstacle, counting back the last time she changed her hearing aid battery.... *Was it a week ago already, I better change it now while I can,* as she reached inside her pocket to take out the package of hearing aid batteries, only to realize that it too somehow had falling out of her pocket.

She was now totally deaf and could no longer hear her own breathing; she had to rely solely on her intuitions to get herself out alive. She fell down against large boulder rocks after rocks and knew she was cut, no doubt bleeding till she noticed the candle's flame began to follow the draft that was once again calling to the flame. Without watching her footings, she stumbled into a hole and dropped her candlestick causing the flame to go out, once again in total blackness. "NOOO," she screamed out as she pounded on the flooring below her. "NO, NO, she kept screaming out. It was at that point she didn't care if she was caught by the Steve or not.

The wide hole she had falling into and knew it came up to, just above her hips, rubbing her legs to make sure that she had no broken bones, she felt the warm dampness around her left knee and knew immediately that she was bleeding. She lit up her fourth match to look for the falling candlestick while at the same time trying to climb out of the hole. Looking around to see where she was and was in total shock when she saw that her fall by sheer luck somehow had just narrowly missed falling down into a very deep blacker cavern below her. She franticly moving the match up higher to see if there were other entrees of some sort and suddenly saw past her the many clay jugs of all sizes and shapes, some were still fully in tacked and some were broken, there on the ground on the other side of her were many artifacts that were spread about till her eyes spotted two skeletons that were lying side by side. Looking around, she realized that she had wandered out onto a narrow ledge that had a hole that she was standing in of some sort and into some kind of a historical storage room.

She quickly looked around to find her candlestick and saw brass reflecting itself against her candlelight. She saw that it had falling over the shallow ledge too far down on the cavern flooring. Looking around and suddenly realized there was no way down to the floor, not with the match halfway burnt down to her fingers. Her fingers began to feel warm from the flame, forcing her to hurry and scan around to find an exit. She spotted a smaller one not more than twenty feet off to the left side of her. After climbing out of the hole and quickly got off the ledge over to the wall side and with one hand on the wall, she moved towards the entrance till the match burned down to her fingertips forcing her to drop the match stick and letting out a loud scream, rubbing it against her chest to dull the burning pain.

In the jet blackness, Madeleine continued to feel her way along the wall till her hand found the mouth of the exit.

Once inside, Madeleine sat down and began to cry hard, sobbing and choking out, "I want to go home, JACK WHERE THE HELL ARE YOUUUUU," screaming out louder into the pitch-black musky air. It was at the point, again, she did not care anymore if the kidnapers heard her or not, she want to be caught and taking back into the security of her, so-called, square dungeon room.

With only one match left in the matchbox, no more candles sticks, a dead hearing aid battery, a tried, extremely thirsty and weak body and she was determined to live to see Jack, her parents, Ginger, her friends and return to 'City Of Lights'! All those thoughts were racing through her tired mind. It was all those thoughts that were trying to keep her alive and she knew it. She was not going to give up, not just yet, anyhow. Her life was just beginning and had too much to live for. Between her sniffling she began to rock herself back and forth till she fell into a deep and heavy sleep till, she heard a voice in her head, *"Run, run hard and don't stop or they will catch up you!"*

She quickly got up on her numb feet and began to feel her way along the mud-caked wall while screaming out loud.

"NOO, noo oh my God, Jack where are you?"

Stumbling and getting up each time all the while praying till she stepped on something soft.

"WHAT WAS THAT, she shouted?" unable to hear herself, but knew that she used her vocal cords.

Quickly reaching down in the pitch black to feel it with her iced cold hand, at first touch, she didn't recognize what the item was and thought perhaps it was some kind of clothing that was left behind, till she moved her hand long, and she screamed as loud and hard as she could, "RAAATTTSSSS."

The Catacombs rats, bats and creeping crawlers have all been the farthest things from her mind till then, like lighting, she bolted screaming and running blindly till she ran into a hard surface wall, bouncing herself backward and onto the ground, leaving her dazed. Reaching out to touch and feel her way along the damp and slimy floor towards the wall, touching whatever was in front of her, suddenly felt something cold and all slimy. She knew it was another wall and turned left, once again, feeling her way along. Her head began to ache even more from banging into too many walls, and the dehydration didn't help.

Finally, calming down just enough, to the point that she was able to think rationally for a minute, to place both hands on her face, and felt the bleeding. Standing up and grabbed the bottom corner of her sweater jacket, bringing up it to her face and she wiped the blood away till it felt dry.

Again she was on the move, blindly with one hand reaching out in case she banged into another wall, the other hand she kept it lower in case she should stumble against a rock. Every so many feet she would stop and rested and breathe in the dank air. Once more on the move again, and again she would fall down hard to get back up till she tripped over rock after rock, she fell hard on her left knee. She could no longer feel her feet. The piercing sharp pain and pounding heart caused her to pass out once more, this time she fell down hard and was caught between the rock and a slimy wall.

When she came around, she was feeling weaker and more dazed. Alarm bells were going off inside her head and she knew that it was still pitch black around all around her. She bravely and weakly stood up only to hit the mud caked low ceiling. The more she walked forwards, the lower the ceiling was becoming, causing her to hunch down to the point that she was crawling on both her hands and knees. *Oh God, where am I going, please don't let me die in this hell hole. Please Jack, show me the way out,* she kept repeating the sentence over and over again till finally she had enough and from the bottom of her abyss lungs she screamed loud and hard, "I HATE NOT HEARING ANYTHING AT ALL," broke down and cried heavy sobs, feeling sorry for herself.

After twenty minutes had passed, tired and exhausted to the point that she could feel ready to pass on to the next world from having no fluids or nourishment, she knew that a human body can live up to a month with no food, but, water was another luxury that was needed. She sat down and took out the last match and struck it against the side of the box, lighting up the area to see what was ahead of her or should she go back instead she noticed the flame on the match was leaning towards a draft. Her intuitions told her that she was heading in the right direction, she pulled herself up on her knees once more and let the flame followed the draft and she in turn followed the flame.

Finally the flame began to burn itself down but, not before Madeleine felt a breeze brush her across the tired face. *What was that,* startling her into thinking of spider webs or was it ghosts?

Quickly searching as far as she could see if there were any more openings she enters into. All she saw were walls and mud. Finally the flame burnt her fingers causing her to let out another loud scream as she began kicking the ground hard with both her numbed feet while she brought her fingers to her mouth to cool down the burned area. "Enough is enough," she screamed out loud from the bottom pit of her lungs to whomever or whatever could hear her.

"Don't panic right now, you need to be strong, you need to get out, now, get moving, go, go, go," she shouted out to herself and was unable to hear if she spoke in a high or low tone.

Breathlessly and crawling on her hands and knees at a quicker pace, through the shallow mucky slime on the ground, she suddenly stopped and noticed the breeze getting stronger. Slowly breathing in and recognized the air was beginning to smell fresher and not as dank or musty as it had been. Staying in that position to try and gain back a bit of her strength from the fresh air or *was she dreaming that she was on her way to the heavens*? How close was she to get out, she had no idea except continued to follow the breeze till she came up against a dirt wall, *nooo, not this again*, she cried out and began with both her fist-pounding hard against the muddy wall.

"There has to be a hole somewhere for the breeze to get through," she said, screaming out loud when suddenly, the wall gave away with a sudden blast of fresh air laying a million kisses in her face, all welcoming her back into civilization.

It was still too dark to see anything and mustered up what little strength and courage she had left in her battered and bloody body, with bare hands, she dug with her broken, chipped and bleeding nails deeply into the muddy dirt, angrily forcing and breaking apart till the hole till it got bigger and bigger. Forcing the hole to become big enough for her to try and slide her weakened body through.

She didn't know if she would fall into another area of the Catacombs or into a deeper hole to die alone, all she knew was that she did not come all the way from Canada to Pairs to die alone. Madeleine made up her mind that was not going to die, not without putting up a big fight first.

Carefully forced her tired body through the hole, it was snug at first, her wiggling had forced the earth to give away more. Finally, she fell out onto her side, exhausted. She rested against the wet and cold ground when suddenly; she recognized something wet was falling on her face, *RAIN,* she whispered.

The rain had been falling down onto her face the whole time that her body was partially out. She gladly let the cold rain wash away the pain, dirty dried blood from her face. The realization had set in, she was finally outside!

"I'm out and I'm and still alive", chocking and crying out loud at the same time forcing the rest of her legs out from the hell hole. Her legs felt heavy as she let them slide down from the wall banks where the hole that she alone had made.

Resting her broken down and tired body on the cold and wet ground, exhausted, she tried to force herself to stand once more, only to stumbled and fall back down again. She sat for ten minutes letting the cold rain stream down her numb body; she knew the rain would help rejuvenate her into getting back up on her feet. But, not until she breathed in the welcoming damp air, letting it remove the dank and earthly air from her battered and bruised lungs.

She felt a need to keep moving; again she got up and tried to run. Her rubber legs buckled from under her, causing her to stumble three feet further away from the hell hole she had just crawled out. Tripped and fell against something hard and passed out from sheer exhaustion, but, not before she barely whispering out his name, *Jack I'm out.*

Friday night at 12:15 a.m.

The gathering of the dark and stormy clouds, suddenly, let lose a split second bolt of lightning along with a thunderous crash, splitting apart a tree. The sudden loud vibrational starling Madeleine awake, which earlier had passed out from sheer exhaustion and was resting her tired body against the trunk of the nearby tree.

In a panic, she jumped and looked around only to realize, that she was finally outside and sitting under a tree. The tree's branches for her umbrella weren't enough to protect her from the harsh weather elements; yet, she was shivering and feeling wet from the cold spring rains heavy downpour.

Her hot tears began to fall and she feebly thought to herself, *oh my God, I made it out, I can't believe it, YES! I'm still alive, ohh the rain; oh it feels so good,* stretching out her weak and feeble hands, cupping them to catch the rain waters, quickly began drinking it in, each time reaching out for more rainwater to quench her thirst, she didn't care if her hands were dirty or not, she needed water.

She hadn't eaten any foods or drank any liquids in the last forty eight hours or so. With water in her belly, she began to wonder if she had to fall asleep or fell unconscious this time. She couldn't tell the time because her watch, a birthday gift from her parents was broken, the crystal glass face had been shattered during one of her recent falls against the rocks and now, the digital time was stuck at seven-thirty in the evening, she just knew that it was much later than that.

Feeling her hot tears spilling over against her cold and bruised cheeks, while feebly thinking to herself, *'oh my God, at last I made it out, and I can't believe it, YES! I'm still alive, ohh the rain; ohh it feels so good'* as she eagerly stretched out her weak and trembling hands, grasping and cupping her palms to catch the rain waters, began quickly drinking and letting the cool water flow down her parched throat, each time reaching out for more rainwater to quench her thirst, she didn't care if her hands were dirty or not, she needed water.

She hadn't eaten any foods or drank any liquids in the last forty-eight hours or was it longer? With just enough water to satisfy her thirst, and trying to remember if she had to fall asleep or fell back unconscious this time.

She couldn't tell the time because her watch, a birthday gift from her parents was broken, the crystal glass face had been shattered during one of her recent falls against the rocks and now, the digital time was stuck at seven-thirty most likely in the evening, the last she remembered it to be, she knew that it was much later.

Feeling her hot tears spilling over against her cold and bruised cheeks, while feebly thinking to herself, *'oh my God, at last I made it out, and I can't believe it, YES! I'm still alive, ohh the rain; ohh it feels so good'* as she eagerly stretched out her weak and trembling hands, grasping and cupping her palms to catch the rain waters, began quickly drinking and letting the cool water flow down her parched throat, each time reaching out for more rainwater to quench her thirst, she didn't care if her hands were dirty or not, she needed water.

The pains in Madeleine body reminded her that she immediately needed medical attention; she knew it was important for her health to get out of the cold rains and fast before she went into shock. Feeling weak and trembling she was unsure if she could stand up and try to make a run before kidnappers somehow, managed to find her. With her back against the tree, she slowly edged herself upright, forcing her rubber legs to stand up, just then, the sudden sharp pain pierced through her left knee.

Gently massaging it and looking through the heavy rains to see where she was. Just up ahead of her, she saw the glow from the city lights, her memory came flooding back reminding her that she was still in Paris. *But, where about in Paris, am I?*

Through the downpour, she immediately looked around for any recognizable buildings or structures of any kind that would stand out to her, disappointed, it didn't. Just over forty-eight hours or so ago, the vast catacombs of Paris's underground networks and the realms of the cavern complexity had plunged Madeleine into total darkness. Her memories came flooding back, to that early morning.

Forcing herself away from the tree feeling dizzy and numb all over, she tried to walk only to stumbling over, falling back down again. She waited till her mind cleared up and catching her breath once more.

Forcing herself to crawl her way over to the roadside, sixty feet in front of her; she couldn't feel her arms or her legs; she only knew that she had to force them to move one in front of the other, one move at a time. With every few paces that she made, she would put her head down on the cold and wet ground, repeating Jack's name over and over to keep herself awake while she continued to make her way over to the edge of the roadside. She made it and waited till she saw a set of lights coming her way. Looking up to the night sky, the welcoming rain continued to wash away the dirt and blood from her face and down on her neck.

Finally, two bright lights were coming down the road towards her. Tiredly, she tried to stand up only to fall back down behind a low shrub, the lights drove pass her. She let out a soft cry, "Nooo, please," feeling discouraged she feebly let out another soft whimper.

"Come on girl, you have to stand up, she told herself," and with all her strength she could mustard, drew in a deep breath and through her hot tears, with all her sheer will power, she stumbled and swayed as she stood straight upwards as soon as she saw another set of headlights shinning towards her..

With weak and shaky legs placing one leg in front of the other, gently swaying and finally stepped out to the road. With both her tired and heavy arms she reached up towards the dark skies, waving to attract the attention of the driver, whoever it may be.

The driver of the older pickup truck saw a figure on the side of the road, he could tell immediately this person looked in need of help and he slowed down, coming to a stop in front of her; the driver didn't get a chance to put his truck into the park mode when she dropped down hard onto the hood of his truck.

In awe he watched her body slide down to the ground. Quickly he jumped out into the heavy rain and ran to her side, kneeled down and just barely heard, "I'm Madeleine Windsor from Canada." At that point she blacked out from pure exhausting.

The driver on recognizing her name didn't waste time calling for an ambulance and the police.

Everything went black as she lost consciousness, spiraling downwards into a deep dark tunnel of the abyss. Slowly, she began to feel her body drift towards a sparkling bright light that was beginning to come closer and closer towards her. The light was warm and welcoming to her as she floated closer and closer while listening to the heavenly music.

CHAPTER 11

Saturday 7:00 a.m.

Madeleine could feel a cool cloth gently dragging across her forehead and over her the sides of her face; she gave a little moan *Nooo*, and fell back into a deep sleep. She had been dreaming that she was still inside the Catacombs and suddenly let out a scream. Startling Jack, who had been by her side since the first day they brought her from the intensive care department to her own private room. As requested, a private room across from the nurse's station.

Wide awake, he dropped the wet cloth and bolted up and was immediately closer to her side, trying to calm her down. He whispered softly into her ear, saying that she was safe. He knew it was of no use, not without her hearing aid on and yet he had hoped that somehow she heard him.

Her dream reaction brought tears to Jack's eyes while the nurses on hearing her moaning out, quickly came in and increased her morphine drip. They stayed and watched while she began to calm down, just enough to fall back, this time into a peaceful sleep.

The rest of the day went quickly and once again she barely awoke to feel a light kiss on her forehead and could tell that she was in bed, thinking she was back on the cot and began to thrash around and scream out loud, *nooo,* when she heard a voice deep inside of her.

"Run, run hard and don't stop or they will catch up you," she felt strong hands pressing hard against her shoulders, holding her down while someone was gently brushing their cool hand across her forehead, she couldn't hear any sounds, all she heard was lull humming tones in her ears and fell back again into a deep sleep.

Sunday 11:00 a.m.

More than twenty-four hours went by and she slowly began to open her eyes, at first all she saw, was a burr, blinking her dry eyes a couple of times and forcing them to clear themselves up.

Glancing around and looked at both her arms and hands all bandaged up, she recognized that she was in the hospital. Looking up, she saw that she was hooked up to the intervention bag. Her eyes were following the plastic tubing down into her arm. She looked to her left and saw Jack sleeping in the chair beside her bed; he was wearing the same clothes the day they entered the Catacombs, he looked haggard and unshaven.

She tried to say his name, but her parched throat and cracked, dry lips wouldn't move, her voice was still too weak. Hard as she tried, to whisper his name, "Jack," he didn't hear her at first; again she said his name a little louder this time, "Jack." Her throat hurt her and she gave a low groan.

On hearing his name and assuming it was one of her nurses calling him, Jack opened his eyes and saw that Madeleine was awake, staring back at him with her tired and teary eyes.

"Maddie," he jumped up from his chair, went over to her side and slid down on his knees, he buried his face into her shoulders crying, "Oh Maddie, darling."

She could feel his heavy sobbing against her shoulder. After a few minutes, she reached over weakly touching his head with her bandaged hand and whispered, "Jack, I made it out, I'm alive."

Lifting his head, not ashamed to show his tear-stained face; he nodded his head, yes, and carefully lean forwards and gently kiss her cracked dry lips.

He pulled back from her face and made sure that her eyes were on his lips to read, "hush darling, don't tax yourself, need to save your strength, we'll talk later, ok."

She did lip-read him and whispered, "I'm so tired and my throat hurts." She closed her eyes and drifting into a peaceful sleep.

Without her hearing aid on, what she didn't hear was Jack saying,

"Yes, Maddie darling, sleep, just what you need, I'm here till I take you back home," while looking over her badly scratched, bruised up face and her matted dirty dark hair. In spite of all that, she still looked beautiful to him. This brave and strong woman was going to be his wife and he was dam proud of her. Earlier, he had sworn to God, if he brought her back to him, alive, that he would forever be in his debt. And now he must repay his debt by forever looking after her.

Still shaking, Jack got up and stepped out the hallway to the nurses stations, using their phone and called her father, with a gentle sob, he told him what he had been anxiously waiting to hear.

"Fred, she just woke up, and yes she is alert but, right now, she is resting."

Fred gave a little choke, "Good to hear that Jack, give her a kiss for us and tell her that we will be right over shortly and Jack, thanks for calling us," said Fred Windsor.

The next call he made, was to Wilbert's private cell phone, on answering, Jack gave him instructions to bring him a clean change of clothing, his shaving kit and he once again, thanked him for remembering to bring over the charger for his cell phone on the first night at the hospital. All he knew was that when Madeleine fully awakens, he didn't want her to see him the way he was. The last call was to Rachel who was staying Canada to run her company till she was well enough to return back to work. Rachel had been jumping every time her cell phone rang; she had been expecting to hear the worst news from France.

When Jack told her of the good news, she quickly replied, "Jack, that is wonderful news, yes, I'll let everyone here know that she is going to be all right," she told him through her tears.

"And Jack, give her my love, will you?"

She told Jack, their Canadian media picked up the news from Paris and it was all over the television and radios, Jack swore out loud. They talked a few minutes more before hanging up.

Jack turned and asked the nurse to inform the doctors and let them know that she woke up and now resting.

The nurse smile and said, "I have already alerted them, all our prayers were answered," Jack smiled. He knew the mysteries of religion were baffling and he didn't dare question it, not right now at least, but, he did have questions for that one man in heaven and that question will have to wait for now.

Going back into her room, he sat down, carefully picked up her bandaged hand and kissed the back of her hand. He could see the blood had been seeping through the white bandages and worried how she was going to react when she finds out that she won't be able to use her hands or walk for a few weeks. He understood that all women put a lot of time and effort into their hair and their fingernails. Madeleine's nails, according to the doctors were badly cracked with one nail completely split down the center and the rest of her nails were broken, *most likely from trying to claw her way out,* thought Jack.

He planned to have someone come to the castle and do a manicure once her nails have healed and she recuperates. He laid his head on the back of his chair and drifted off the sleep for he too, had a long harrowing experience missing his Maddie.

Sunday 5:30 p.m.

When Madeleine woke up, she saw both her parents standing at the foot of her bed, the three doctors on her right and Jack who has since changed his clothing, was sitting in the chair by her left side and still holding onto her hand. She looked peacefully at him and he kissed her hand, and pointed to her mother. She could see that her parents had aged a few years from worrying about their missing daughter.

When Jack made the call the night she went missing, just before the media picked up the story, together they flew the first jet out to Paris; now, they were staying at Jack's castle.

Courtney held up Madeleine's hearing aid for her to see, she pointed to the battery case and she immediately understood that her mother had changed and put in the new hearing aid battery for her. Courtney went to her bedside and very gently, she moved away from her matted dry hair and carefully put the ear mole snuggly into her right ear, Madeleine automatically reached upwards to push in the mole further inside the ear canal, and look terrified what saw that it was not only one but both of her hands that were bandaged with blood seeping through.

Jack carefully grabbed both her hands into his, and closing them together, he kissed them, looking into her eyes telling her, its ok.

After Madeleine had her hearing aid in, she reached up automatically and tried to turn up the volume, realizing she couldn't. It was her mother that turned it up till Madeleine move her head aside, indicating, loud enough for her to hear once again. The first sound she heard was the beeping of the heart monitoring machine and heard Courtney's voice, "is that better my dear?"

Glancing at her mother she whispered a feeble "yes."

Fred came around and gently kissed his daughter on the forehead and looked directly at her.

"You have given us quite a scare my dear and we missed you Madeleine, I want you to take it easy for now and soon, you will be back to old yourself again."

Jack knew that Fred had lied to her, but understood, it was for her own sake, with the condition she was in; he knew that she was going to be in the hospital for a long while yet.

The main doctor in charge of her cleared his throat and signaled for everyone, all but Jack to leave the room while he checked out his patient. He knew with the parents listening, their reactions normally caused the patient to be more upset or worried than they needed to be.

Jack stayed sitting in his chair, with her parents gone and the door was closed, the doctor pulled back her blankets, Jack gasped out loud when he saw Madeleine's legs. Her legs were mostly scraped, bloodied along with black and blue marks all down both her legs, there was hardly any clean bare skin left to see on her. Just below her left knee was large blood-soaked bandage that was covering a deep gash where the doctor had closed it with stitches inside and outside.

Jack watched while the doctor removed the bandages to inspect his stitching handiwork. The doctor pointed out other cuts to him while looking over her legs for any signs of infection, satisfied none had shown. Next, together Jack and the doctors all inspected both soles of her feet and could see both had the cuts and bruises; Jack noticed what looked like a couple of toes were broken and she had torn out a couple of her toenails on the other foot. Jack cried quietly inside himself known that the pain she must have suffered with.

The doctor began checking around each of her toes and the cuts for signs of infection, satisfied all look clear, for now and after the decisions with the other doctors who were all there for the learning experience, he ask the nurses to rewrap with more antibiotic creams and clean bandages. Next, he put gentle pressure on her ribs, and she gave a soft cry. After writing his notes in her chart, he told them in English, the x-rays showed that most of her ribs were badly bruised up, no doubt from her falling onto something hard. "Luckily no major breaks."

Next, he listened to her lungs with his stethoscope and Jack turned his head the other way, giving her some privacy. He had explained to the doctor when she was first brought in that he didn't think that she had not yet, laid with a man, the doctor only nodded his head in acknowledgment, and promised to be extra careful with her.

After his assessment, he ordered the nurse to take more blood examples; he wanted to be sure her electrolytes were back up to normal and to make sure there were no signs of blood poisoning or infections. What Madeleine didn't know was that on her arrival she needed a blood transfusion, but, a couple of bags had been order up from the lab. A couple of the deeper cuts had been bleeding out profusely by the time she arrived at the hospital.

When the head nurse left to call down and order the blood workup, the doctors closed her bedroom door to give them some privacy. He knew that he was going to be talking a bit louder. He knew she was waiting to hear what happened to her and he wanted her to hear what he was about to tell her.

Sitting in the chair by the right side of her bed and facing her, so she could lip-read him, if needed, "Miss Windsor, am I speaking loud enough for you to hear me?"

She nodded her head, yes to him.

"Good, my name is Dr. Jacques; I am your attending physician, now, I don't want you to talk for a few more days yet, your vocal cords in your throat are strained and slightly damaged, no doubt feeling raw and yes, they will get better with time, but only if you rest them!"

She understood now why they were sore; she knew it was from all her screaming that she did while inside the Catacombs.

"Your ribs are very badly bruised; did someone punch you in the ribs at all?"

She shook her head, no, and was about to tell the doctor that she had fallen, but, he quickly put up his hand to keep her from talking.

"In any case, your ribs bruising are equivalent to a boxer's bruised ribs."

She only shook her head and whispered that, she fell on too many rocks and into holes.

Looking at her very seriously and remarked, "Then, that makes more sense."

"You have a lot of cuts and bruises all over you and it will take some time to heal itself, the soles of your feet are very badly lacerated, a couple of them are deep. You have broken off a couple of your toenails two of your toes are broken," pointing to her feet that were all bandaged up.

"Don't worry, the nails will grow back in."

"It's beyond my comprehension how you managed to walk; you can tell me about that later, when your throat is feeling much better, my dear."

"Also, you must have to fall onto something sharp, the inside of your left knee has a very deep, laceration, we managed to clean it up and put in stitches, whatever you cut your knee on, it just barely nicked the main artery, that was one of the reasons that you lost some blood."

"All I can say is thank heavens the driver who stopped to assist you called for the ambulance when he did. When you first arrived, we needed to give you a blood transfusion; for now, we'll need to keep an eye on your blood work."

"As for your lungs, they are still strong and no signs of infection yet, it's a real miracle considering the damp and moldy air you have been breathing the entire time, we put you on one of the newer types of antibiotics, and it seemed to be working. There are no signs of infections anywhere and that itself is a real miracle."

Looking at Jack, he cleared his throat, "just for your own personal information, you were not raped."

He saw her looking at him in shock, he quickly held up his hand, "oh don't worry Miss Windsor, I had a female doctor check you out.

It's a standard procedure for the to police for someone in your condition. By the way, I ordered her to put in a tube into your ureter, it's a hook to the bag by your bed, so you won't need to get up to use the washroom, just until your feet are completely healed and you are able to stand on them, ok?"

She knew that she had not been raped but, felt relieved that it was a woman and not a male that did the internal examination, with her face flushed, she nodded a thank you.

"Now, I'm guessing you want to know when you came to go home, am I correct so far?"

She only nodded her head in agreement.

He sternly looked to Jack and back to her, he hated to tell her the truth.

"Let me put it this way, you will be our guest for a while."

She looked at him with a frown, and he understood, like most of his patience, she wanted to know why.

He shook his head, "Miss Windsor, there is no easy way to say this, there is, by far too much damage done to your body, you have been very traumatized and you need time to heal your cuts. As of today, I'm going to keep you here for at least a week or even two. Let's take it one day at a time, shall we?"

When she heard how long she will be in and the amount of damage, tears spilled down her cheeks and Jack got up and carefully sat on the edge of her bed, with a tissue. And he wiped away her tears, telling her, that he will be with her till the day she walks out. Again, the good doctor advised them to take it one day at a time, and said that he will check in a bit later and give them an updated review on her new blood work results; and quietly left the room, closing the door behind him, leaving the couple to themselves once more.

When the doctor stepped out to the hallway and saw the reporters all hanging around for information on his patient, he quietly asked the nurse to find and take her parents into his private office down the hallway. He knew he had to give them what they have been waiting to hear. They had not been told the severity of her battered and bruised body.

Once settled in, the Windsor's listened to his medical reports, Courtney let out a stifling cry and Fred swore out loud. The doctor assured the Windsor's that she will make a full recovery but, it will take some time and that she will be giving the best care during her stay.

"For someone who is hearing impaired and came through hell, she was one brave lady, if she were my daughter, I would be extremely proud of her!"

When Madeleine asked Jack in her soft whispering voice, how long she had been in the hospital for, he hesitated and thought she best know the truth, he held up his fingers and quietly told her four whole days, and that she was unconscious and close to death when the ambulance brought her in.

Her next question was, "And the kidnappers?"

With a scowl on his face, he told her, "We got them both; they were connected to Gregory, and get this, were hired by Professor Burnet."

"Apparently, they were after my Golden Medallion, the dam thing, I wished I had never dug it up in the first place and none of this would have happened, it has brought me nothing but bad luck!"

Madeleine's eyes widen and she whispered to him.

"Did they get all of the men?"

"Oh those bastards, Inspector Dupert had all the Catacombs en-trées staked out including the newest one you came through. They caught coming out through one of the older entrées; the policed nailed them on the spot. The Inspector questioned your where-about, they told him, that you had escaped somewhere into the Cat-acombs, and they tried to find you and just gave up, how do you like that, just given up, just like that uh?"

Madeleine laid her tired head back down on her pillow, she knew then, they had left her for dead and for that, she, too was upset.

"Maddie, I think you have had quite enough information for to-day. Look darling; it's after nine o'clock at night and you should get some sleep, tomorrow is another day."

As tired as she was, sleep would not come to her, Jack stayed by her bed watching her, he had vowed that he would never let her out of his sights again and a dull ache in his heart had him worried that she may want to return back home to Canada after the hell she had been through.

He could see that she was having trouble with sleeping.

"Would you like me to lie down beside you, I promised to behave myself," giving her one of his famous smiles.

Looking into his soft hazel eyes, nodded her head to him, with a lazy smile. Before he lay on the bed with her, he questioned her.

"Would you like to have the lights left on or turned off?"

He saw his answer when he saw a horror expression in her eyes and he knew they both were in for a long recovery.

"The lights will stay on for as long as you want them to be, dar-ling."

Carefully, he laid his head down on her pillow with his body lying next to hers, and put his right arm gently across her waist, "Is this ok or am I hurting you?"

She shook her head, and she immediately fell off to sleep. He listened to her even rhythms of breathing in and out, and he knew she was at peace.

While he listened to her breathing, he made up his mind that when she was well enough to travel and once back at his castle, he was going to wait on her hand and foot. But, first things first, he planned to hire extra security, since the second day she went missing; the media pick up the news and posted the title across the front page *'Canadian Woman Lost in Our Catacombs, Will She Be Found?'*

Jack, earlier when the word came to her parents, that Madeleine had been found alive on the side of the road and was on her way to the hospital. They were told the bad shape that she was in, and to prepare themselves for the worst.

It was Wilbert who drove them immediately to the hospital but, not before Fred swore a blue streak in the car when their daughter was well enough to travel, they were going to bring her back to Canada with them, regardless of what Jack had to say. Wilbert knew better than to say anything to them; he was just as concerned for Madeleine as they were.

When her parents were brought directly to her intensive care room, Jack was standing there watching the action through the glass window and leaning against the emergency intensive care door. Hearing Fred's voice, he wiped his eyes dry and turned to face them and began to quickly explain what was happening and what was taking place behind the doors.

"Madeleine is unconscious and the nurses behind the curtains were giving her a quick wash down, the doctors and a couple of surgeons are also in her room, they just are conferring over her charts at the moment."

Jack explained to them that they are going to do some x-rays and blood workup and suggest that the three of them go for a coffee while we wait for the reports. After agreeing, Jack told the head nurse in the French language, and asked to be notified when she was awake or if one of the doctors needed them.

The police had cleared away the hallway filled with the Media and some of the braver ones who badly wanted her story to stay hidden out of the way. The Inspector's second in command, rounded up the rest of them and ordered all the Medias to leave the hospital immediately or face heavy fines of obstruction.

After they picked out a quiet corner spot in the hospital's cafeteria, and Jack had settled his nerves with a few sips of his strong black cup of coffee, he told them both the whole story in between their quiet sobbing. He told them,

"Near as anyone could piece together, she had founded her own way out of from the Catacombs."

Jack explained to them the uncharted area that she came through, was never known about or even marked out on the Catacomb's maps. She was the first to have found it. He also mentioned, the police talked with the driver who found her on the road, a precautionary to make sure he had no connections to her kidnapping. The driver gave his alibi and it checked out, the police were satisfied.

"Better brace yourselves; the driver was shooting his mouth off to the media."

"Apparently, the Media are saying that he is a hero, can you believe the jerk!"

"We both know dam well that Madeleine is the real hero here, she saved her own life by braving the Catacombs, and she will have a real story to tell our children," sniffled Jack.

Fred looked at Jack with his somberly look, "Jack, when she is able, we are bringing her back home with us, where she belongs. I believe she has had enough of Paris, wouldn't you agree?"

Courtney shook her head in agreement with her husband. And Jack made up his mind earlier, whatever Madeleine wanted that he would be ok with it. He had visions of her wanting to return to Canada, but first, not without a fight, he was not going to let her back out of his life, even if he had to move to Canada, regardless of what her parents had just said.

By the time they were back up to her room, the doctors were just finishing up with her. On seeing Jack, Dr. Jacques had asked them to follow them into a more private area. Once there, Jack introduced her parents to each of the doctors where one was speaking in clear English and the others in broken English.

Each of the doctors began to tell them of their assessments and their recommendations. And by the time the doctors had left them to absorb the impact of her severity, both Jack and her parents were in total shock.

The echoes of their words had impacted their minds with, "In learning of the seriousness of her condition, had it been anyone else, they would have been long ago, died. Your daughter, sir, is a living miracle; one of her Saints must have been looking out for her."

It took the three of them a little while for the information to sink in and when they regrouped themselves, they worked up the courage and not expecting what to see, they slowly and quietly went into

Madeleine's room. The head nurse, who was by her side, gave them a stern look, to be quiet and not to disturb her sleep.

She whispers to Jack, "She really needs it; she is one brave miracle lady," and walked out to leave the three of them alone with Madeleine.

Courtney on seeing her daughter's face gave out a loud gasp while trying to stifle her cry, "Oh my God."

Fred on seeing beautiful daughter's badly bruised and scratched up face quickly bought his wife closer to him and allowing her to place her head on his shoulders while she cried quietly into his suit jacket, while his stoned ridged face made up his mind, she was returning home to Canada.

And Jack whispered to Madeleine, "What have they done to you my darling?" And he made a promise to himself when he came face to face, with Gregory that he would beat his face to a pulp. At the same time, Fred quietly whispered to Courtney, that, "when the judgement day came, I vowed to be at the courthouse to witness the court judges throwing the books at the lot of them."

Jack heard Madeleine when she gave a low groan, he gently laid his hand on her shoulder to let her know that he was there with her; he knew that she didn't have her hearing aid on and that it would be no use for him to talk to her. He spoke anyway, just in case, "Darling, you are in the hospital, I'm right here with you and I'm not leaving your side, you need to rest, hush, darling, sleep, hushhh."

She gave out another groan, this time she tried to move around. Fred ran out to the hallway to get her nurse who was already on her way in, to carry a needle, she quickly injected the fluid into her inter-venes tube.

Jack quickly spoke up, "what are you giving her?"

"It's ok Mr. Holt, doctor ordered the low dose of morphine, it will help to keep her shock stabilized, poor girl, and she is dreaming that she is still in the Catacombs." She waited till Madeleine was calm, and went back to her station writing out her reports.

Jack cursed out loud; "I'll never set foot in that dam Catacombs for as long as I live."

Fred walked over to her bed and brushed a lock of his daughter's hair that had falling down over the bridge of her nose. He was shocked to see that she had a cut above her hairline and counted three stiches. Kneeling down closer to her face, he gently kissed her cheek and noticed that she was feeling a little flushed. He worried that her cuts and marks had become infected.

He asked Jack, if he would mind asking the nurse, how much longer before she would be awake. And Jack agreed, it was the least he could do for the Windsor's known that he was the reason for her condition. When he returned, he saw that both Fred and Courtney were in deep discussion, *probably planning her return to Canada*, he thought.

Jack told them, "She may not fully wake up for at the most, twenty-four hours, the doctors want her body to rest as much as possible and there is nothing that any of us can do right now, except to pray for her speedy recovery."

Hearing the news, "Otherwise, we may as well go back to your castle, are you coming too, Jack?"

"No, I am staying with her till she is fully awake and when she does, she will need me, and I hope you will understand."

It was agreed that her parents would wait till Jack called them with the good news, at least for now she was out of immediate danger. It was a matter of her regaining consciousness. They said their good byes and Wilbert drove them back to the castle.

Sunday 9:15 p.m.

Jack was alone by her side when the head nurse brought over a newspaper for him to see, "You might want to read this, Mr. Holt."

Jack thanked her and quickly scanned the French Star's front page only to translate the words, "Canada's Miracle Lady Survives the Catacombs on Prayers."

Jack spent the rest of the afternoon reading and rereading all about Madeleine Windsor's heroically survival; with each group of survivor guides speculation how she did it.

Then he read about the people who were responsible for her misfortune, the news also stated how upset the people of Paris were; it showed pictures of people placing numerous bouquets of flowers around the hospital gates. He was even more surprised to read about their engagement. The paper showed pictures of the media trying to question the doctors and nurses walking in the hospital's parking lots that were trying to get into their cars to head for home.

Pages after pages, headline stories of Madeleine, a well-known Canadian designer, the report went on about her business with their Parisian suppliers who gave their opinions on this great lady, saying how sweet and kind she was. Jack thought *they are almost making her out to be a saint; "she is my saint,"* he whispered.

Jack spent the rest of the day and night, sitting upright by her side and quietly waiting for her to wake up, leaving her, only to quickly grab a bite to eat or use the washroom, each time cursing that he had to leave her side. And when the doctors came in, on their orders, he would quickly put on a hospital sterile gown whenever they needed to check on her vitals or change the dressing on her wounds, checking for any signs of infections. The doctors, satisfied there were no fevers or infections, and a few encouraging words to Jack, once more, left the couple alone.

It was getting late and Jack wonder where he was going to sleep, he made it his mission that he would not leave the hospital till she was also, ready to leave. Just then the night head nurse walked into the room carrying a folded-up cot, a pillow and a blanket under one arm.

"Here dear, you can sleep on this, in the morning someone will fetch and put it away for you, I brought you a pillow from the linen storage room, try and get some sleep tonight, tomorrow's day will be much longer!"

Jack thanked her and quietly set up the cot a few feet away from Madeleine's bed, he knew the doctors and nurses would be in and out most of the night, he left just enough room for them to get by. He wanted to be able to hear her in case she needed him, exhausted as he was; he fell into a deep sleep himself.

Monday 7:30 a.m.

He woke to a sunny room, with flowers everywhere and a few teddy bears and wondered where they all came from. The day nurse had noticed that he had awake, and with a slight chuckle she whispered, "We nurses had a bet, which one of you would be the first to wake up, and I won the bet!"

Jack only smiled at her and pointed to Madeleine, "Did she sleep the night through?"

"Yes, she, slept peacefully, the good Lord is at her side."

And Jack pointed to the flowers, "Who sent all this?"

"Let's see, our president, her Prime Minister of Canada, her parents and her office staff members as wells as her business associates."

Jack took it that she meant her suppliers and he planned to look at the flowers and read the car later but, right now he wanted to see Madeleine.

She was still sleeping, in the sunlight in her room, she looked like an Angel. He needed a break to stretch his legs and after using the washroom in her room he left to go down to the cafeteria to grab a quick bite to eat. Once he stepped off the elevator, he was confronted by a swarm of reporters who somehow, snuck their way into the front lobby, past the security guards. The noise of the reports all asking questions at the same time was deafening to the point, the security guards heard them and came running to clear them out of the hospital. Jack had to stay back in the elevator while the guards ushered the reporters back outside. And once the hallway was cleared, he stepped off the elevator and he continued on his way to the cafeteria, he noticed, a lot of hospital staff members were all starring and seemed to be watching his every move.

At the counter Jack order his breakfast meal to go, along with some fresh fruit for snacks. The server handed Jack his bag of food and when he ask how much money he owe her, she said, " No charge, Mr. Holt, the hospital said, while you are here, you are to get all your meals for free."

This generosity stunt Jack who was at lost for words.

He put a mental note on the back burner to remember to make a good sized donation to the hospital. He thanked her proceeded back down the long hallway to the elevator; while Jack waited, he felt his tears welling up as he thought of humanity's nature to be a giver in time of need.

When Jack returned to her room with his breakfast, the head nurse suggested he eat his meal by the waiting area as the doctors are with Madeleine. He agreed and found the area cleared and sat down to quickly gulp down his food without tasting any of it. His mind was on Madeline. Once he finished his coffee and tossed out his garbage into the can, next, he headed to the nurse's station, the two nurses informed Jack, according to the doctors, Madeleine was beginning to awake at any time and they suggested in the future, he stayed close by. One of the nurses offered to go down to the cafeteria and bring up his meals. Their generosity would allow Jack to be there when she woke up.

Monday 9:00 a.m.

He knew the waiting part was always the worst time, after that, the recuperation would be the next step and had it in his head where, when and how she was going to recuperate.

The doctors came out of her room into the hallway and Jack stood by them listening to the prognoses.

"So far there are no signs of infections yet, her cuts and bruises are healing nicely and we all here have determinate to cut back on her morphine.

"Let me warn you Mr. Holt, she will be very weak; and it may take her a few more days before realization on the nature of her extending injuries."

"So is she out of the woods, will she fully recover?"

"We don't see any reason for her not to, other than physiologically, it may very well take her some time, don't forget, she just came through the Catacombs of hell!"

Before Jack could ask any more questions, he heard Inspector Dupert's voice, "I'm glad I caught you all together, is there someplace we can talk?"

The doctors show them to the staff's boardroom that was sitting empty, the five of them sat around the table and Inspector asked the doctors how Madeleine was doing. They each briefed the Inspector their same prognoses as they told Jack.

"Glad to hear that she is coming along nicely, now, what I am about to tell you all, some shocking news!"

Jack was not so sure he wanted to hear anything more at this point. The doctors on the other hand were always ready for whatever gets thrown at them, always on guard and ready.

With the three doctors and Jack listening to the Inspector's telling them about his findings and theories of how Madeleine Windsor surveyed the Catacombs and he warned them, the news was soon about to hit the media and how he wanted them to be the first to hear him out.

In his serious business-like tone, the Inspector began to give the details.

"I met with the search party leader this morning and this is what they found, so far, Madeleine had bent forwards to tie up her sneakers, it shows that she was dragged behind a wall. The men broke through that wall and found an old cloth laced with Chloroform, they figured it out that was why, you Jack, did not her here scream. They followed the footprints to a small room; the door was very thick, no way for anyone to hear her. She did have bottles of water, food and used an old creamery can for a toilet. At least she was well taken care of in that respect."

Jack, on hearing about the room, started to curse, while both his hands turned into great balls of the fist, but the Inspector put up his hand, "Let me finished Jack, the worse of it is yet to be told."

"The search party was surprised to see where she broke out through the wall and began to follow her footprints but, not till they ordered more water, foods, more men and more lighting equipment. Once that was made available, they carried on and followed the rest of her footprints; they left behind a trail of ropes and markers in case they too got lost."

The Inspector took a break and continued with the rest of the story, "They followed her prints out of the safe area in the Catacombs till she veneered from the corridor, she somehow found and unknown entrees, she must have broken though the wall and they could see where she lost her candles along the way. Before venturing further along, they continued to mark the area, just in case they somehow can't find their way back. Believe it or not, they found a skeleton hanging, no doubt she saw it hanging by the neck, because, according to them, she spent the night there, I'm guessing she may have passed out, poor girl."

When he heard the last sentence, Jack banged both his fits on the table and he immediately got up from his chair and started to pace back and forth while cursing out loud.

"Ok Jack, calm down, do you want to hear what else Madeleine went through with or not?"

And Jack sat down crunching both fits harder and the doctor sitting next to Jack patted him on the shoulders, helping him to calm down.

The inspector pick up where he left off, "she somehow managed to find her way into a new cavern and from what I hear, it's the biggest one yet, they could see that she must have dropped into a hole and dropped her candle below, it was sitting on the very bottom and there was no way in hell, she would have been able to retrieve it, there was no way down to the flooring!"

"I'm told that, she crawled across a very thin ledge which led to the next corridor; by the way, the ledge broke up when the last of the search party made it across just in the nick of time before the entire ledge collapsed away from the main wall. From that point on, the party knew they would have to continue to find their way out, just like she did! With her having no lights of any kind, she simply did what she had to do to survive, she crawled her way out!"

"Oh my God, Madeleine," whispered Jack, as he suddenly saw the visions in his head of her crawling around in the dark and not able to hear anything at all."

The Inspector once again stopped to take a breather before he continued on with the story, he noticed the doctors and Jack were all teary-eyed and they should be.

"The search party could see where she fell and got up to crawl, they found a dead rat that she must have stepped on because it was freshly killed and saw that she ran for a way till she ran into a wall. They found her nail scratches, like she was trying to dig her way out. And yes, they found her dried blood stains on rocks and small boulders that she must have fallen against. They continued to follow her footprints and could see where she ran further along into a shorter tunnel as it becoming narrower, that was why she took to crawling along, she did come to a dead-end, and it was, die or try breaking through soft dirt wall and that, is just what she did. When the party stepped outside, they could see that her footprints led to a tree and she did rest there in the rain. They followed the prints to the roadside, the rest is history. For your information, she crawled her way there too," emphasizes the Inspector."

"Well, you know the rest of the story, all I can say is that, she is one hell of a determinate lady you have there, Jack. And there has not been a story this big since Napoleon days. I wouldn't be a bit surprised if the movie companies pick up on this for their award-win-ning movie!"

"Bye the way Jack, Madeleine found old pottery and bones that must go way back in time, the archologies are already settling lights up everywhere, The Catacombs are closed down to the public till they finished their work, God knows it could be months or even years before they reopen again. You should know, Jack, whatever her findings, she will be getting a share of that money for whatever it might be worth, who knows, she will be Canadas next millionaire."

"I'm not so sure Maddie would want anything to do with it, but thanks for mentioning it though."

All was silenced and he noticed that both Jack and the doctors were in a state of shock. He knew that once the media leaked out the real story, the whole world was going to be in shock too.

The Inspector got up to leave them alone, till he thought of something, turning to face Jack, he said, "Jack, she must love you very much to get through the Catacombs of Hell eh? You know the old say, to hell and back, well that is just what she did. Had it been anyone else they would have given up. I do hope you appreciate that woman!"

In his soft voice, "We love each other but, her parents are saying, that she is going back to Canada with them, that is, when she is able to, I'm afraid, I may have already lost her, Inspector Dupert."

"I wouldn't bet on it Jack, from what I'm guessing, she was try-ing to get back to you, I think she is your soul mate for life, in any case, I'm sure she will use her own discretion, she is not a lady to be told what to do and I hope you keep that in mind for the future," chuckled the inspector while he walked over to look out the window and looked below.

"Better come and see this," he told everyone. They all got up at the same time and walked over to the window and glanced outside. They were stunned to see so many people singing songs, and some were waving place cards, while others were simply dropping off flowers by the gateway. Some of them were tying up balloons to the hospitals fencing. The area surrounding had policemen on horses trying to keep back the crowds while doctors and nurses were making their way into and out from the hospital front entrances.

Jack was amazed to see so many people showing their support for Madeleine, it warmed his heart.

After thanking the inspector for his in-depth information, he went back to be with Madeleine who was still sleeping. Thanking the nurses who stayed with her.   He looked down on her, she was still sleeping peacefully and he sank down into his cold leather chair, once more staring at the woman he was going to marry.

Jack mentally cursed the Professor and his hunch men and began to plan what he was going to do with them, should the courts be too soft with them. He planned to bury them at the bottom of his lake.

He spent the remaining day by her side and said his prayers while doctors and nurses dropped in and checking on her vitals every three hours. They would make small talk with Jack and kept him in the loop on their prognosis.

Monday 12:15 p.m.
Finally, she opened her eyes and tried to talk, she felt her throat was still a bit raw and hoarse, and she restored to whispering.

"Jack, have you been sitting here all that time?"

Jack seeing and hearing her soft voice, quickly got up from his chair and gently took her wrapped hand into his and with a wide grin, "there is nowhere else I rather be darling, then here, welcome back my love." smiling at her.

"What about your business and the stores?"

"Don't fret darling, that's what my managers at the winery are being paid for!"

She smiled at him, the first smile since that day at the Catacombs. He took it as a sign that she was getting better.

"Welcome back, Darling," again, he told her.

She tried to shift her body on the bed and gave a quince at every movement she made. Jack got up and carefully helped to shift her to comfort.

"Would you like me to raise your bed up a little?"

She nodded her head and braced herself for the pain and when Jack pushed down on the mechanical button, slowly the bed began to rise till, and she whispered 'stop' and came around to the head of her bed and carefully, he fixed her pillow, then he pulled up his chair closer to her bed and sat back down in his chair. He could see that her cheeks were beginning to gain some of its coloring.

"Maddie, when we get you back home, I want you to rest as much as possible, I mean there will be things that you won't be able to do for a while and I am going to hire you a private nurse, to help you out for the time being."

"I won't argue with you on one condition, she better be much older than you," she said and quietly chuckled.

"You got it darling, besides, I wouldn't worry about their ages, you are the only one for me, ten women, all younger, wouldn't be able to do what you did to survive!"

Jack gave a small frown at the last word he had just said, "Speaking of surviving, what kept you going, darling?"

"I kept hearing your voice in my head encouraging me to escape."

"Really, and what did I say, I hope it was encouraging?"

"It was, do you want the exact wordings?"

 Darling I want to hear what you went through to survive!"

She understood what he meant, "I kept hearing, "Run, run hard and don't stops or they will catch up to you."

Jack looked at her and said, "Yes that would have been something I would have told you. You know darling, it truly amazes me what fueled you to stay focused long enough to find your way through the darkness of the Catacombs and your capacity for life surprises me even more. As desperate as you were, I'm just glad that our love was the motivation enough for your survival otherwise, had you died, I know I would be lost without you in my life!"

She could only smile at the man she loved, she understood that he too must have gone through hell waiting to hear if she was alive or not.

With a stern look on his face, "Now, let's concentrate on getting you better, so we can get the hell out of here, what do you say, Mrs. Windsor, soon to be?"

Jack wasn't sure if this was the right time to tell her of her parent's plan they had for her but, he decided to take his chances anyway.

"Darling, just so you know: your parents have mentioned, once you are well enough to travel, they plan to take you back home with them to Canada!"

"Humm that is not going to happen, especially after what I went through to get back to you Jack, I remember, I had a dream or rather I saw a vision of us, we were married and had a boy and a girl, don't ask me why."

Jack picked up her hand and plant a gentle kiss on her fingertips, we will have as many kids as you want darling. And, on each of our anniversary, I will shower you one thousand kisses!" saying with a smile.

The following week was much of the same for Madeleine; all she could do was rest, eat and take it easy. She took the vitamins the doctors had ordered for her.

On the other hand; Jack read her the French newspaper stories what the media were all saying about her heretic escape. He ordered television for her room even though it was all French-speaking and he helped her with her French. By the time she was released from the hospital, she knew more than a few French words.

And every second day, along with her parent as did Wilbert came to the hospital with a fresh clean change of clothes and many updates on his winery and coffee houses during her sleeping times. He also told Jack quietly out in the hallway of the trespassers they have been catching on their property and the many phone calls from the umpteenth reporters. Jack told him to contact the inspector and see what else they could do about it.

Once satisfied with her slow recovery, both her parents went back to Canada but, only after her protesting that she was in good hands. And Courtney, knowingly her daughter had found the man of her dreams. She had to encourage Fred to leave and head back home to Canada but, under his terms, which she kept in contacts, daily via internet viewings.

As for Wilbert, he was kept plenty busy with his travels back and forth to the hospital bringing whatever the couple needed.

Even though it was against the hospital's policy for overnight adult guest unless of course it was a mother and her young child, the board approved of Jack's stay for the duration till Madeleine was released. Impressed with the emergency teams, he became a new member of the hospital's donation list.

And the media, they all camped out in the hospital's small park under watchful eyes of the law. They would rise early in the morning, spending all-day waiting to be the first ones to take her picture and publishing the photo in their newspapers, hoping for the all –time, photographer's award-winning photos.

In the second week, all her stitches came out and bandages came off to allow the cuts to heal and breathe. The doctors were amazed at her quick healings, given credit to a newly founded antibiotic that made it into the Medical Journal of the year.

During last week, while Madeleine was resting, Jack would hold his meetings with the prospect nurses in an empty bedroom next door to hers. The head nurse, Jack earlier learned her name was Martha and she was kind enough to help Jack wean out the better qualified retired nurses, till Jack suggested that she come for a couple of months or till it would take her to heal properly, but, stating that he would pay her handsomely and she would have the room next door to Madeleine.

He stated to her, "After all, you know more about her injures and she feels more comfortable with you attending to her 'womanly' needs."

The hospital granted Martha's request for the absence of leave till, Miss Windsor was well enough to be on her own, of course, with the hospital hoping for another sizable donation.

By the time Madeleine was well enough to leave the hospital, she was able to stand barely on her two feet for a very short duration of time. She would exhaust very easily. Jack knew that he had his work cut out for him and he was looking forwards to his time with her. With sunshine and fresh air by the lakeside would bring the woman he loved back to her normal self. Still a knot in his stomach reminded him that her parents might have something more to say.

One afternoon after all her tests came back normal, the head doctor told them the good news they both had been waiting to hear. Madeleine was finally going to be released, it was a matter of how, when and where she could leave without drawing the reporters attention. It was Martha, who was also in their room, who came up with an idea.

"May I suggest that Miss Windsor leave by helicopter, away from prying eyes, I mean, the helicopters are always landing and taking off from our hospital rooftops, the reporters will only think it's another emergency pickup?"

"That is a very brilliant idea, Martha, but, I'm sure once the reporter sees her, they will know," suggested the doctor.

"No, I don't think they would be able to recognize her, not if she was fully under the blankets with a surgical cap on and we rush her inside the copter," said Jack.

"And what about you Jack, they will recognize you," pointed out the doctor.

"Not if I am dressed in the doctor's lab coat, glasses and fake mustache, they won't." he smiled at the trickery of it all, anything to get back at the trespassers.

After they all agreed to the stunt, the doctor asked Jack if, somewhere on his property the helicopter could land. Jack thought it over and told them there was plenty of room down by the lakeside.

And so the planning and scheming came together, the Holt's castle employees were all set and waiting for Madeleine. Nurse Martha had her bags packed and they were all on the rooftop watching the helicopter land. Nurse Martha covered Madeleine's entire face and while Jack, who was dressed as a doctor, rushed alongside her stretcher with his head bending downwards.

Once the three of them were securely inside the helicopter, it quickly lifted off the roof, up into the air; Jack quickly scanned the hospital grounds and was shocked to see the media. To him it looked like a war zone.

The helicopter ride took just an under a half hour to get to Holt's property. And Jack, for the first time got to see just how big his property looked from the air. As they were hovering over the lake and Jack pointed to a couple of his men waiting on the grounds, he point out the area for the pilot to land his helicopter.

Jack did notice that no one was parked in front of his gates, and he knew that once the word was out, the gates would be swamped with reporters and well-wishers.

Wilbert was standing by the lake's edge with a wheelchair for Madeleine.

As the helicopter made its safe landing on Jack's property and as quickly as they all worked together, Jack lifted Madeleine carefully from the hospital's stretcher and carefully stepped out of the helicopter and carefully seated her in the wheelchair in no time. It was Wilbert and Richard who skillfully wheeled her up the slight hillside and around the side door into the greenhouse with Jack and Nurse Martha with her suitcase following closely behind. By the time they got inside, the helicopter was already on its way back to the airport hangar.

Courtney and Fred, who arrived back from Canada on hearing their daughter being released, greeted their daughter and congratulated Jack on a fine helicopter scheme.

Jack pointed out to Fred, that it was Nurse Martha's idea.

Before Fred could say anything, Nurse Martha asked to see the bedrooms and suggested they help Madeleine get settled in so that she can immediately check on her vitals, and Madeleine began to protest.

"Unless you want to go back to the hospital, dear, I suggest you get some rest; because, once the media gets wind of what really went down, there is going to be hell to pay, do you get my meaning, Miss Windsor?"

And so they got Madeleine settled into her room and Nurse Martha check on her cuts and checked her vitals, all was well considering the excursion she has been through.

Satisfied, Nurse Martha went to her room to put away her own things; Jack was finally alone with his finance at last.

Sitting on the edge of her bed, he took her into his arms and gave her a long and slow kiss. The two spent the time talking till Fred and Courtney knocked on her bedroom door, Jack shouted to come in, thinking that it was Nurse Martha.

Madeleine's parents stepped inside and they were surprised to see the couple hugging each other and quickly apologized for the interruption. The knot in Jack's stomach got a little tighter when he saw the look in Fred's face, he knew why they were there, he only prayed that his and Madeleine's love was strong enough to fight off whatever they were going to say to their daughter.

"Darling, I'll take my leave and let your parents have some private time with you, I need to go down and talk with Richard about the vineyards and I'll see you in a bit, ok?"

Madeleine nodded her head but, she knew that he didn't want to leave her, nor did she want him to leave. The two and half weeks they spent together in the hospital were blissful in spite of the pain she had endured, but, their love for each other outshone the pains. With Jack out of earshot and her bedroom door closed, Fred cleared his throat.

"Your mother and I would like to take you back to Canada next week if you are able to, I can make all the arrangements and we will have our own doctors inspect your wounds, and."

Madeleine in her, serious voice interrupted him before he could finish his sentence.

"Thank you both, but you are forgetting something, I am engaged to Jack and I plan to marry him in the fall. You know and seen for yourselves; I have been very well taken care of, there is no need for any more doctors."

"I think what your father is trying to say dear is, it's time to return back home where you belong. Let's face the facts here, you've been kidnapped and lost in the tunnels and you have been a very sick lady. How more can you take?"

"Thanks for your concerns but, I am staying here and when we are married, I'll come back home to get my affairs in order."

"Are you telling us, that you are going to marry and spend the rest of your life, here in France, where all this tragedy took place?"

"Yes father, I am and I do hope that you and mother will come to visit often, Jack is planning on giving you both a whole east wing section of the castle, all to yourselves, for when you come for a visit. You will be able to spend as much time with us as you like and when our children come along, you can help us out."

The Windsor's were at loss for words, they knew they both have lost Madeleine to Jack, this time for good. Known that she had a mind of her own, nothing they could say or do, could change it.

Jack bounced down the stairs, three steps and a time; he had heard every word they have spoken, while he stood and listened through the door that he left slightly ajar. The knot in his stomach magically disappeared into thin air. He was proud that she stood up to her parents, *remind me in the future, never to mess with wife,* he told himself, chuckling.

The Windsor's stayed at the Holt's castle for the two weeks that it took her to get well but, not for lack of trying, getting their daughter to return back home with them.

And the media got wind two days after that she had already had left the hospital in the helicopter. The group of reporters being annoyed, immediately drove to hang around the Holt's front locked down gates.

They all were trying to get through the trees a tiny glimpse of the couple sitting on the bench down by the lakeside. Jack doubled his security team when Wilbert told him how many more people and reporters had gathered around the gates, even the food supply delivery trucks were having a difficult time, getting through the gates without first being hazard by the reporters. Bold and brazen as some were, one reporter asked the driver of the delivery truck to take his camera along with him and take some snapshots of Madeleine, he even offered to pay him a vast amount of money, the driver, of course refused such a request for fear of losing his reputation along with his other customers.

With the security being tight, the people and reporters finally gave up but, not before they cried foul and not fair that, they did not get the story of the year.

CHAPTER 12

The Windsor's gone back to Canada but, not before Fred, had a man to man talk with Jack. And he was glad they finally left. The two weeks went by fast but, not fast enough for him as he was running out of ideas of how to keep his guests entertained.

It wasn't till after the Windsor saw the castle's spare east wing where they would be staying during their future visitations, and saw how he dotted on Madeleine, with that, their attitude towards Jack had completely changed and known how much she was still in love with Jack in spite of her harrowing escape... were they able to return back home.

Jack hired a wedding planner to help the Windsor's with the wedding preparations which were quickly put together and the invitations had been ordered.

The plan was to have a traditional Thanksgiving wedding and dinner on Jack's property under a large wedding tent. The ceremony was to take place by the lakeside along with all the floral decorations. And Jack ordered extra security and parking attendants. He wanted their wedding to be special for his bride.

Madeleine kept in close touch with Rachel and Hugo regarding the making of her wedding gown as well as, hearing how well her business was doing. Donna who was going to be her bridesmaid and Rachel being the Matron of Honor, they planned to arrive in Paris a week earlier to put the final touches on the wedding and to Madeleine's gown. They wanted to have a long visit with their friend and future sister-in-law whom they already missed.

Nurse Martha stayed with Madeleine till the doctor who did his weekly check signed off he released her duties with the understanding that once Madeleine was well, she would return back to the duties at the hospital. The patient did make a speedy recovery.

Both Jack and Madeleine took their daily slow walk down to the lakeside and around the property like two people who were madly in love. Jack always made sure his bride ate well and kept her warm as the doctor's per orders.

Since she left the hospital, she had made an amazing recovery except for a few nightmares. A couple of times, both he and Nurse Martha both ran into her room when they heard her screaming, they knew that she was having a bad dream.

It would be her mother who would slide into her bed and spend the rest of the night by her daughter's side, gently rocking her, till morning came.

Courtney had a long talk with Nurse Martha, on what to do, should Madeleine happen to dream again, after her leaving for Canada. She wanted to make sure that it would be Nurse Martha who would take her place and not Jack. "Call me old fashion, I don't care." She smiled.

There had been of couple of nights Jack race to Madeleine's bedside, beating the nurse, who stumbled in later. He would calm Madeleine down with his smooth-talking voice and the nurse would try to encourage Jack to leave the job to her. He paid no heed to her and one night he actually repeatedly ordered her out of the room a couple of times.

And after he calmed Madeleine down, with the lights left on low, he would lay by her side, cradling her till she fell into a deep sleep. And very carefully, he got up to sit in the big chair by her bed; he would stay awake watching over her till morning when she woke up.

And Nurse Martha, after being ordered out, would stay out in the hallway watching Jack and Madeleine, once she saw that he was in the chair, she would go back to her room but, with the door left ajar. She knew that Jack had every intention of doing right by her till the two of them were properly married especially after hearing the nurses at the hospital; she knew all about Jack's previous reputations, still, she was happy for the couple.

One warm and sunny day while sitting on the bench by the lake, they spotted someone standing by the group of Birch trees. Jack seeing the camera's reflection immediately knew it was a reporter and he was furious.

"Dam them, where the hell is the security team and why can't the reporters leave us alone?"

"I think dear, the only way to get rid of them is to give them what they want!"

"Meaning what darling?"

"By, telling them my experience of being lost in the Catacombs!"

"I'm not sure if you are up for the game, you are just now sleeping the night through, I don't want you reliving all that chaos again?"

"Unless you want to put up with the reporters hanging around, I'd say, I'm ready to tell the world my story; besides, I do believe it would help me to put a closure in it!"

Jack would do anything for his bride, feeling perplexed, he waved and called out loud for the reporter to come and join them. The reporter ran as fast as his legs would let him, stopping in front of the couple, out of breath, he immediately began introducing himself.

"My name is Perry Chambery and I am a reporter with the Paris Star paper. Miss Windsor, can I please hear your side of the story and with your permission I to be the first to have it published in our papers?"

Before Madeleine could acknowledge, Jack interrupted.

"First of all, how did you get through the security, I thought the security was heavy enough?"

Sir, I climbed over the fence a little further down past the end of the wall, no one saw me." Feeling red-faced that he had been caught.

"If we give you the story you want, will you and all the rest of the reports, at least leave us alone, you can see that Miss Windsor has a lot more recuperation to do, still?"

And Jack mentally made up his mind to have the wall extended further down to each of the ends of his property before the special was to take place, he didn't want reporters barging in on their private wedding.

"Yes, Mr. Holt, we will leave you alone. But, please can I explain what a lot of people don't know?"

Jack nodded his head for the reporter to go ahead.

"What people don't know, once her story is published in our newspapers, all other reporters will contact our office for more information. You see, we keep back a few details to share with other Parisian newspaper companies. It's a custom among us, we help each other to keep our jobs, I don't know about the rest of the world, how they get their story out but, in Paris, this is the way we do things."

"Fine, I will give you my story, but first, let's walk up to the Greenhouse to have some coffee, I am feeling a bit tired sitting out here," Suggested Madeleine.

The three of them walked slowly up to the Greenhouse and Perry couldn't help but notice Madeleine was walking with a limp, for her sake he slowed down his pace to keep up with her and Jack.

Wilbert, always one step ahead of everyone, met them at the Greenhouse carrying a tray with coffee and tea for the three of them, setting the tray down on the little table by the bridge way, Madeleine's favorite spot. He turned to face the intruder, giving him a disproval look, and then he took his leave, leaving them to themselves.

After they all had their refreshments and made small talk about the greenhouse, Perry turned on the recorder setting it on the table closer to Madeleine.

Under Jack's watchful eye, she began to tell her story, day by day from the moment of her kidnapping to breaking through the Catacomb's walls falling out into the rainy night. She told him how she managed to crawl her way to the roadside and gave the driver her full name.

"After that, I don't much remember anything till I woke to see Jack asleep on the chair by my bed."

"You are a very lucky lady, Miss Windsor, many people had died trying to find a secret stash of gold that was supposedly hidden away many, many centuries ago by pirates and you found it!"

"Well, I don't know anything about this so-called loot; I was trying to find my way out alive, I mean, I did remember seeing clay pottery and a couple of skeletons."

"And you didn't once look into the clay pots out of curiosity?"

"No, I was busy trying to stay alive."

Jack had quietly been watching the report's reaction while Madeleine told her story, he did not once interrupt. He could tell that Perry was emotionally upset during her story-telling and knew that in a once sense of way, her relaying the story, was therapeutic for her.

Seeing that she was getting tired, he stood up and politely asked if the reporter had enough information as Madeleine was tired and needed to rest.   Perry thanked them both and wished them well; he also told them if ever they needed anything to get him a call. He handed Madeleine his business card.

"Remember, anything at all, any time, day or night, call me and I will take care of everything."

Their wedding date suddenly occurred to Jack, "Well there is one thing you can do for us, that is if you would like to?"

"You name it and considered it done."

"Would you be interested in taking pictures and covering the story of our Thanksgiving wedding?"

"Really, why, I would be honored to do it, thank you for asking me," hardly containing his excitement.

"If it would be ok, can I mention your engagement with this story?"

"You have our blessings," smiled Madeleine, she knew that he was a kind-hearted man who was trying to make a living and not like some of them, very pushy and bold.

The reporter thanked both of them once more and took his leave, again leaving the couple to themselves. And Jack had suggested that she rest up for dinner while he tended to the vineyard business.

"Jack, may I ask, why did you ask Perry to cover our wedding?"

"Because by knowing that with one official reporter covering our story would mean that all other reports must stay away and wait for his news!"

In the Paris Star the next day, the story of her Catacombs ordeal as well as their engagement was announced to the public. As promised, the reports left them alone and Jack released his security team. With the understanding they were to return for their Thanksgiving wedding with extra pay.

Things were finally back to normal and as the days and months came and went Madeleine made a complete full recovery to the point where, she was able to go into Paris with Jack to see if her French citizenship was excepted or not. Her application was immediate, granted. The government were prepared for her request and didn't hesitate in giving in to her. She was access to their country with her fashionable designs. They also approved of her parents' applications as well, known full well, they would be visiting often. To the world it made France shine everyone's eyes.

And Jack kept in close touch with his lawyers regarding Professor Burnet, along with George and his hunch men. With the city being in such an uproar, the trio got many, many years of jail terms.

Between the four of them, the jail term added up to well over a lifetime of sentencing.

Jack had the gardener keep up with the gardens looking beautiful all summer and he managed to include colorful fall plants as well. Inside the castle, some of the walls were given a facelift of Madeleine's choice of paint colors. Wilbert and the cook hired on a couple more staff helpers, now that Madeleine had fully moved in with them but, kept her own bedroom till her wedding night.

One night in the Greenhouse, Jack and her had a long talk and decided to wait for their wedding night before making love. Madeleine told Jack, what he had suspected a long time ago, that she had never laid with another man before. And Jack respected her decision.

Her parent's parcel posted her requested few items that she needed. At her request, they sold her condo and the rest of the contents had been packed and forwards to Jack's spare guest condo in Lansing. Rachel and Courtney unpacked and set up some of Madeleine's personal contents as per instructions through emails. The rest of her items went into storage for later sorting when they came back to Canada to visit.

The Windsor's arrived four days before the wedding to help out the Thanksgiving preparations. When they first arrived, Madeleine and Jack opened the oak front door to welcome their guest only coming face to face with 'Ginger,' who was held by Courtney. And Madeleine immediately took her from her mother's arms cuddled her in her arms telling her how much she had missed her.

"Jack, I would like you to meet Ginger," turning to face him.

"Ginger, meet Jack, he is also going to be your new master too."

"You two are going to play nice, no biting, scratching or hissing at each other," Madeleine laughing out loud.

"I'm sure we would get along just fine, won't we, Ginger, she is as pretty as her master is," as he reached to pet the top of her head and Ginger gave a soft purring.

He looked to Fred and said, "Glad you both made it safely and thanks for the new addition," pointing to the cat.

"Told you Jack, the cat comes with the package," chuckled Fred.

Wilbert, always one step ahead as usual, already had the new cat litter box ready for Ginger's arrival, he set the box at the far corner of the Greenhouse. Her food and water dish was in the kitchen by the back door and was the cook's new responsibility, to feed and change her water dish every day. With the cook's understanding, Ginger had free reign of the household.

Rachel, Hugo and his male companion all arrived two full days before the wedding, the men stayed together at the Grande` Hotel in Paris, they rented a convertible sports car to do some sightseeing during their long-overdue week's holiday. Rachel stayed at the castle to help with the wedding party and put the final touched on Madeleine's wedding gown. Donna and her husband Greg Walters both turned down the offer of staying at the Holt's castle and stayed at the local hotel in the town of Chalons-en-Champagne. Wilbert would pick up Donna and bring her to the castle to help with the wedding and return her back to the hotel. Greg brought his paperwork along with him to keep himself busy. They spent the evenings touring the town and its famous landmarks, the many champagne vineyards.

It was a beautiful fall day for a Thanksgiving wedding on the Holt's property, according to the weather reports, with no rain in sight for the next two weeks. The early morning of the wedding day, Madeleine was excited and nervous couldn't eat her breakfast till Donna finally enticed her into eating by saying that she didn't want her best friend back in the hospital again.

Jack came down to have a late breakfast with the family till Richard came to collect him, Fed and Greg. The women teasingly told all the men they had to leave.

Jack laughed to see the sights of the women having fun and he understood that he was not allowed to see his bride before the wedding.

And Richard encouraged all the men of the wedding party to come over to the vineyard warehouse. They had their own private celebrations till two o'clock when it was time for the wedding ceremony to take place by the lakeside.

Jack with a wide grin was standing by the flowered covered arbor, along with his best man, Richard the foreman of Holt's vineyard whom he had taking a liking to the first time he met him. Greg Walter Donna's husband was also one of the groom's men as well.

The band began to play the wedding music just as the bride's maid and matron of honor stepped out through the Greenhouse doors. Fred came out next and held out his right arm for Madeleine to place her arm through his arm. He smiled and told her how lovely she looked. Together, slowly they walked to the wedding music and all eyes were feasting on the bride, she looked stunning with her Ivory full-length silk gown that gently hugging her body and fell loosely around her flat ivory silk matching shoes. Her dress had capped sleeves that followed the lines of a sweetheart shape slightly revealing her soft cleavage and her veil was of the same color, long to her heels with very small sparkling sequences that were hand-stitched carefully on the material. With the Sun's glare dancing on the sequences; it revealed diamonds glittering all down on her veil. Her hair was swept up away from her face and she wore very little makeup.

Jack's heart swelled with pride on his first sight of this woman who was his beautiful bride and she was full of glory and had true grit for living, especially for a lady who was hearing impaired.

The closer she walked towards him, the more in love he felt for her. He could see that she was flushed from excitement and nervous, both at the same time. When Fred handed her hand to Jack, he kissed Madeleine on the cheek and turned to Jack, he whispered quietly to him, "Take good care of her or you will answer me."

Jack only smiled and whispered back to him, "With my life."

And lifted Madeleine's hand up and kissed her fingertips whispering, "My darling, you look very beautiful, I'm a lucky man and I love you."

Madeleine, as nervous as she was could only smile and said,

"And I love you too, Jack." And together they turned to face the priest to be married. Earlier Jack had a chat with the priest and reminded him of her hearing impairment.

Fred went over and sat by Courtney who was having a hard time finding a tissue in her small clutch purse till, Fred pulled out a hanky from his inside his jacket and handed it to his wife.

The small groups of people were mostly from local and Perry Chambery, the reporter was there with his photography camera snapping away as many pictures as he could mustard of the wedding and its party.

When they put their rings on each other, and the priest's announcement of husband and wife, Jack gave Madeleine a long and tender kiss, looked lovingly into her teary eyes, and whispered, "we did it darling," and gave each other a gently hug. They turned to face their guests, who all stood up to applause the newlyweds.

Wilbert and the cook watched the wedding from a short distance and when the vows were exchanged, they quickly went back inside the castle to make sure the glasses were filled with only the Holt's Champagne and all the hor'dur food, were ready to be served at the right moment. The servers dressed in white and black, in a single file marched out with silver trays to serve the champagne to the guests.

The atmosphere was lively while the band played soft jazzy music most of the late afternoon into midnight. The newlyweds, walked arm in arm while they associated with their guest. Rarely were the couple seen separated, Madeleine could tell that Jack was happy and attentive with all her needs. He held out her chair when they were seated for dinner in the tent under the stars. The toasts to the newlyweds were made by Richard and Fred, Donna and Rachel did their speech as well. But, all made sure to face Madeleine.

After the lights dimmed, another set of lights that were mounted on a nearby tree began to keep rhythm with the music. Fireworks began to fly over the lake, keeping rhythm with the music as well. The lights began to sparkle, setting the area to look like stars and diamonds swirling around the grounds where Jack and Madeleine had their first dance under the stars in that night sky.

While they slow danced to the music, Jack faced Madeleine and whispered, "Do you remember this music?"

She nodded her head, "I do, and it was our first dance at the nightclub in Paris."

Everyone applauded the couple and when the music started up again, couples all joined in the next dance which was a Waltz and Jack slowly danced Madeleine down to the edge of the water and carefully sat her on the bench. With his arm around her shoulders, he pointed out the full moon and other stars. He placed his hand on her face, tilting it to face his, and gently gave her a kiss and asked her if she had any regrets in marrying him, to which she responded back to him, a firm, no, and she kissed him.

The rest of the wedding evening came to life with a younger band that took over from the first Jazz band. Everyone was having a great time; the Holt's wines and Champagne were flowing, people were dancing and some danced without partners. Even Perry Chambery set down his camera and joined in with the dancing group.

By twelve-thirty, Jack could see that Madeline was getting tired, "tired darling?" in his husky voice to which Madeleine only nodded.

He flagged Wilbert; a signal was given to bring around the car to the side so that everyone could see them off.

With the help from Rachel and Donna, had earlier, the two had packed up the couples clothing and items and secretly put them into the car at Jack's request. Wilbert brought the car around and Jack who was watching gave him a head nod to let Wilbert know that he was ready to leave.

Turning to face Madeleine, "Darling, let's say or goodnight to everyone, I like to take you for a drive under the stars and we will return in a couple of hours and by that time, everyone should be gone.”

"Oh that sounds nice, I should go inside to change and put on something comfortable.”

He could tell that she was a bit nervous about their first night together in coming.

"No need to change, you look beautiful and I want this night to last forever.”

Madeleine was surprised about the drive and agreed; together they said their goodbyes and thanked all the staff members. Rachel and Donna helped with her wedding gown getting carefully into the car. Everyone was tossing a small handfuls of rice while the couple drove away.

With Madeleine sitting closer to Jack, he took his time and drove them around the outskirts of Chalons-en-Champagne and once he found a perfect parking spot up on a sloped hillside, he parked the car and turning off his car lights. He turned to Madeleine as suggested they get out of the car and check out the stars in the night sky. After agreeing, Jack came around to Madeleine's side of the car and held open the door for her while she got out. Together they walked arm in arm till they came to a large bolder, while looking up, he pointed out the big dipper and as she looked up, he gently kissed her. Unexpectedly, his kiss took away her breath. With the moonlight, he could see a tear trickled down her cheeks. He kissed her cheek and in his husky voice he asked her if she was alright.

"Yes, dear, I am ok.”
"Why these tears, darling?”
"Because, I have never been this happy before, oh, Jack, everything has been so beautiful and it's been so hard to believe that just

a few months ago, I was kidnapped inside the Catacombs, I didn't think, I would ever find my way out, especially when I lost the candles and everything was black inside, I feared for my life, I didn't think I would see you again."

"Maddie my darling, I went crazy when I turned around and you were gone, I was frantic, I even went to my car and said a prayer that we find you in time."

''We belong together, Jack."

They stood hugging each other till he felt her trembled.

"Are you cold?"

And she responded that she was and Jack took her back to the car and helped her with her wedding gown. He got in and turned on the heat, it was the last thing he wanted was for her to get sick, he pulled out onto the road from where they parked and then turned onto the highway, driving towards the City of the Lights, Paris.

This surprised her, "ummm, Honey, I'm still in my wedding gown, surely you don't think we should be going into Paris like this?"

"We are not going to parade ourselves through the city, although, if I had my way, I would take you up to the Eiffel Tower, gown and all to show the world how beautiful my bride is."

"Jack!"

"No darling, he chuckled, I'm taking you to our condo to spend our first couple of nights alone. Surely, you don't think it would be right to spend our first night together with our families listening through the walls back at the castle, do you?"

Madeleine felt herself blushing at the thoughts of her parents being in the same area.

"I agree with you but, what about the things that we need for the morning?"

"All taken care of my Love, Rachel, Donna and Wilbert all packed up the car while we were down by the water," he told her.

"Those three never cease to amaze me; I have to admit they work well together."

"With Donna married and someday I pray, Rachael will find the right man to settle down with."

"I believe she has already found someone!"

"Oh really, this is the first I have heard of it, who is he?"

"Ummm, it's someone you already know."

"You are a real tease, tell me, who is he, please?"

"Ok, believe it or not, it's Wilbert."

"WILBERT, surely you don't mean your butler??"

"You mean to say, OUR butler, that I do darling, you see, Wilbert has had a crush on my sister for as long as I can remember, and I suspect Rachael has known it for a while too."

"Then why didn't she didn't she give into their feelings, I mean, is it because of their age difference?"

"I have no clue what their reasons are, after all, Wilbert has never confined in me about his feelings for her and I have always stayed out of her affairs and may I kindly suggest you to stay out of it."

"Whoa dear, what is this, our first argument already," chuckled Madeleine.

"Not our first real argument, just a suggestion and besides, I would never be able to win an argument with you anyway!"

"Oh really, and pray, tell me why not dear?"

"Because my dear wife, as long as you live the rest of your life safely, I will let you win all our arguments."

"Oh Jack, you have a way with words and tell me one thing and I promise to leave it alone, how did you suspect Wilbert had a crush on her?"

"Because of the way he watches her every move and the way he is always one step ahead of her, my dear nosy wife."

"In that case, I hope they both find what they are looking for, without any interference, I might add."

Just then, Jack pulled into the side street and makes a sharp right turn into the underground parking of their tall condo. He pulled into his reserved parking space next to an empty parking space. Shutting down his car, again, he got out and came around and held open Madeleine's door. He helped her with her gown so that she didn't let it touched the cement flooring.

Together while carrying the two suitcases and Madeleine's smaller one and they walked over to the private penthouse elevator. Jack was glad there was no one else in the garage; he knew Madeleine would feel embarrassed being caught in her wedding gown. After Jack touched a button, the door immediately opened.   They entered into the elevator, again Jack pushed on one of the green buttons for his penthouse. He turned and smiled while he was admiring her standing in the corner all by herself, staring back at him. He could no longer resist the temptation and seductively walked over and lean forwards, giving his new bride a long and sweet kiss for as long as the elevator took to reach his floor, leaving Madeleine feeling breathless and wanting more.

Hand in hand, they walked out in the hallway where the three other tenets share the same hall, stopping in front of the tall double-wide doors and setting down their suitcases on the floor. With his access card, he swiped it through the mechanical lock, automatically unlocking the door; he reached inside and turned on all the lights. Turning to face his new bride, he very gently scooped up Madeleine into his arms and she wrapped both her arms around Jack's neck while he carried her across the threshold. Madeleine was feeling a little nervous and excited at the same time.

Looking deeply into her eyes, he whispered "Welcome to our home away from our country home," he told her lovingly.

With his eyes locked onto hers, he carried her to the wide-open living room but, not before setting her down, gave her another long and tender kiss. In his husky voice, "You have no idea how much I love you Mrs. Holt," and set her gently down on her feet. Madeleine, felt weak at her knees and felt a little shiver run through her body as she watched Jack slowly walk over to bring inside the suitcases, locking the door behind him. He turned to take in her beauty and could see in her eyes that she was flushed; he wanted to calm all her fears, for he planned to let her come to him, ready and willingly, whether it took her two hours or forty-eight hours. He has been patiently waiting for her all this time and waiting a bit longer won't hurt him. He wanted her to feel secured and comfortable with him. After all they had their entire lives to explore each other, tonight was not a night to rush through their first time in making love.

"Darling, shall I uncork the Champagne?"

"That would be nice, is the Champagne from your vineyard?" She was hoping her nervousness didn't show.

"As a matter of fact, yes, it is from 'OUR' vineyard, my dear, Mrs. Holt."

Madeleine was surprised to see the Champagne was already chilled in the ice bucket and waiting to be served. She looked around the apartment while Jack dimmed the lights. Picking up the lighter he lit up some candles, put on soft piano music and uncorked the Champagne pouring it into their tall fluted glasses.

She noticed the apartment was very spacious and modernly decorated with tasteful paintings hanging up on the walls. She walked over to the floor-to-ceiling windows and noticed the city lights below.

Jack came over to join her, setting down the glasses; he unlocked and opened the patio doors so they could step out. He took a plaid blanket from the nearby sofa and wrapped it around her shoulders; today had been long and stressful for his bride who is still recuperating from the Catacomb incident. He picked up the two glasses and invited her to step out on the balcony and she gracefully did. Jack handed her the glass and he made toast.

"May both our businesses be successful, may our marriage last forever and may we have many children."

And Madeleine was not quite sure how to respond to his toast, she simply said, "And I agree."

Jack smiled at his bride; he knew that she was also inexperienced in toasting as well. He had his work cut out for him to introduce finer things of life that he planned to shower her with.

They drank their Champagne and together they admire the Parisian city lights. Jack was right the city of Paris never sleeps.

She felt a sudden chill in the air and Jack noticed her shivering, he took it as a sign that she was becoming more nervous and suggested the she go back inside. At first she hesitated, then he leaned forwards and kissed her lips, very softly and enticing her to relax. She did.

Once inside, he closed the doors and locked them and together walked over and sat on the sofa, looking at his bride.

"Darling, can I ask you something?"
"What's on your mind?"

"I don't mean to embarrass you, but, have you ever made love to another man?"

"That is an odd question to ask your bride?"

"I apologize, I wanted you to feel we could talk about anything and if you are experienced, then we will take it slow."

"Umm, no, I have not, why?" She felt her cheeks on fire from his personal questioning.

"Because I can see that you are nervous and that is normal for any bride. If you are not ready, we can wait for the right time, if you would prefer?"

"Thank you for noticing and yes, I am nervous, I mean you are far more experience than I am."

"I won't deny that daring, I know we have known each other a short time but, I feel as if I have known all my life, if you rather, I will take the guest room and you can have our master bedroom."

"Thank you and yes, I will take our room but, only if you share it with me," surprising Jack.

"Are you saying what I think you are saying?"

"I'm saying let's take it one step at a time, please, be patient with me."

Jack leaned towards her and gave her a long tender kiss and she responded back, he helped her to stand up and he quickly scooped her up into his arms, with his lips still on hers, he walked into their bedroom and carefully set her down on the king-size bed.

Madeleine felt breathless and her body felt flushed while she watched Jack slowly walk over to the light switch and dimmed all the bedroom lights; he slowly removed his suit jacket, placing it over the back of the chair and took off his shoes. He came back, standing tall before her and carefully lifted up her foot, one at a time, and slowly removing her wedding shoes. With his strong hand he gently massaged her small and tired feet.

He could see that her cheeks were flushed with fever, it made him want to take her right then and there but, being the gentleman he was, he planned to let her play by her rules, just for tonight.

In his seductive voice, "Darling, would you like me to lie down beside you and hold you in my arms?"

She could only nod her head, yes.

And he carefully laid his body down on the bed by her side. Together they lay, cradled. They talked about how the wedding went and the people that were there till Jack gave her a long and slow kiss; his tongue met hers and he could feel her tremble and she was breathless, kiss after kiss; till finally, he knew that she was begging for more. She was ready and willing as he had been from the first moment he laid eyes on her out on the hotel's balcony in her blue dress.

And so, the rest of the night was blissful for the newly married couple. That night they fully consumed their marriage and officially made themselves, husband and wife. They spent the next few days at the condo exploring and getting to know each other till it was decided they should return back to the castle where Jack's work was waiting for him. Madeleine had plans to open a new dress shop in town. But, what she didn't know was that Jack had secretly bought the building on the main street. With the help from Rachel and her friends, Madeleine's new shop was about to open for business. And Jack had a new sign 'Madam's City of Lights' already placed above her new shop.

As they drove through the double gates up to the castle, she couldn't help but, noticed the walls on both sides of the gateway had been extended further down to the ends of their property. She looked questionably at Jack and he explained to her that while they were at the condo, he had bricklayers working twenty-four-hour shifts, building the walls day and night till it was finished.

When they arrived at the castle's oak front doors, Wilbert stepped out to welcome them both home.

"Welcome home, Mr. and Mrs. Holt," he told them.

"Thank you Wilbert," said Madeleine feeling a little bit embarrassed.

From behind Wilbert a little collie puppy followed him outside, surprising Madeleine. She stepped away from the door and reached out to pat him.

"A puppy, oh my goodness Wilbert, is this your new puppy?"

"No madam it is not." Looking towards Jack and waited for him to take over the rest of the conversation.

"Darling, the puppy is yours," smiled Jack.

Madeleine turned to face her new husband, "Why a puppy and what about Ginger?"

"Oh, that, I'm sure they will get along fine, right Wilbert?"

"Yes sir, Ginger has already let him know who the boss is of this household," he chuckled.

"You see Darling, I ordered you the collie pup and hopefully you can train him to be your hearing ear dog, I was told that collies are well known to be protective of their owners. Besides, I wanted you to feel safe at all times especially when I'm out of the country on business, I'll feel better known that you have someone to talk to and I hope you don't mind, if you don't like him we can always trade him up."

"I don't think so Jack, I do like him, besides he is so cute."

"Now, we have to give him a name, what would you like to call him and please don't call him Rambo?"

"Honey, you are right, he does need a real name. I have an idea, why don't we call him, 'HUGO."

Just then the collie pup lifted his head, perking up his ears. He looked directly at Madeleine and scampered over and stood closer to her. He began to lick her out stretched hand.

"See, I believe he does like his new name, don't you, Hugo," trussing up his ears with both her hands.

"Then it's officially 'Hugo, is his name and I just hope the real Hugo in Canada don't mind us using his namesake," he said while eyeing Madeleine.

The three together, laughed out loud while the little collie pup ran around in circles and in and out between their legs while giving them his puppy barks.   Madeleine could have sworn the pup was laughing along with them.

End of story!

9 781087 993720